Gemini Heat

'Slow down, Dee,' he whispered, taking her busy hands off him and holding them still in her lap. 'I've waited too long for—' He paused and smiled boyishly. 'For something like this. . . I want it to last. I want to savour it. Just the way I've always imagined I would.'

This was a deviation from the fantasy pattern. Both with her, and by all accounts, with Deana, Jake had been swift in the taking and pleasuring of his woman. In each case, of course, circumstances had dictated there be haste, but somehow slow leisurely sex was not what she associated with Jackson Kazuto de Guile.

Gemini Heat
Portia Da Costa

Black Lace books contain sexual fantasies.
In real life, always practise safe sex.

This edition published in 2008 by
Black Lace
Thames Wharf Studios
Rainville Rd
London W6 9HA

Originally published 1994

A catalogue record for this book is available from the British Library.

www.black-lace-books.com

Typeset by Palimpsest Book Production Limited, Grangemouth, Stirlingshire
Printed and bound in Great Britain by CPI Bookmarque, Croydon, CR0 4TD

ISBN 978 0 352 34187 7

The Random House Group Limited supports The Forest Stewardship Council [FSC],
the leading international forest certification organisation. All our titles that are
printed on Greenpeace approved FSC certified paper carry the FSC logo
Our paper procurement policy can be found at www.rbooks.co.uk/environment

1 3 5 7 9 10 8 6 4 2

Contents

Dedicated to ISIS ...
... who makes my mind fertile.
THANK YOU

1

The Art Lovers

I can't take much more of this heat, thought Deana Ferraro, watching the condensation run slowly down the side of her glass. It was only May – the thirtieth to be exact – but the temperatures, both outside and in, were already becoming impossible.

Sweat ran freely in the crease between her buttocks, caressing them like an unseen lover, and she imagined it sizzling as it trickled and pooled in her vulva. Her entire body felt as hot as the steamy air in the gallery, but down there, in the peach-soft groove of her bottom, the conditions were almost volcanic.

It's this bloody exhibition! she thought with feeling. It's enough to make a celibate, librarian nun boil over, never mind a poor sex-starved creature like me.

'Visions of Eroticism – the de Guile Collection' the glossy brochure announced with some pomp, but 'eroticism' was putting it mildly. The collector in this case was an out and out pervert, a connoisseur of fine art as well as true-blue porn, and Deana had drawn enough nude studies in her life to know that a singularly inspired creation could easily be both. When it had happened to her though she'd hidden the result in the 'special album' she kept in her knicker drawer. It seemed that J. K. de Guile, however, the owner of this particular Rabelaisian collection, was quite happy to have *his* secret masturbation file put on show to the general public.

There was everything here. Solo sex. Couples. Groups. Explicit penetrations. Byways and fetishes. Every dark, kinky concept from a wild man's wildest dreams and more.

A wild *woman's* dreams too, thought Deana, moving uncomfortably and wondering if anyone could read her thoughts. There were times when she loved how she felt now: the congestion in the pit of her belly, the heat in her dark, secret crevice, the swollen sensitivity of her clitoris. But it was no fun in public, alone, and with no chance of relief on the horizon. She sipped her wine in the vain hope it might quench her lust as well as her thirst, but it had no effect. She had a lunatic urge to touch herself, here, in the middle of the gallery. To satisfy – albeit temporarily – the dreadful aching yen for sex that had been plaguing her since she'd told Jimmy their fling was over.

It's your own fault, Ferraro, she told herself, sipping again and trying to concentrate on the subdued strains of a Mozart trio playing in the background. Only an idiot or a masochist would come to an exhibition of erotic art when she was dying of frustration. But what else could you do when you were alone on your birthday and fed up?

Delia was the one who should have been here tonight, of course; it was her name on the invitation. Letting Deana come in her place was just a sisterly way of saying sorry ... Sorry for not sharing their birthday as they'd always done.

Deana wasn't angry with her twin. If anything, she was sorry for her. Even though it was murder on the libido, viewing the de Guile Collection was infinitely preferable to dining with slimy, odious Russell. What the hell did Delia see in him?

Weaving her way through a swarm of chattering celebs, Deana moved on to the next exhibit – then almost wished she hadn't. It was a floor to ceiling full-colour photograph of a man and woman making love. And not one of those airy fairy things with tactfully placed shadows either. The couple in the brushed steel frame were actually doing it, copulating for real, and their glistening, tightly nested sex organs were 'wham bam, thank you ma'am' right in the centre of the photo.

'Good God,' whispered Deana, taking another sip of wine. As the crisp, chilled taste flooded her mouth, two thoughts occurred to her. One, that this was her third drink and she was tipsy; two, that the photo above her made her feel worse than ever. Or better, depending on which way you looked at it. Wine and sex were inseparably linked in Deana's mind, and suddenly she wished she hadn't been so hasty about Jimmy. She stared up longingly. She needed what *they'd* got so badly, and even if Jimmy was an unimaginative so-and-so, at least he was good at plain, hard and consistently orgasmic sex.

Drawing on her artist's ability to 'image', Deana put herself into the picture before her. She saw a slim, shapely woman with dark hair, dark eyes and a warm apricot complexion. An earthy girl with a good figure and a face that was dainty and heart shaped, eyes that were big and bright, and a mouth that was small, but naturally red and with a pout that begged to be kissed.

Smiling at her own vanity, Deana succumbed to preening. She smoothed down her thin black dress over her narrow waist and the soft, curving flare of her hips.

An otherwise ninety-nine per cent perfect fit, the black cotton frock was just a smidgeon too tight across her breasts. She'd known that when she'd seen it on the market stall, but she'd loved it and tried it on anyway. The stall holder had peeped at her through the curtains of his makeshift cubicle. He must have known from the dress's cut that she wouldn't be able to wear a bra with it, and that he'd get a free show. But somehow, Deana hadn't minded him seeing her bare breasts. She'd enjoyed it because in many ways, she *liked* being looked at. Especially by cute-looking rogues like that stall man.

She couldn't imagine Delia feeling the same though. Or even liking the dress, for that matter. Second-hand Indian cotton with fringes and mirror beads wasn't her sister at all, and with a sudden pang of misgiving, Deana wondered if she should've tried a bit harder to look like the woman she was supposed to *be* tonight.

Facially, it was easy. She and Delia were identical twins, and their alikeness was so uncanny that even their parents had sometimes had problems. Nowadays though, their radically different tastes in clothes and styles made differentiating between the Ferraros simpler. At a function like this, Delia would've worn something subtle, neutral and very Jean Muir. Her hair would've been groomed to within an inch of its glossy life, and *not* in a turbulent, nut-brown tangle like Deana's. What's more, sensible Delia would've been drinking Perrier water with a slice of lime in case her boss of all bosses turned up – not swigging down glass after glass of Frascati as if sobriety were going out of fashion.

The bonking bodies in the picture were suddenly too much for Deana and she decided to move on. Perhaps there was something blander to look at somewhere, something that wouldn't make her feel so needful?

But as she flicked through the catalogue, she felt the most curious sensation surround her. On the back of her neck, the tiny downy hairs stood to attention all at once, and she saw a vague, dark shadow slide into the left-hand periphery of her vision. She gasped when a presence of some kind seemed to reach out and stroke her. Fondle her slowly and with complete familiarity, like phantom male fingertips sliding slickly across the tissues of her sex.

As unobtrusively as she could, she turned and looked to her left.

There was a man standing in front of the next exhibit, studying it closely. A man so dark and erotically gorgeous he could've been one of the exhibits himself. Schooling herself not to ogle, Deana concentrated on her catalogue, her mind's eye struggling to 'image' again...image *him* this time, not herself.

Gripping the shiny pages 'til her knuckles went white, she wondered why she felt suddenly 'on display' too. It was as if the man were perusing her intently through the veil of her dress, examining her naked body in the closest of detail even though to all intents and purposes he was looking at a small sepia-work sketch of a woman masturbating.

You're imagining things, Deana, she told herself. You're drunk. He's probably nothing special and not even interested.

Even so, her skin glowed hotter than ever and the blush from her face and throat flowed insidiously down to her sex. Her self-awareness doubled, trebled and quadrupled, and her breasts seemed to swell and look lewdly obvious beneath the skimpy top of her dress. She felt as if someone nearby was playing an X-ray beam across her body and taking salacious pleasure from the fact that – because of the heat – she was wearing precious little in the way of underwear.

Suddenly, she could smell herself too, even though she'd lathered herself in rose-scented skin balm just before she'd come out. With that sombre shadow just inches away, her body smelt musky, sexy and sweaty. A huge blast of pheromones had swamped her feeble perfume, and seemed to be drifting around her like an invisible, mate-calling fog.

As soft footedly as she could, Deana strolled away. The rush of adrenalin had made her dizzy and she needed to find a cloakroom or something where she could spray herself with cologne and try and let her body cool down. Only then dare she come back and find her dark, disruptive stranger. Taking another glass of wine, and resolving to drink cautiously from now on, she scanned her surroundings. There was no obvious sign indicating a ladies room, but she did see a spot she could escape to.

The gallery was a rambling modernistic affair, and what no-one else seemed to have noticed was a balcony, on the first floor, which – judging by its elevation – would have a commanding view of the whole room. From the floor where she stood, Deana could see very little of the upper level, but above the featureless white parapet, the tops of a number of picture frames were visible. There was obviously more art displayed on the wall beyond, so Deana decided to find her way up to the balcony and look at it.

It took her several minutes to find the right stairs, but when she arrived on the balcony the view was disappointing. True, when she stood at the waist-high wall and looked over, she could see the whole of the gallery and its gaggle of smartly dressed 'art lovers', but Mr Tall, Dark and Handsome was stunningly conspicuous by his absence.

'Oh well done, Ferraro,' she muttered, 'he's gone. You should have chatted him up when you had a chance, you twit!'

'Chatted who up?'

The voice from beside her was soft and light with an insidiously husky catch. Pure sex, filtered through human vocal cords, and Deana knew exactly who it belonged to. Slowly, almost reluctantly, she turned around.

Her moments-only impression hadn't done him justice. She'd formed a sketch in her mind but what stood before her was a masterpiece, a living composition more fine and sensual than anything in this mad, bad collection.

'Who were you going to chat up?' her vision in black persisted, but for several seconds all Deana could do was stare at his smiling lips, his large dark eyes, his hands, his body, his crotch. His narrow black eyebrows lifted in enquiry and amusement, and after what seemed like a century she recovered her voice.

'You,' she said sharply, making a split second decision to be her usual unflinching self. He was raw eroticism on two legs, but she wasn't frightened of him. She wanted him, yes – instantly and unequivocably – but she didn't fear him. Although a small voice inside her said she ought to.

'Yes,' she went on as she faced him. Panicking, creatively she said the first thing that came into her head. 'Although "chat up" is purely a figure of speech. You seem to be one of the few people here who is genuinely interested in the exhibits. So I thought it would be nice to "chat you up" and get your opinions. I'm an artist myself and I wanted to compare ... compare my reactions with someone else's.' She paused, flustered, realising that she was rabbiting on and that he was still smiling his slow, indulgent smile. 'You are interested, aren't you?'

'Of course. It's my speciality.' He accompanied this cryptic utterance with an elegant flip of his fingers. Deana noted the slenderness of his hands and how beautifully kept they were, and suddenly she imagined them slipping knowledgeably over her body, seeking out the most sensitive places and stroking her to climax after climax. She could almost see her own juices on his narrow toffee-coloured fingertips.

'Is that a fact?' she answered pertly, feeling the blush rise again, then fall as it had done before, to the place that now yearned for this strange dark man. 'Are you an artist yourself? Do you paint? Or draw?'

'No, sadly I have no talent. I merely observe beauty,' he replied, his eyes roving almost crudely across her body. As his gaze returned to meet hers, Deana met dark, electric-blue fire and was shocked. Not just by the blatant desire there, but by the fact that with his colouring she'd been expecting brown eyes, or grey ones like hers.

The shape of his eyes was unusual too. In a caucasian face, they were slanted, oriental, almost cat-like. Wide-set and with thick, sooty lashes, they had a slight overfolding of the lids at the inner corners. Mr Mystery here had the East not too far back in his heritage, and his eyes bore the epicanthus to prove it.

His hair was also eastern. Steel-black and straight as water, it was smoothed back closely against his head and caught at the nape of his neck in a pony-tail. Its hard, unruffled shine reminded Deana of a seal's coat, but almost instantly, she revised her assessment. Seals were cuddly and playful, and this man just wasn't. He was a shark or a king cobra, hovering to strike or kill, smiling and deadly. Suddenly, she *knew* she should fear him.

'Me too,' she said, responding belatedly. He must think I'm a complete ninny, she thought, annoyed by her own inability to impress. 'Why don't we get together?'

It was a fairly innocuous remark, and yet the dark eyes before her seemed to spark and court her as if she'd asked him to strip naked and take her. 'It'd be a pleasure,' he purred, gesturing towards a nearby painting with that same exotic grace that had affected her so powerfully a moment ago.

Dear heaven, the man's a cliché, Deana thought, as she fell into step beside him. An erotic cliché. The classic 'man in black', posed like an icon against the featureless white walls of the gallery. A dark and handsome stranger who scored ten out of ten for both technical merit and artistic expression – although on closer inspection, there were some minor but telling idiosyncrasies.

8

He was tall, certainly. Using her own five foot seven as a yardstick, Deana estimated him to be about five foot eleven. He was dark, too, not only in his hair and eyes, but also in his skin; which was as smooth as polished wood, its ambery-olive tint another indicator of very Far Eastern origins.

Handsome? Yes, but not in any bland, conventional sense. Her beauty-loving friend was a beauty himself, the near perfection of his features flawed only by a thin white scar that scored his left temple from brow to hairline. This and his strange slanted eyes – so oriental in a western face – set an unassailable new standard of maleness; as did his reddish, rather full-lipped mouth and a nose that was strong and straight, but with an ever-so-slight and impish up-turn.

Almost without thinking, she glanced down towards his groin, wondering what his cock would be like. She'd never set much store by old wives' tales, but with his long slender hands and that bold, pointed nose, she imagined he'd have a penis with similar characteristics. Long but slender, and with a naughty probing glans that would go soul-deep inside a woman and caress her right at her core. He was wearing a pair of tight, narrow-cut, black leather trousers, and where they skimmed his crotch there was a substantial, extenuated bulge that tended to lend credence to her ramblings.

Of course he had to catch her looking . . .

Flicking his gaze down to his own leather covered loins, her companion then panned upwards again, slowly and infuriatingly. His smile was faint but disgustingly and complacently a man's. Without shame, he was cataloguing her charms as thoroughly as she'd checked out his. More so. And for all his beauty and his sensual chemistry, Deana could have quite happily punched him in the mouth.

Men. They were all such vain swines . . . Even if they had every cause to be so.

'Seen enough?' she retorted.

'No. Not really. But then again, the night is young...' The slight smile became a broad bright grin that hit Deana square in the solar plexus – as well as in some other more critical areas. She felt herself heat up. Melt. Run.

'Come along, my dear,' he said, reaching out to take her free hand. 'Let's look at some art instead. The very best exhibits are up here, and you and I have got them all to ourselves.'

He started with surprise when their fingers touched, and Deana smiled, enjoying the tiniest of advantages.

'You're so warm,' he said, taking hold of her hand and stretching out her arm. He seemed to study it as a curious artefact for a moment, then he ran the fingertips of his free hand all the way up from her wrist to her bare shoulders in one smooth, continuous caress. The long stroke felt deliciously soft and cool, but she knew that to him, her flesh would feel hot. 'Do you have a fever? Or is it something else?' His dark blue gaze bored into her, as if ordering her to say *he* was the source of the heat.

Deana didn't give him the satisfaction. 'I have a higher than normal body temperature. It's a family trait. It's nothing to do with you, if that's what you're thinking.' Realising she was still clutching her glass of wine, she raised it to her lips for Dutch courage.

But before she could drink, her companion took the glass from her, and proposed a toast.

'Here's to heat then,' he murmured softly, 'especially hot women.' He took a sip of her wine, his brown throat undulating voluptuously as it went down, then he held the glass to *her* lips, touching her mouth with its chilly rim and forcing her to drink down its contents.

Something went flip in Deana's belly. Men never treated her like this, they were usually slightly in awe of her. But this dark stranger had bent her to his will in the simplest of ways within only a few minutes of meeting him. She drank obediently until the glass was empty, then stood like a doll as he swooped down, placed it on the floor beside them, then stood up again just as quickly and wiped her lips with a flick of his fingers.

'What's your name, fellow art-lover?' he asked, his velvet voice far more potent than the wine.

'D—' She almost said it, but in the micro-second before she completed her name, her interior alarm bell started clanging. Maybe it didn't matter, but wasn't she supposed to be 'Delia' here?

'Dee,' she answered after a momentary pause. 'People call me "Dee".'

It was true, she did get called 'Dee' – and Delia got it too, especially when people weren't quite sure which twin they were with.

'And people call me "Jake",' her companion replied, sliding his arm around her shoulders before she could stop him and turning her bodily towards the nearest exhibit. 'So, Dee, what you do think of this?'

'This' was a frighteningly beautiful oil painting; the best thing she'd seen in the gallery and by far the most disturbing. Especially now, here, with this audacious Jake who was stroking the tender skin of her shoulder as if they were lovers and had been for years.

Against the Parapet showed a masked woman, bent from the waist over a low, white plastered wall, and being taken from behind by a dark-haired, broad-shouldered man. His rumpled jeans indicated that he was unzipped in front, but otherwise the man was fully clothed. The woman, in contrast, was bared from the middle of her back to her ankles, her soft red dress bunched ruthlessly at her shoulders and her panties a crumpled blur and still draped around her feet. Her pale thighs and buttocks, where they could be seen behind her assailant, were criss-crossed with thin streaks of pink – implying that she'd been recently and cruelly beaten. She was handcuffed, and her thin wrists, crossed at the small of her back, seemed to command the eye more than any other part of the painting. It wasn't clear if she was being buggered or simply screwed. It didn't seem to matter.

'Glorious, isn't it?' said Jake from behind Deana, his fingers drifting from her shoulder to the warm bare skin of her back. She felt the cuff of his silk shirt brush delicately against her, then his hand slide slowly around the curve of her rib cage to settle on her breast like a feather.

Deana registered both his touch and the smoky arousal of his voice, but her attention was still claimed by the painting. The woman's face was barely sketched, but her attitude was not one of suffering. On the contrary, her willowy body was supremely sensuous and the marks on her smooth white skin were more like marks of pleasure than of pain. The man who was taking her was a cipher – a dark animal form, an accessory to the woman's enjoyment rather than a protagonist in his own right.

And yet, somehow, the black shape seemed familiar. She didn't dare turn and look at him, but Deana could almost imagine that the long, dark marauder was Jake.

The pressure of his fingers on her nipple dragged her rudely back from her imaginings. He'd taken the stiffly swollen stalk between his thumb and one finger and was swirling it slowly but determinedly. Deana could hardly believe what was happening. Or that she was letting it happen. Or, worse still, that she was responding to it purely on instinct, her hips slowly weaving as the pinching of her nipple transferred itself directly to her aching clitoris – the sensation remote but identical.

'Does it arouse you?' Jake asked, his warm breath flowing across her neck as his free hand lifted her hair and his mouth settled lightly on her shoulder. She felt his teeth against her skin, very hard and deadly, then a single touch of his tongue. But just when she thought he was going to bite her, he let her hair fall back into place and reached around her to enclose her other breast.

'Does it arouse you, Dee?' he repeated, gently kneading her, cupping the soft weight of her flesh, and holding both nipples in his fingers now. She'd no idea whether he meant the painting or the way he was holding her, and she didn't much care. She heard herself sigh 'yes' in the affirmative to either.

'Good,' he whispered, and in a move of total vulgarity, he pressed the jut of his erection into the cotton-covered cleft of her buttocks.

Deana knew she should try to break free, but instead her body swayed backwards to caress him, gripping at his hardness with the cheeks of her bottom, the gesture as gross as his had been. Under her thin dress she wore only a G-string, and as Jake's penis poked rudely at her rear, she could feel a single strand of furled silk being rubbed like a goad against her anus.

She whimpered, trapped between two powerful poles of sensation: his brisk workman-like mauling of her sensitised breasts and the slower, richer, more subversive stimulation of her bottom. He was bouncing her on himself now, and as she gasped and put her hand to her unattended crotch, she heard him laugh like a devil in her ear.

'Yes, Dee, do it,' he urged. 'Stroke yourself, you know you want to. The picture's turned you on, hasn't it? Touch yourself, Dee, touch your clitoris. I can hear your pussy crying for it ... Go on, Dee, caress yourself. Do it!'

His words compelled her as much as her yearning body did.

The situation was unreal, surreal, not of this world – and in this altered erotic state, there seemed no valid reason to defy him. Bunching the cotton of her dress, she drew it up past her knees, her thighs, then her belly. Clutching it inelegantly at her waist, she put her free hand to her groin and pushed her fingers beneath the lace of her G-string. Her sex-lips were puffed open in readiness and the whole of her groove was awash with hot wet slickness.

'Are you wet, Dee?'

Weak at the knees, she nodded and stirred gently at her own thick fluids.

'Show me.'

She felt her sex pulsate beneath her touch, then shiver with need as she raised up her fingertips and held them shimmering before her own face and Jake's.

'Taste yourself,' he ordered.

Her flavour was pungent, salty, oceanic, and as she licked her fingers hungrily, she was astounded how much she savoured it. She'd tasted her own juices before, but never with such relish, or for a man.

'Now give *me* your taste.'

She reached down again, scooped up her nectar on two fingers and lifted it this time to Jake's lips. He leaned forward, his chin over her shoulder, and as he sucked the aromatic offering, she caught an intoxicating whiff of his cologne – a heady floral blend that for a moment even drowned out the odour of her sex. She smelt lavender and lily of the valley, so strong and stupefying that she swayed backwards, pressing harder against him, her nether cheeks dividing around the unyielding bulge of his prick.

'Yes,' he purred, then sucked like a baby on her fingers. Almost swooning, Deana had no way of knowing if it was her flavour he was applauding or the pillowy caress of her bottom. As he ground himself against her, she felt his tongue move mockingly against her fingertips, licking and darting in a sly imitation of cunnilingus.

'Look at the picture, pretty Dee,' he whispered as he reached up, took her hand, and drew it back down to her groin. Guiding her, he made her touch herself again, press her fingertip against her clitoris as he slipped two fingers of his own into the swimming channel of her vagina. 'Look at it. Isn't that what you want? Right here? With me?' His fingers waggled slightly and she moaned, the sound echoing betrayingly along the narrow balcony. Any second now some curious soul might turn the corner onto this deserted level and find a woman being vigorously masturbated, a man's hands moving at her breast and her sex.

This was bizarre. An hallucination. It had to be. She'd met this man literally minutes ago and now she was fingering her own body for him, rubbing herself at his command, giving herself pleasure to please *him* – while his own fingers were deep inside her. She rippled around him while her mind fought to believe what was happening. Her clitoris leapt beneath her touch, a throbbing blip, a promise of even better things to come.

'Yes, Dee, you do want it.' His voice was very quiet but utterly triumphant. The tiny, beautiful pre-orgasm had given her away completely. 'And you shall have it, my sweet girl. There against that little wall over there. Just like in the picture.' He lifted his hand from her breast to her chin, tilting up her face so she could do nothing but stare at the unbearably stimulating painting. 'Say yes, Dee,' he cajoled, flexing his supple wrist and plunging even deeper into her.

Her mind, her better judgement was screaming, 'No! Break

away! Slap his face and run!' But she heard herself sob a faint, broken 'Yes'. Nothing else seemed possible . . .

'Come with me then.'

She expected him to remove his hand, take his fingers out of her body. But she blushed with mortification when he led her to the parapet just as she was: still penetrated, still immolated. Edging her towards the low wall, he almost steered her by her sex, his thumb taking control of her clitoris, using little dabs of pressure to guide her.

It was humiliating, but she couldn't help responding. Responding with a fervour she'd never felt in her more egalitarian sexual encounters. She'd always had the upper hand with her men, either by her wiles or the sheer force of personality. But here, with Jake, she was simply a hungry female creature he could manipulate. An object. A body. Flesh for his amusement. She'd never felt more alive and ready for sex in her life. She was sandwiched between his hand and his prodding erection and both of them enflamed her.

'Lift your dress,' he instructed when they reached the waist-high, white-painted barrier. Below them the glittering assembly still laughed and drank and tried to be blasé about the red hot art on the walls – all the time totally oblivious that a far more outrageous tableau was being enacted above them.

Someone was going to look up, she was sure of it; and even if they could only see the upper part of her, the motion of lovemaking, the jerking, the leap of a body being thrust into, were all things that were impossible to mistake. How long, she wondered wildly, could she and Jake hope to remain alone?

'Please, no,' she pleaded, her voice hoarse.

'Please, yes,' he hissed back at her, a core of steel in the soft, sibilant sound. 'Lift your dress, Dee. You know it's what you want.' She made a murmur of protest when he reached down to begin the process himself; but nevertheless, she took hold of her full flowing skirt and raised it hesitantly to her waist.

'All of it, Dee.'

Handling the cloth clumsily, she managed to get it all out of the way, deeply embarrassed that the minuscule G-string was her only garment beneath and that the fruit-smooth rounds of her bottom were now on full display.

'Sublime . . .' She felt a fingertip trace its way across one full globe, dip into her uncovered crevice, then slide out again and delineate the other firm cheek. Without warning, he hooked his thumbs through the elastic at her waist and began teasing it downwards. In a couple of seconds he had the silly, ineffectual garment right down around her knees, and with his own knee, he nudged open her legs, stretching the scrap of black lace into an obscene elasticated bridge.

In her mind's eye she saw her own silky-skinned bottom, gleaming pale and nude like the woman's in the picture. There were no cane marks on her, but already she felt branded in other ways. This man had laid hands on her, had his fingers in her, and deep in some secret recess of her heart she knew she could never be the same again.

She felt a simmering heat both without and within her; her sex-flesh was naked now and shining wet. A trickle of love-juice ran like honey down her leg, and she could feel its slow explicit track as it crawled across her skin. Behind her, Jake would be able to see it, dribbling in plain sight down the smooth inner sweep of her thigh. She'd never seeped like this before, and she knew – without knowing why – that Jake himself was fully aware of the fact.

He was light on his feet, but she sensed him step closer. His hands gripped her bare buttocks and mounded them, just as he'd mounded her breasts.

'Beautiful,' he sighed into her ear, squeezing the taut resilient flesh, then shifting it and massaging it in slow insulting circles that made her weep with shame . . . then climax with forbidden excitement. The sensation peaked unbearably when he opened her cheeks almost painfully wide and seemed to peer at the rose of her anus.

'Beautiful,' he whispered again, the word so tangible it seemed as if he'd touched her there, right on the tiny quivering hole.

She knew then that the woman in the picture was being buggered. It wasn't shown, it was just ancient female instinct that told her. The same instinct that told her Jake knew it too, that he had some special knowledge of the painting and its origins – and that he wanted to reproduce it, make it real on this balcony.

'No! Oh, please,' she gasped, but he was already too close, already unzipping: the sharp rasping sound a raw threat. 'Please, not that! Not here!'

As he leaned over her back, she was forced forward against the parapet and had to take her weight on one hand because the other was still clutching at her skirt. Beyond speech, she made a tiny mewing sound, a squeak of perfect fear.

'It's all right, my sweet Dee,' he reassured, his gentle tone more menacing than harshness would have been. 'Not here. Not now. But soon though . . .' She felt his penis sliding across her soft rear furrow, teasing the orifice that trembled in terror of his entry. He felt so big, so slippery . . . The velvet skin of his glans was hot even to her, the one who should've felt it as cool. Repeatedly and wickedly, the rounded bulb probed impudently at her bottom, and as the mass of it pressed and almost entered, then slid away down her long juicy niche, she felt an irrational twinge of regret.

She'd been so scared he'd bugger her, scared of the pain, and even more scared of the huge loss of dignity; but now it wasn't going to happen she almost wanted it. It had been some years since she'd been a virgin, but suddenly with this strange new man, this vision, this presence from out of nowhere, she wanted something fresh to give. Something new and untouched that Jake could have the first bite of.

But before she could properly analyse her feelings, he was taking her, his long stiff penis forcing its way into her vagina, her satin membranes yielding exquisitely to his hot living bulk. Inclining her body forward, she felt faint, disorientated, aware only – for several long seconds – of his member pushing in, in, in; its entry long and sweet and total as his fingers crept down across her belly, then plunged into her bush, seeking and finding her clitoris. Her flesh jumped around him as he touched it, her inner walls twitching and caressing him of their own accord. She suppressed her groans, came softly, and felt the deepest, most female jubilation when he gasped against her ear in his pleasure.

'You're a hot little minx, my Dee,' he whispered, rotating his hips once, then sliding his fingers to and fro over her bud. She tasted blood in her mouth from sinking her teeth into her own lip. What he was doing was too great to be borne in silence, and yet she could not and must not cry out. The people below were waiting for her screams, waiting for her to moan out her ecstasy as he tantalised her tiny clitoral bead, worked it clear of its protecting hood, and flicked and pinched it until she wove her hips helplessly in response.

He was cooing softly against the back of her neck, gentling her in the way a skilled horseman would calm a restive filly. He was quieting her and soothing her, murmuring encouragements to pacify her, and all the time his fingertip moved relentlessly on the intimate nexus of her pleasure.

Deana felt as if her body was disassembling itself and breaking down into its constituent fluids. Tears trickled down her cheeks, sweat pooled in her armpits, between her breasts and in her groin, and her love-juice was running so freely around Jake's rigid cock that it overflowed out of her sex and seeped down her legs in silvery, slow-moving streams.

'I . . . I can't,' she whispered, her voice barely audible but what there was of it broken and panting.

'Yes, my Dee, you can,' was his answer as his fingertips rocked inexorably. To her dazed astonishment, she realised he'd barely even moved inside her yet; he'd entered to an unbelievable depth, stretching her tight, clingy passage in a way she'd rarely, if ever, experienced, but since his first long slow thrust he'd been still. Stock still, as if better to enjoy *her* spasms.

'Yes, you can, Dee,' he repeated implacably. 'I'm going to screw you now. And you're going to climax and you're going to want to yell and screech and howl.' He swirled his pelvis, and Deana had to drop the folds of her dress and cram her fist into her mouth to stop herself shouting. Sliding his free arm around her middle he pulled her back against him and sideways, then lowered their still joined bodies to the floor.

Pitching forward, elbows on the polished wood surface and her sweating face pressed against her forearm, Deana bit down on her own flesh as Jake began to thrust hard and fast. He was holding her hips steady to brace her, and it didn't seem to matter that he wasn't now touching her clitoris. Every push, every heave, every shove of his penis inside her seemed to impact on a screaming knot of nerves.

Climaxing hugely and continuously, her womb beating and pulsing against the marauding rod that possessed her, Deana felt her soul rise up and soar free. In that magnificent, almost crystalline moment, it no longer seemed necessary to cry out. She was floating like a star in a world of silent white glory, quite detached from her thrashing body and the dark force that was over and in her . . . Across the vastness of space, she heard Jake cry out very softly and felt his penis throb deep inside her.

It was the first time she'd really *felt* a man ejaculating inside her, felt his balls tighten at the moment of exquisiteness, and her mind came spinning back from the void to give it her whole attention. He was inundating her body with rapturous feelings, his jerking throbbing pleasure blending with hers and creating an entirely new beast altogether. She allowed herself to sob, to groan quietly, to whisper absurd thanks to her violator even as his weapon pulsed slowly inside her.

As they drew apart, she imagined a picture: two black clad forms rutting furiously on a polished wood floor, the most erotic image in the gallery, living sex, a command performance. She no longer cared if they'd been seen or heard; in fact she was surprised, as she struggled to her feet, to find that they were still alone. Pulling up her G-string she cringed at the wetness of her vulva. The juices. The sweat. She was awash, and she could feel it all flowing down her legs. Her silly flimsy underwear was soaked and she'd have to find somewhere private to clean herself.

Her legs weak, she turned towards Jake. He was leaning with his back against the parapet, his leather trousers still unzipped, his soft, gleaming cock still exposed. Seeing it for the first time, Deana blushed irrationally, then grabbed for her shoulder bag that had long since fallen to the floor. The swish of her skirts, as she straightened up, seemed to wake him from a post-coital stupor, but he said not a word, his thin, conqueror's smile bringing home the full enormity of what she'd just allowed to happen.

God, I must be mad! I've let myself be used by a total stranger for a moment's satisfaction . . . I'm a whore. A slut. A pick-up. And an easy, available screw.

'Excuse me . . . Please . . . I'm sorry,' she babbled, wondering what on earth she was apologising for as she virtually ran along the balcony towards the stairs. She was searching for a sanctuary from Jake's sated and mocking smile, but she knew there was no such haven. Nowhere to hide from the bare reality of a penis still wet with her juices.

It took some time to tidy herself up.

Jake's essence slid out of her as fast as she could wipe herself, and in the end she crumpled her ruined G-string into a ball and took comfort that her long full skirt would hide the evidence of her sins: her wet, pulpy quim, her swollen labia and the semen drying stickily on her thighs.

Deana didn't usually need much make-up, but what she had put on tonight had been ruined. Her mascara was all over her cheeks and she'd chewed off her last scrap of lipstick. Taking more time than she actually needed, she reapplied everything, working slowly and meticulously to delay the moment when she'd have to leave this opulent bolthole and face the man who'd possessed her.

But when she did finally emerge, he wasn't there to be faced.

As discreetly as she could, she searched the balcony, the corridors, and the main body of the gallery. A couple of times she imagined she saw him – a lean sleek figure in black silk and leather – but it was just as much an illusion as the exhibits themselves were.

The bastard, she thought, hating him as passionately as she'd enjoyed his hard, dark body. He's gone . . . He's had me and now he's buggered off and left me!

Bereft of its most truly erotic component, the gallery full of dirty pictures had suddenly lost all its charm. Wine was still being served, but Deana felt repelled by even the thought of drinking. Rolling up her catalogue, she made her way slowly out into the hot night air.

As she stood on the pavement, debating between a taxi and the Tube, a strange and perplexing thought occurred to her...

Somewhere in this crazy, boiling city was a man called Jake who'd made love to her. She touched her fingers to her lips, remembering the orgasms and the pleasure, and realised that not once during the whole insane experience had he put his mouth against hers and kissed her.

2

A Prince in the City

I'm being possessed by the Devil, I must be! thought Delia Ferraro in the darkness.

Behind her tightly closed eyes she saw a handsome, yet indistinct face, the long bronzed column of a man's strong body, and – as it loomed above her – the beauty of his full, naked sex.

Soundlessly, like the dream of perfection he was, the man slid in between her wide open thighs, found the tropical place that wanted him, then thrust deeply and surely inside her. To the hilt. The bulk of his flesh was considerable and he stretched her, but with a broken sigh of pleasure, she lifted up her hips to encourage him.

Don't speak! Oh, please, my Prince, don't speak! she begged him silently as he started to move. Her body was quickening, soaring up the slope towards orgasm, but as the elusive silvery heaviness formed around his sliding organ, she knew that any second it could be snatched away from her. Dissolved by words. Her need to climax was like a rage in her flesh, but it was delicate and friable too. If her lover spoke, her pleasure could be torn clean away, dismantled, destroyed. She'd be high and dry, left hanging – unmoved.

But the spirits smiled, just as they'd done last night, and the inner image of her gorgeous dark Prince stayed clear and strong and true. And for the second time in a row, the amalgam of her own mind and physical reality obeyed her. The toiling man above her groaned and gasped and moaned, but didn't speak. He murmured with satisfaction as he worked in deeper, but mercifully the sounds remained guttural.

Two grabbing hands held her bottom in a spasmic grip, and as the pace of thrusting increased, Delia felt a moment of pure panic. She wasn't quite ready. It was too soon. The Prince's face faded to a featureless blank and the curtained harem of her fantasy wavered and grew faint.

No! Not now! Don't leave, she begged, aware on a more cognisant level that she was pleading with her own imagination. Wriggling in her lover's hold, she pushed her fingers down between her sweating body and his and sought out the cleft of her labia. There was a grunt of disapproval in her ear, but Delia ignored it. With a giant effort of will she summoned her sweet dark secret fantasy to her bosom, then pressed hard on her own throbbing clitoris – pounding at the tiny wet bead with a ferocity that made her corporeal partner redundant.

As her fevered flesh leapt she made a small sound of relief, and in her mind, the finger in her furrow became the Prince's. After a couple of seconds, it turned magically into his tongue, pointed and moist, flickering and dancing for her pleasure.

The pictures she saw were clear and unbearably sweet. Before they'd been simple interior visuals, but now their texture was totally integrated. She could hear words now, but they were coming from within. 'Sublime' a soft voice purred, and on the screen behind her eyes she got a micro-second flash of her dark lord's face. It was the first time she'd seen it so clearly, and the image was so erotic that she almost climaxed. It was gone again before her pleasure-soaked senses could imprint it though, leaving only an impression in its wake: a fancy, a memory, one of her sister's sketches ... and crazily, an odour. An intoxicating blend of heavy blooming flowers that came not from the room she was lying in but from the harem of her mind and her dreams.

And as orgasm drafted through her, her last sense gave up its gift. Clamping her knuckle in her teeth to keep in her screams, she tasted not her own hot skin, but the unmistakable flavour of man – the pungent tang of stiff sexual flesh and the fluids that leaked and flowed from it.

For one instant, as she came, she could have sworn that she'd tasted the Prince.

Russell hadn't liked it. He hadn't liked it one bit. And as Delia stood in the shower, sluicing her body with water and still feeling hot, she realised that a lot of her heat came from anger.

What on earth was wrong with him? Most men went wild for enthusiasm in bed, but not her Mister Prissy Russell. He only seemed to like it when she was passive. In the beginning it hadn't been a problem; they'd seemed so well suited in other ways that the less than glorious sex hadn't been high on their agenda.

But sometime in the last few weeks, Delia had changed. Or her libido had. She couldn't pin down the beginning of this metamorphosis, but all she knew was that now she wanted good sex and lots of it. She wanted orgasms aplenty. She wanted exciting, active bed-play and all the noise and histrionics that went with it, and every dreary uninspiring event she shared with Russell only made her crave mayhem even more.

She'd sought the advice of her sister, of course. Deana was fifteen minutes younger but several millennia ahead in sexual experience, and she had given two simple pieces of advice. The first was a blunt 'chuck the miserable bastard!' – a drastic measure that Delia was rapidly beginning to consider. The second was that Delia should fantasise more, both in bed and out of it. She'd embraced this idea immediately. Hence the arrival of the 'Prince'.

He was a classic stereotype, she realised, but he worked so well for her that she didn't worry about it. Her macho cliché of sexual fantasy could inject far more thrills into her than Russell's real life penis had ever done. The Prince was tall, dark, undefined maleness: lean-bodied, large-sexed, phantasmagorical yet strangely real when she opened her mind to him. Following Deana's instructions, she thought about him before sex, during sex, and after sex ... and at a lot of other times in between. She'd never once – except for that one split second this morning – seen his face, but she knew every last nuance of his erotic *modus operandi*.

The Prince liked a noisy orgasmic response and went out of his way to evoke it. He used his hands and mouth on her body and sex for hours and hours and hours before even suggesting he penetrate her. The time dynamics of fantasy were conveniently accommodating, however, and this delicious preparation could be miraculously compressed into the few minutes it took Russell to get through his usual in-out-shake-it-all-about.

And that's what'd happened this morning – in the degrading quickie that Russell had unexpectedly wheedled out of her before work. He'd muttered something about 'giving her oats for her birthday' and to keep the peace she'd succumbed, then reached out for her fantasy.

Tripping on her new-found drug, Delia had had the Prince in bed with her, the Prince sliding like a god into the hot, slick depths of her vagina; and she'd cried out, made a fuss, and had a huge, mind-bendingly toe-curling orgasm.

But she'd got the cold shoulder afterwards and that had made her angry, so angry. She'd had sex when – initially – she hadn't wanted to. She'd made herself late for work at a time when punctuality and super-efficiency were crucial, and all the thanks she'd got was a fit of the sulks.

Oh God, this was no good! Anger at Russell was rebounding inside her in the strangest of ways. She felt aroused again. Hot. With no conscious effort, she summoned the Prince again and bade him share her steamy shower. The weather was crazy for May, and even though it was only seven-thirty in the morning she could feel herself sweating into the water. It felt like she was melting from the bones outward, softening in the heat, both within and without. Her whole body felt loose and malleable, the only areas of tension were the places where the Prince was sovereign: her aching nipples and the heavy, puffed up place between her legs. With a moan of resignation, she reached down to touch herself. She'd be late anyway, so she might as well be hung for a sheep etc. etc. As her sticky sex yielded open its flower, she received a small malicious pang of extra pleasure. If she stayed in the shower masturbating, she'd make Russell late too.

It's just you and me, my Liege, she murmured, bowing open her thighs, and letting the Prince lend magic to her own long fingers. As she stroked lightly at her clitoris, it was his gracious hand that stirred her, his dexterity that took the breath from her body and all shred of reason from her mind. She leaned hard against the streaming shower wall, pressing her breasts and belly to its sheeny surface, then tilting her hips to jam her fingers in harder between her legs. She could no longer believe it was her own hand moving at her crotch; the vulnerable flesh itself said it was the Prince's long, bronzed body she was shimmying against, his strong chest that stimulated her nipples, and his swollen penis that was pushing between her sex-lips and rubbing her.

Surging against the ineffectual coolness of the tiles, she summoned up his final fabulous outrage. With her tender bud still caught between her fingertips, and her breasts still flattened and crushed, she curved her free hand around between the cheeks of her bottom. In her glorious eastern dream, the Prince fell to his knees behind her and began sucking voraciously at her anus. As she feathered the tiny aperture, it was her dark invader that licked and pushed and stabbed with his tongue, boring it inside her as if intending to meet and mate with the pleasure in her pulsing clitoris.

'Oh yes, oh yes, oh yes,' she whispered, water running into her mouth as she slid in a heap down the wall, her fingers still working, working, working . . .

Delia was later than she'd feared. Late, out of sorts and feeling far less than immaculate on a day when she should've looked faultless.

As she'd steered her car through the morning rush-hour traffic, she'd felt grubby already in spite of her extended shower. The fact that she'd been dragged out of a clandestine afterglow by a peevish Russell had only added insult to injury. Finishing with him was an unpleasant task to be faced, but as she finally negotiated the lifts and corridors of the de Guile Tower, it slipped in her league of pending problems. Top of the list was the fact that due to Russell and his 'birthday dinner' she was wearing the same work clothes as yesterday. Obsessive about a daisy-fresh outfit each day, this had never happened to Delia before. She wished to God now that she'd put her foot down last night and gone to the art exhibition as she'd intended. Or at least insisted on going home after sex!

On any other day, she would've nipped out mid-morning and gone home to change. But today wasn't just any day. The big boss was in residence. The boss of all bosses, visiting his UK holdings. Jackson K. de Guile – the 'de Guile' in de Guile International and the de Guile Tower. Even now, he could be perusing her personnel file in his penthouse office – the near-mythic eyrie that sat atop the imposing structure in which Delia worked. Her own office was several dozen floors below, but she could be summoned skywards at any moment. 'Random informal interviews of key personnel' was the word on the grapevine and Murphy's law predicted that Delia Ferraro, Divisional Administration Manager, be called in just when she was wearing yesterday's suit, no tights and some distinctly uneasy-making underwear. Taking a grateful swig of the coffee her secretary had ready for her, she dove straight for the women's rest room as soon as she arrived on her floor.

Appraising herself in the mirror, Delia saw that all things considered, she really didn't look too bad.

Her hair and make-up were as neat and cool-looking as this insane weather would allow. Luckily she kept a small supply of toiletries at Russell's for the rare occasions when she stayed over. With these she'd been able to paint, perfume and deodorise herself to her usual fastidious standards. She was fortunate too, in that even though her conker-coloured hair was riotously thick and wavy, she had an inborn 'knack' for taming it. She could always coax it into one or another of various sleek, 'power' hairstyles, and today's was a coil at the nape of her neck. With a slight, clever twist in the pull-back, she'd smoothed in all the wayward tendrils without the need for any lacquer or spray.

Oh God, why was it so hot? Taking a small pressed powder compact from her bag, Delia dabbed at the faint traces of shine on her brow, her upper lip and her chin. It was a nightmare staying fresh when it was like this. She felt sleazy and used; faintly animalistic, as if the unnatural heat were putting her 'on heat' too. Was it a coincidence that her new cravings for sex were matched by the record-breaking temperatures?

Staring at her slightly flushed face, Delia wished she could sometimes be more like Deana. Sister dear didn't bother about conventional bandbox turnout at the best of times, but when it was hot she'd just fling on some skimpy old vest-like frock, or maybe a semi-transparent skirt and camisole, then blithely sally forth with just the tiniest pair of knickers underneath. If that! And even though this just wasn't Delia's 'thing', she had to admit that her feckless, free-wheeling twin always ended up looking like a goddess. A new age nymph, as laid back and sensual as it was possible to be, and always, repeat always, ready for sex.

Sex! Oh damn! Not that again! Delia smoothed her fingers over her navy blue linen skirt and wondered what the heat-wave was doing to her hormones. Here she was, on possibly the most important business day of her life, with a pivotal interview ahead, and she was already having carnal thoughts again. Carnal in the form of a dusky mental intruder who both improved her sex-life with Russell and showed her how utterly pathetic it really was.

And that was another thing! For a fairly sexless sort of man, Russell had surprised her with a strangely salacious birthday present: a gift she'd had to wear this morning because she had no clean underwear to put on.

It felt very peculiar to be wearing a pair of lemon silk cami-knickers beneath her tailored suit, instead of the usual M&S cottons. She was disturbingly aware of its lace-encrusted bodice delicately stimulating her nipples; and worse still, the feel of a fragile popper-fastened gusset working its way slowly but insidiously into her sexual furrow. Every movement seemed to tighten it against her inner lips and clitoris and she hardly dare imagine what state the garment might be in. It was so flimsy and she was sweating and already lightly aroused again. Not to mention the fact she'd had sex twice in the last twelve hours ... She was just about to slip into a cubicle and make some intimate adjustments when there was a sharp panicky rapping at the cloakroom door.

'Delia! Please! Come quickly,' squeaked her secretary, Susie, almost tumbling into the room. 'De Guile's PA just called. You're next! He wants you upstairs now for your "informal chat".'

A million ominous thoughts occurred to Delia as she ascended in the lift, and most of them were self-recriminations.

Why hadn't she had the guts to go home and change? Surely she could've cooked up some excuse? What on earth had possessed her *not* to go to the big man's art exhibition? It was another of de Guile's disquietingly 'random' things, but he was bound to ask the recipient of his invitation what she thought of his collection. Unfortunately for Delia, only Deana could answer that question!

Most of all, why hadn't she done herself a favour and found out a bit more about the mysterious de Guile himself? He owned the company she worked for and was one of the wealthiest men in the world, yet she'd no idea what he looked like or even how old he was.

She tried to imagine him while she waited outside his office. To picture someone so powerful and so unthinkably rich. Logic suggested he'd look like Ross Perot or one of those silver-haired tycoons from the glamorous 'soaps'. But the only image Delia could summon was—

'He'll see you now, Mizz Ferraro,' murmured de Guile's bland, super-competent secretary.

Delia's heart started bouncing and her bloodstream flushed with adrenalin. This was stupid! He was only a man, and probably a boring old stick at that. She was good at her job, superlative in fact. What the devil had she got to worry about? And even if he did ask about the flaming exhibition, it wasn't a hanging offence to give your invitation to your sister, was it?

The office she entered was immense. From where she stood, it appeared to run the entire width of the building, and its sole occupant was a man sitting reading at a large and distant desk. A dark-haired man, who seemed engrossed in a file that lay open before him. A man whose eyes were masked by a pair of gold-framed reading glasses and whose height and body were obscured by both his clothing and the wide expanse of leather-topped wood in front of him. A man who by all that was sane and understandable in the world, should've been a total stranger...but it was the man who Delia had kissed and caressed and been possessed by in virtually all her waking dreams for the past few sex-obsessed weeks.

And as 'The Prince' rose elegantly to his feet and walked smoothly towards her, holding out his hand in welcome, Delia felt the same old instant sexual response she always felt.

For several seconds, she could neither think, speak nor breathe, and afterwards she often wondered how she had been able to stand.

The man wasn't real but he was *here*. This was the hard, bleak prosaic City, not the sumptuous harem of her fantasies – but it was still *him*. It was his face she'd seen in that split-second this morning; and in a notion of pure outrageousness, she knew that if she knelt at his feet now, unzipped his perfectly tailored trousers and sucked him, it'd be the same flesh she'd tasted in her fantasy.

Before her stood the stereotype, the cliché, the archetype of everything that had ever been tall, dark and handsome. A man with the mouth, the hands and the body which had initiated the entirety of her sexual pleasure since the very first moment she'd dreamed him up.

'Delia Ferraro,' he said softly, his intonation familiar in every meaning of the word. 'How do you feel today? You look a little surprised to see me.'

Delia's head was whirling. This was crazy. He didn't know her. They were *her* dreams, not his! How could he know what he was to her?

'I...I'm sorry,' she muttered, feeling genuinely dizzy. 'You're...You're not what I expected. I—'

The rest wouldn't come out because great puffs of soft white light seemed to be exploding between her and de Guile. The morning heat was murder already, even in this air-conditioned haven, and suddenly it all seemed to swirl up and envelop Delia. She was definitely going to faint in the next few seconds, but just as the swaying started and the carpet seemed to tilt precariously, she felt herself being swept up off her feet and carried effortlessly across the width of the room. Almost before she could analyse precisely what had happened she was set down on a big squashy leather sofa that stood to one side in a kind of 'conversation' area; a set of opulent modern couches and armchairs arranged around a glass-topped coffee table, and standing by a breathtaking, window-on-the-city view. With her vision still impaired, much of this was lost on Delia, but in a couple of moments, she felt a glass of water being put against her lips, and a strong hand sliding behind her head, encouraging her to drink.

The water was cool and had a faint mineral sparkle – and it was this subtle effervescence that returned her to her senses. Blinking furiously, she managed to focus on the man who was now sitting beside her, his dark, besuited knees almost touching her bare and stockingless ones.

'All right now?' de Guile's light, velvety voice was as incredible as his looks. And as familiar. Delia had a manic, almost unbearable urge to ask him to say the word 'sublime' for her, but as her wits returned she thought better of it.

'Yes, thanks, I'm fine now,' she said as calmly as she could.

'I'm sorry about what happened just now, Mr de Guile. It's this heat . . . I can't seem to get used to it.'

'Mr de Guile?' Jet black eyebrows shot up in amusement – although for the life of her, Delia couldn't work out why. It *was* his name when all was said and done!

'How formal we are today, Mizz Ferraro.' He chuckled quietly, then without warning reached out to take the glass from her shaking hand. When he'd put it aside, he took hold of the hand again, and ran his thumb in a slow, sensuous circle around the centre of her palm. 'So warm,' he whispered. 'But it doesn't say anything about this in your personnel file, Dee, does it?' The thumb stilled and slid away, and as it did de Guile raised her trembling hand to his lips and placed a kiss on the area he'd stroked.

As moisture spread across the hot landscape of her palm, she felt it in other places too. Between her legs, her sex rippled against the soft constriction of the camiknickers, and though her mind seemed temporarily unable to function, her hormones were firing and flowing. De Guile's tongue moved and she moaned, transported instantly back to fantasy and the Prince. She was lying on a bed, her hot back pinned against silk, as the Prince pressed his face between her splayed thighs. The dream, and the sensations, were so real that she shuffled on the leather seat, unconsciously sliding her slim skirt up the naked length of her thighs. Making ready . . .

'Mr de Guile! Please!' she squeaked, and snatched back her hand. He'd started sucking her palm and it felt obscenely erotic. 'I . . . I thought I was here to talk about work . . . About my performance ratio . . .'

'My sweet Dee,' he breathed against her hand, 'I know all I need to know about your performance.' He paused then and straightened up, pulling off his golden glasses and placing them on the coffee table.

Delia suppressed a gasp of surprise.

In her sexual dreams, she'd always had the impression that the Prince had brown eyes – to match his coal-black hair and his richly swarthy skin. Jackson de Guile had both the dark, lustrous locks of her phantom lover, and his toasted coppery complexion – but she saw now that his eyes smashed the pattern completely. They were blue. Deep deep blue. The blue of a storm-tossed eastern ocean and glittering intensely.

More than this, they were a curious shape too; long and almond-shaped, slanting up at the outer corners and slightly hooded at the inner. She knew his middle name was Kazuto, but she'd not expected his Japaneseness to be so physically apparent.

The total effect was shocking. He'd first locked himself into her fantasy then visibly deviated from it. Suddenly she felt lost. Out on a limb. Adrift in a strange sexual land where the signposts were rapidly disintegrating.

'Didn't you realise I wore glasses?' he enquired, blinking once as if to emphasise the exotic submarine brilliance of his gaze. 'I wear them for reading. And I've just been reading your file, Dee. Very carefully.'

'Why?' she asked, unable to disguise her stare, and wondering why on earth he kept calling her 'Dee'. The company personnel files were fairly comprehensive, but to her knowledge they'd never listed nicknames. There was something very weird going on here, she decided, but faced with the living embodiment of her dreams, she felt powerless to shape proper questions.

But he was more than the dreams. And different . . . He had all the beauty that was *de rigueur* for a sexual fantasy, but had the Prince had that thin white scar on his forehead? Had his hair been so long it needed tying back in a pony-tail like that? These new variations only made him more alluring, though, and he was as erotic in a two thousand guinea business suit as he'd been in his rampant nakedness. Even as she watched him, he threw back his head and laughed at her question. His brown throat was a long bare elegant line emerging from his sparkling white collar and Delia could've wept at her aching urge to kiss it.

'Why?' he repeated, reaching out and pressing his cool fingers on her cheek. 'Because I want you, Dee. I'm intrigued by you. You're exactly like your file, and yet you're a complete surprise too. It's like being with two different women.'

As his fingertips skated slowly across her cheek and jaw, then on and boldly down into the long, steep vee of her neckline, a bright, flashing light popped on in Delia's mind. A hazard warning beacon.

Deana! The erotica exhibition! Last night! Of course! De Guile had been at his own art show ... and he'd met Deana.

And now he was touching *her*, Delia, like *this*. Talking to her intimately. Indecently. What had Deana *said*, for heaven's sake? What had she *done*?

But as Jackson Kazuto de Guile began unfastening his Divisional Admin Manager's severe suit jacket, the answer was obvious. He was undressing her now because he had last night. Or he believed he had.

Choices and emotions whirled in Delia's brain as the sensations roiled in her body. The sensible, rational side of her said 'Tell him now!' Explain it all now before he strips you naked and you can't turn back.

But then another voice spoke up. A louder voice. The voice of her senses and her dreams. The voice of her yearning sex.

He's mine! it cried. He's mine, Deana, and you've stolen him! Goddamn you, sister, he's mine and I want him back!

It wasn't sensible and it wasn't rational. But as de Guile's clever fingers flicked open her jacket buttons, Delia's own hands rose up to help him.

Sanity made one last rally, 'Mr de Guile, please,' she panted as he pulled open the dark lapels of her suit and exposed her lace-encased breasts.

'"Jake"...I told you, it's "Jake",' he said, locking his navy blue eyes with her pleading grey ones. He cupped her breasts and kneaded them with a roughness that made her gasp but was exactly what she wanted. 'My God, Dee, you're lovely! I had to leave last night, but I wanted to stay. I woke up this morning and the first thing I thought about was your body. I had to touch myself because I couldn't touch you! I brought myself off imagining how your breasts would feel and look when I made them naked. Remembering what it felt like to slide myself into your luscious flesh. How wet and hot and ready you were. I went crazy wondering how you'd taste...Do you realise something, Dee? I haven't even kissed you yet.'

All this was whispered against her cheek, the instant before he inclined her face towards him and word became deed.

Without conscious thought, Delia opened her lips beneath his for that first sweet foray into her mouth. His tongue was cool, moist and flexible inside her hot wetness, and she met it immediately and boldly. As their mouths duelled, she let her mind run ahead, imagining the taste of his skin and his sex. She imagined every intimate flavour and texture of his body, then felt his hands – both of them – take an imperious hold of her jacket lapels and slide the garment down off her.

Pinioned like a slave-girl, her arms were caught against her sides while her throat, her shoulders and her breasts were his to command. Somewhere in her fantasy, his tongue pushed in deeper and subdued hers – while his fingers took possession of her breasts. Delicately, almost tentatively, he pinched her nipples and rolled them this way and that. An exquisite tugging pressure shot straight to the tip of her clitoris and as he pulled at her sensitised teats, her vulva throbbed out its answer. The flesh down there was so excited she almost climaxed without contact.

She wanted to cry out his name, call him 'Your Highness', 'My Liege' and a million other fantasy titles but her mouth was stuffed with his tongue. Pushing her body towards him, she offered him her breasts more freely.

Her offer was instantly taken. With the deftness of great experience, he flicked down the spaghetti straps of her camisole top and exposed her. Delia gasped then, aware of the preposterousness of what was happening to her. They were sitting before a blind-less window in broad daylight; this office was unlocked and open to any intrusion; a secretary or typist could walk in at any second ... and she was being kissed and her breasts were naked.

'But Mr de Guile,' she murmured against his mouth, her own vulnerability thrilling her. *He* was still fully and immaculately dressed while she was bared to the waist, her arms virtually immobilised by her own bunched-up clothing.

'My name is "Jake",' he said, swooping down and putting his lips to one swollen breast, '"Jake",' he repeated, taking the nipple between his straight white teeth and biting it ever-so-gently.

Delia's hips bucked towards him, the movement involuntary, her whole sex shimmering with soft, wet tremors of yearning. She wanted fingers down there, touching and pressing. A tongue licking ... A cock pushing and stretching ... Anything. Anything of his, there between her legs to assuage her roaring hunger. And as he chewed delicately on her stiff, sensitive nipple, she moaned and wriggled, her bottom sliding helplessly on the leather of the sofa.

'Patience.' His breath fanned her breast. 'We won't be disturbed. There's plenty of time. And there's so much I want to do to you.' He shifted his mouth to her other nipple, first sucking, then blowing, using his tongue to anoint the dimpled aureole with saliva, then flick at the peak itself.

The pleasure was very precisely granted, very carefully measured; an exercise in building arousal and raising it to a new and as yet unachieved height. Until now, Delia had always coasted during sex, accepting stimulation as it arrived. She'd never thirsted and craved as she did now; never needed a man's touch so desperately that she thought she might die if she didn't get it. Needed it like a junkie needed dope . . . Never before had her breasts and vulva ached like fire, gnawed from within because she wanted every sexual part of her to be caressed and sucked and fondled all at once and as roughly and savagely as possible.

With a final sequence of long cat-like tongue strokes, de Guile made both her breasts wet all over, then lifted his head and reached out to take hold of her hands.

'Hold yourself, Dee,' he ordered quietly, shaping her fingers with his, and fitting them around her own body. She felt uncomfortable, and hindered by the tangled jacket, but still she obeyed him. Her own engorgement was warm against her palms, and she felt his spittle as a thin moist film. As he closed her fingers and thumbs around her own teats, she gasped, then whimpered. Below, her body was already betraying her . . .

He'd made her come. Brought her to climax. He'd touched only her breasts, and yet she'd had an exquisite orgasm. Floating half-way between fantasy and the heat of the city, she surrendered to a cresting wave of pulsating sensation and heard a cry bubble helplessly from her lips. She squeezed hard on her own nipples and sobbed: then heard de Guile – who was suddenly and utterly 'Jake' – laugh archly as she squirmed before him.

'I knew you'd be like this,' he said, sliding neatly from the couch and dropping down to kneel at her feet. 'When I first saw your picture in the files. Your eyes . . . I knew you'd come easily for me. That you'd be beautiful and melt and flow with the slightest of handling. I knew when we met that you'd *perform* for me.'

Delia – who'd never performed or come easily in her life – was desperate to touch her quim. It was fluttering and beating like a second heart. It was crying out to be fingered and stroked. But she felt paralysed. Only Jake could give her leave to caress herself.

When was it that he'd taken control of her? The exact moment eluded her but suddenly he *was* her master. The Prince, alive in the city and complete in the sovereignty of his title; and in the power to give her effortless pleasure.

Slumped back, eyes closed, her breasts still held in her hands, she sensed him shift his weight slightly, then felt his fingers on the hem of her skirt. Without the slightest hesitation, he pushed the slim tube swiftly up her thighs and shuffled it over her hips, using the thin satin lining as a slider. Delia lifted her bottom off the seat automatically, and within moments she was as displayed below as she was above – with everything that should've covered her bunched crudely in a bundle at her waist.

She didn't dare look down, knowing that the thin silk crotch of her camiknickers was twisted and lodged between her labia. She could feel the empty air warm against her exposed pubic floss and the long bare expanse of her thighs – and only a narrow sliver of sheer yellow fabric kept her sex from his compelling blue gaze.

'Sublime . . .'

For a few seconds Delia's shivers had nothing to do with sex. He'd said it. Said the dream-word. Blue eyes or not, he'd come straight from her fantasy, and her near-naked body was dying for him.

Moving purely on instinct, she undulated her pelvis before him, wafting it and lifting it like an Egyptian belly dancer. It was the lewdest thing she'd ever done but there was no way now she could stop herself.

'Sublime,' he murmured again, his touching fingers tender on the inner slope of her thigh.

She shuddered again when he plucked at the worked-in strip of silk, then dragged it rhythmically back and forth against the swollen tip of her clitoris. The sodden cloth clung wickedly to her flesh, dragging on her most sensitive membranes, and Delia felt a hot, wet flush. Her thighs scissored wildly as she came again, but almost before it had begun, she felt Jake push his fingers between her sex-lips and ease out the thin piece of fabric. There was a sensation of pulling and tugging, then he was folding up the two detached halves of the gusset and baring her shining folds to his view.

'Agh! Oh God!' She grunted low but loud as a finger pushed into her vagina. He did it with ineffable gentleness but it was still a violation, a delicious shaming rudeness. The very core of her speared on a stranger's slim digit.

His face was so close to her now that she could feel his breath on her moistness. 'Relax, Dee,' he whispered, 'let me in.' A second finger slid in beside the first and their combined thickness swivelled inside her.

'Oh, Jake, please!' she sobbed, aware that she'd used his given name for the first time. She didn't quite know what she was pleading for, but even as she did, her clitoris leapt in the empty air. It felt bigger and more blood-filled now than she could ever remember, and seemed to beg, mutely, to be masturbated. Opening her eyes at last, fighting what felt like hugely weighted eyelids, she looked down at the man crouched lithely between her thighs.

His concentration on her sex was somehow almost religious, and in spite of her distractions, she found a moment of lucidity to admire him, and marvel at his densely black, perfectly groomed hair.

She'd never seen hair before that lay so thick and straight and vital against the head. At first she thought it was gelled, but when she reached out – awkwardly – to touch him, she found only silkiness and the lush soft tactility of a healthy animal's coat. Feeling her fingers upon him, he glanced up for a second, and the narrow feline gleam of his smile only served to reinforce the impression. He *was* an animal. A beautiful, hard-glossed prey-seeker, a clever gentle woman-eater who was there between her bare legs to feed.

She could no longer close her eyes now. Rapt, she watched him smile again, then put out his long pink tongue and lower his face to her crotch. She sobbed as she felt a soft, wet touch connect divinely with her quivering clitoris and nudge the tiny nub of flesh into another almost heart-stopping orgasm. Her sobs turned to broken, mewling screams as he flapped his tongue rapidly against her, piling on the glorious stimulation when she'd already had as much as she could bear. Even so, her naked loins rose up again to meet him, and as best she could in her makeshift bonds, she grabbed hold of his dark, elegant head and pulled his cool face closer to her sex.

Suddenly it was all too much. At least far more than Delia was used to. Still deep in orgasm, she felt a great, soft blackness engulf her and sweet oblivion descend to save her sanity.

But just at the very last second before she drifted away, she felt her name 'Dee' whispered right around her still-throbbing clitoris ...

* * *

As Delia woke up, she remembered a dream. A voluptuous, impressionist dream in which the Prince had given her ultimate pleasure. With mirror-like clarity, she recalled his fingers on her flesh, and then his mouth there too. These acts were as sharp and true in her mind as anything that had ever happened to her, but there were other erotic fragments that were less so.

She seemed to remember his hand upon her ankle, caressing it and raising it up, stretching her thighs into a open arc that tautened and displayed her sex. She remembered his lips kissing her foot, his hands sliding up and down her leg, then his fingertips opening up her labia like the petals of an orchid.

There'd been the rustle of clothing then, she seemed to remember, and immediately after, a steady, probing pressure against the entrance of her vagina.

With that came a long and very male sigh and the invasion of an erect penis into her body.

But that seemed to be all she could remember.

Sitting up cautiously on the deep-cushioned leather settee, Delia ran her fingers down the seam of her skirt. Then frowned.

She checked the neckline, and the snugly fastened buttons of her jacket, and frowned again.

Had it happened or hadn't it? She was most definitely in Jackson de Guile's acre-sized office, but as to what had occurred in the last half-hour or so, she couldn't truthfully be certain. Glancing towards the huge executive desk at the far end of the room, she ascertained that at least the man himself was no dream. He was talking quietly into a slim portable phone, and although from the tenor of his conversation he seemed to be engaged in some fairly important negotiation or other, he was smiling in *her* direction. Even as she watched him, he winked roguishly and blew her a fingertip kiss.

Dear heaven, it *had* happened. At least some of it ... Yet, unaccountably, she was dressed again: covered up, buttoned up, and even – she discovered when she shifted her thighs experimentally against each other – poppered up. She was primly and properly clothed, but had no recollection of getting that way herself!

De Guile – or Jake, she supposed she should call him now – appeared superbly cool and unruffled. If he *had* actually made love to her, outwardly he showed no sign of it. Snapping his slim phone closed, he slid to his feet and walked soundlessly across the carpet towards her, as immaculate as a *GQ* model and ten times as smooth and glamorous.

As he sat down beside her, a primal womanish fear made her cower ever-so-slightly away, and this made him smile. With a slick, almost reptilian swiftness, his long hand whipped out and cupped her feverish cheek.

'You're so exciting, sweet Dee,' he murmured, leaning forward and feathering her lips with his. It was a chaste kiss, almost nothing, yet in the heart of it his tongue moved delicately on her skin. 'I'd like to spend the day with you. Keep you aroused for hours and hours. Play with this hot little body ... his fingertip slid from her face and cruised down over her jaw to her throat ... until you beg for me. But alas, I've a meeting in ten minutes which I'll have to attend, even though I'm still excited.' Taking her shaking hand in his, he laid it against his erection, straining in the containment of his underwear. Even to her, and through his clothes, he felt warm – a great hard mass that pulsed and throbbed even as she held him.

He made a throaty sound as she unconsciously caressed him. Had this strong bar of flesh been inside her? she wondered, frantic at not truly knowing. She'd dreamed of it, yes, but it could've been just that. A dream.

With obvious reluctance, he removed her hand from his body and rose gracefully to his feet. 'Later, my gorgeous Dee,' he said, his voice intimate even though he was already withdrawing from her orbit. 'I have to go now.'

Her distress must have shown on her face, she realised, because with a look of almost compassion, he stepped close again, took up the hand that had held him and dusted her fingers with a kiss.

'Take the rest of the day off. Go home, relax, and I'll collect you tonight at eight.' And then he was moving again, going, leaving her with little apparent regret. For all it seemed to cost him, they could've just finished a discussion on staff performance statistics – which was what she'd been expecting before he'd taken hold of her life and turned it on its head. 'Wear something stylish, Dee. Dress to impress. I know just the place to take you.' With that, and no other word of farewell, he was gone – leaving the long airy room without once looking back in her direction.

Stunned, she sat on the warm leather settee for minute after minute after minute. Jake's secretary would come in to investigate soon, wondering why Delia was still here when her boss had gone.

And yet the gigantic question still plagued her. Had he or hadn't he? He'd touched her, pleasured her, sucked her even...But had he been *in* her? She tried and tried to remember.

It wasn't until she finally rose to her feet that she received a conclusive answer. When she straightened up and twitched at her lapels and smoothed down her skirt, she felt a slight but very telling sensation. The physical evidence.

As she walked slowly towards the door and the sexless world

of office normality, a thin skein of her fluid trickled out from beneath the soft, loose leg of her camiknickers.

'Damn you, Jake! Damn you!' she whispered, both hating the man and already missing him.

3

The Gemini Game

'Deana! Where the hell are you? I know you haven't gone to work!'

At the sound of her sister's angry voice, Deana sank down beneath the surface of her tepid bath and submerged her head to shut out both the voice and the prospect of facing its implications.

But when she popped up again, her streaming hair clinging to her face and neck, the sounds of a sibling on the warpath were still there and getting louder.

She knows! thought Deana climbing from the cooling water and wrapping her nude body in a towel. Somehow she knows about Jake ... God, I hope he's not someone important at work!

Deana dried herself slowly for a number of reasons. The first was that even though it couldn't be much later than midday, it was already too hot for hectic activity. The second was to give herself time to frame what she could say to Delia. The third was because the action of the towel on her naked skin reminded her of Jake and the way he'd touched her and taken her. And even though his disappearance had been as intensely infuriating as it had been sudden, she couldn't stop reliving what had happened with him!

She'd never had sex quite like it, but it was certainly a kind she would've liked more of. If I'd been able to get it, she observed silently – as irate knuckles rapped at the locked bath-room door.

'Deana!'

'Yes?'

'I know you're in there! Get dressed and come out at once!'

Narrow, tapping heels receded furiously across parquet flooring outside and by the time Deana had tucked her towel into a makeshift sarong, then unlocked the door and poked her head out, Delia – the righteous avenger – had gone.

When she padded gingerly into the lounge, Deana got something of a surprise. Her sister, always a cautious drinker and never one to partake during the daytime, was cork-screwing open some white wine. Two glasses stood on the coffee table – one in front of the couch and one in front of the armchair – and Deana got the impression that a summit conference was about to begin.

'Sit down, Deana.' Delia's voice was calm as she poured out the wine, but Deana wasn't fooled. Sister dear was well het up about something – the more reasonable she sounded the worse it usually boded.

The wine, for once, did not make Deana relax. This was cheap and cheerful stuff she was sipping, but it still made her think of the brew that she'd drunk last night, the cool smooth nectar that had softened her up for Jake.

'How was the exhibition?' enquired Delia ominously. 'Anything unusual happen?'

For half a second Deana considered lying, but realised just as quickly it was useless. She and Delia weren't the uncanny type of twins who could mind-read, but they were certainly close enough to tell when one another were fibbing.

'Er . . . Yes, there was something actually. A man. I met this man.'

'You "met" a man?' It didn't take all that many words to condemn her. And as she looked into the face that was so magically like her own – yet in many ways so different – Deana knew she would have to tell all.

'It was more than that ...' After taking a deep breath, then a deeper drink of her wine, she slowly and haltingly began.

As she outlined the extraordinary events on the balcony, she didn't dare look at her sister. Instead she studied her glass like a crystal ball, and in its several times refilled depths, she saw the dark, almost samurai face of Jake. Her handsome, outrageous, insatiable Jake.

'So,' prompted Delia when Deana finally dried up. 'This man you let fuck you? And you think he might be part-oriental ...'

'Yes,' whispered Deana, as shocked by her sister's language as by anything. Delia never ever used the 'f' word.

'Well, that's rather a coincidence, Deana ...' Delia topped up her own glass, drank from it, then piling on the tension, paused to kick off her shoes and unfasten the buttons of her jacket.

For an instant, Deana was surprised by her sister's rather glamorous underwear. Then she forgot it again as Delia continued her deadly calm discourse.

'Yes, it's very odd indeed. I met a half-oriental man this morning. One Jackson Kazuto de Guile. *J. K.* de Guile, that is. "Jake", as he likes to be called.' Delia's glass went down onto the coffee table. Very carefully. Very precisely. 'He's my boss, Deana, and you dropped your knickers for him twenty minutes after you met him. What the bloody hell were you playing at? I asked you to keep a low profile!'

'You also said there'd be no-one from your section there, so it didn't matter that you'd given your ticket away!' Deana felt indignant herself now. If Delia was going to take on about this, she had to understand it was partially her own fault. If she'd had the good sense to attend the exhibition herself instead of going out with Mr Yukky Russell, the whole situation wouldn't have arisen.

Suddenly, Deana felt almost queasy. If Delia *had* gone to the art gallery, *she*'d have been the one on the balcony with Jake! 'What ifs' and consequences began to stack up like cards, and on top of them all was the realisation that Delia *had* now met Jake.

'What did he say? Did you tell him? What did he say about us being twins?' said Deana.

'Not much. No. Nothing.'

'What are you on about, Delia? What do you mean?' The dizzy feeling came back and Deana gulped down more wine, trying to wash away her forebodings.

'Just what I said.' Delia's voice was odd; she sounded as confused and disorientated as Deana felt. 'He didn't say a very great deal. And because I didn't get a chance to tell him we were twins, he doesn't know.'

The bottle was empty now, so Deana twisted a corner of her towel nervously instead of drinking, aware that although the heat was steadily increasing, she suddenly felt cold and shivery.

'So he thinks it was *you* he had last night?'

'Yes.'

'*Delia* Ferraro?'

'He calls us "Dee".'

'And did he ... Was he?'

How to ask? What to ask? A man had come into her life last night and changed her in a way she was hard pressed to describe. She'd been given a glimpse of a whole new sensuality and then had it snatched away just as quickly. But now there was a chance again. A backwards-about-chance, fraught with complications and pitfalls.

'What did he say about the sex?' Deana blurted out at last.

Delia's face was a picture. In spite of everything, Deana's fingers itched for a pencil to capture such a subtle combination of emotions. Her sister was confused, yes, but also full of excitement, mischief and wonder. Her anger was still there, but fading now; replaced by a curious complicity.

'Well,' Delia said at last, 'he's a man of action, isn't he? Not words . . .'

Deana felt her own emotions surge and swirl and rise up to choke her. 'The randy bastard!' she cried. 'He's had you, too, hasn't he?' She couldn't properly tell whether she felt jealousy or admiration. And if it was admiration, was it for this potent, beautiful, philandering de Guile? Or was it for her cautious, self-possessed sister, who'd done something utterly disgraceful at last? Good grief, it was only just after midday. They'd have to have done it at the office!

Suddenly the two Ferraros were hugging each other and sobbing in a huge, cathartic release of tension. Firing garbled questions at each other, still faintly, mutually jealous, but more than anything, excited. They'd shared boyfriends in their teens, and played tricks on those boys, swapped places without telling them. They'd made up their own private game and seen just how long a swain could be hoodwinked into believing there was just one girl . . .

But this was the first time in their adult life that they'd shared a man – and the first time *ever* that they'd both had that same man as a lover. To Deana it felt like a bizarre but strangely apposite rite of passage.

'What are we going to do?' she asked when they'd settled down and – in an unprecedented move for her – Delia had shucked off her severe jacket and was curled up on the sofa with her skirt all scrunched and her bosom half revealed by an extravagant yellow silk camisole.

'I don't quite know,' replied Delia, absentmindedly fiddling with a shoulder strap, 'but whatever we do, we've got to make a decision by tonight.'

'Why?'

'Jake's coming to collect "Dee" at eight.'

'Oh hell!'

'Quite!'

'You want him as much as I do, don't you?' Deana said quietly, knowing she didn't really have to ask. The twin sitting with her was a brand new Delia, a vibrant, sensual Delia quite different to the suppressed and single-minded girl who'd been stifled by the awful Russell.

'Yes ... I'd like to say "take him and good luck". But I can't, Deana, I just can't!'

'Neither can I, love. So there's only one thing for it ...'

'Oh, Deana, we haven't done it since we were fifteen!'

'It's the only way. Do you have a coin?'

As she watched her sister reach for her bag, open her purse and take out a ten pence piece, Deana was shaking. She mimed 'heads' but couldn't tell whether she wanted it to come up or not.

With a deftness that Deana envied, Delia tossed the coin, caught it neatly, then exposed the face. 'The Gemini Game. Round One. Deana Ferraro to play,' she said with a shrug and a half-envious, half-relieved grin. 'Come on, we'd better sort you out something to wear. He said dress to impress, Deana love, and I don't think you've a single impressive item in your whole wardrobe!'

'Bloody cheek!' replied Deana affectionately, jumping to her feet and following her sister from the room. It was a matter of taste, she supposed, but for once, and for the purpose of going out with one Jackson Kazuto de Guile, she knew that Delia was most probably right ...

At ten to eight, Deana's senses were turbo-charged, and even though Delia said she did look impressive, to her own eyes she wasn't so sure.

From their combined wardrobes – and cosmetic resources – the two Ferraros had created an accumulated persona called 'Dee'. A woman who was both wild and smooth, and who – with luck – could fell any man on earth. Even half-Japanese billionaires with a penchant for quickie sex.

In the narrow antique mirror that stood in the hall of their flat, Deana surveyed the potential slayer and felt a small surge of confidence.

The top was hers; an iridescent sequinned bustier which Delia had been somewhat dubious about until Deana had showed her its bona fide designer label. It was eyecatching but tasteful and clung faithfully to Deana's braless breasts. De Guile would appreciate the body beneath and he had no way of knowing that the sparkly garment that covered it had cost just fifteen quid at a Saturday second hand market.

Bearing in mind 'their' date's fondness for leather, the girls had chosen a straight black skirt made of buttery high-gloss hide. This was Delia's but not something she wore often. She liked the skirt but rarely went to places that it suited. Even so, its sophisticated two inches above the knee length, and skimming rather than clinging shape, reflected a far less 'obvious' sense of style than Deana's. The same good taste that had insisted on smoke-grey stockings, not bare legs, and made Deana take off virtually all the jewellery she'd put on. She scowled now at the simple beaten silver button-shaped earrings, and the thin bangle which was the only other item she'd been permitted. She'd complained at first, but now had to admit that her sister was right. And about the hair too, a sensuously coiled topknot with just a few wayward tendrils that drifted around a lightly made-up face. Unbeknownst to Delia, though, Deana had slicked on a coat of darker, plummier lipstick at the last minute and changed her sister's plain grosgrain court shoes for a pair of three-inch high black patent stilettos – another magic find from the markets.

'You look good, kid,' she whispered to herself, adjusting a strand of her coiffure. 'But for how long?'

Delia had said de Guile was taking 'Dee' somewhere, but in both their experiences so far, he was far more likely to want her body almost immediately. Deana felt her breasts prickle in the scrunchy containment of her top as she imagined those long dark fingers upon her: stroking and exploring, and this time reaching areas that he'd not reached before. The bustier fitted neatly, but would make very little of an obstacle if de Guile wanted to handle her bosom. And the skirt, whilst tapered, was an easyish fit with a super-slidey lining. A narrow hand, such as the one that had touched her in the gallery, would be slipping up her thighs in no time and discovering her sparsely covered loins.

But, Deana, it's what you want!

It was true, of course, and as she opened the door a chink, and saw a long shadowy shape come gliding up the drive, the whole of the surface of her skin – both covered and uncovered – began to quiver in hot anticipation.

Delia would've shut the door again, but Deana was too eager and impatient of subterfuge. Walking boldly out, she waved to the as yet unseen occupant of the approaching limousine, and wondered if her sister was watching. Peering from the window of their neighbour's flat – where she was hiding out of sight.

As the sexy black car trickled to a halt, the driver's door swung open, and a man – but not de Guile – got out.

Deana hesitated, then stepped forward again as the chauffeur

– a tall, unsmiling blond dressed from head to foot in unrelieved black – came round to the rear door nearest to her and opened it without speaking a word.

The dour servant unnerved her, but not nearly as much as the relaxed figure who half-reclined on the spacious back seat.

'Dee ... How beautiful you look,' murmured Jake as she slid in beside him, 'and how refreshing not to have to wait for you. That's the mark of a truly sensual woman, my sweet. Instant readiness. I cherish it.'

Instant readiness. She wondered if he knew how true his words were, then remembered his uncanny sexual insights in the gallery. Of course he knew she was on heat and ready for him! What woman wouldn't be with a man like Jackson de Guile. His beauty almost dazzled her as she let her hot hand be taken in his cool one and conveyed to the velvet of his lips.

Dress to impress. Dress to impress. Dress to impress. From Delia's 'briefing' it echoed at her in an endless repeating loop. And she'd done so with some degree of distinction. But no way could she match this incredible creature beside her.

It was leather trousers again, although clearly not the same pair. This time there was a slight but discernible texture to the hide and the cut was slightly closer. With them, and as if to temper their macho stud-ishness, Jake wore the fullest and softest of white silk shirts. Its sleeves were floating and Byronic, and it had a narrow, stand-up collar, which he wore unfastened. His face was pure amber against its snowiness and Deana felt her libido riot and betray her. As the car door clicked shut, all she could think about was lying on this broad, soft, leather-covered banquette with her body exposed and ready. Her body laid bare. Her body wet and flowing to receive this male god in its heat.

He saw it too, it seemed.

'Only this morning, eh?' he whispered, his eyes like blue lasers in the soft dark light of the limousine's opulent interior. He kissed her hand again, turning it slowly within his grip and licking long and lingeringly at her palm.

Deana remembered in panic where that mouth had been this morning. What he'd done to her sister ... And even as she imagined the act, she empathically received its resonances. She felt her own sex flutter as if he were mouthing it, and she felt a quick hard dew of moisture flow out onto her thin silk panties. Oh please, begged some wanton inside her. Do it again! Do it now! Do it to *me*!

And she felt powerless as he placed her hand – like some inanimate object – on the leather of the seat beside her. Her only awareness was waiting. Wanting. The car was cruising along the main road now, but it could've sprouted wings and be flying them to the moon for all the interest she could muster in the world rushing by outside.

'Yes, you are ready,' Jake observed, his voice amused. He looked down at her breasts, rising and falling beneath their shimmering armour, and at her thighs which were revealingly parted. She sensed him choosing somehow, eyeing her up like some choice dish or delicacy. Selecting which tasty portion to sample first. He moved closer and almost touched his lips to hers, then put a finger up to her jammy lipstick, dabbing at the glossy crimson coating and then studying its trace on his skin.

'Too nice to spoil.' Leaving her make-up inviolate, he pressed his lips to her throat, licking again and tasting, his hand taking possession of a sequin covered breast as his mouth browsed languidly on her neck. He nipped the tender skin there, and simultaneously pinched the stiff peak of her nipple. The small, sweet twin-centred pain made Deana writhe and whimper.

Unable to stay still, she glanced frantically at the blond man visible through the glass in front of her – and as if reading her mind, Jake straightened up and locked her frightened eyes with his.

'We're sound-proofed, Dee. But don't worry, Fargo's seen far more than just kisses in his time . . .' His fingertips twisted slightly and she wriggled again. 'Yes, that would be good, wouldn't it, my sweet?' His light voice took on a vaguely contemplative cast. 'I'd like to see you aroused before a crowd. Your loins naked and pumping, giving pleasure to many, not just one. Your sex wet and engorged. My fingers at work in you while an audience watches and drools . . .'

'No! That's awful!' Lies! Lies! Lies!

But he knew . . .

'It isn't and you know it,' he purred, both hands working now, tugging at the tips of her breasts in a slow, wicked rhythm. 'You were walking around the gallery, looking at my pictures . . . and you were even more on show than they were. Why else wear a dress so thin, and be so nude beneath it?'

She made a token noise of dissent, her nails gouging deep into the seat when – without warning – he took hold of the top of her bustier and rolled it right down to her midriff.

'And this morning, so chic,' he went on suavely, just touching her exposure very gently, a forefinger rubbing at each hard peak in turn, as if to make sure they stayed stiff. 'That pretty business girl suit on a body that was hot for sex. There are words for you, Dee—' He studied her naked nipples for a second, then dropped both hands to the hem of her skirt and started pushing. Inexorably. 'You're wanton, my darling. You're rude. You're easy. You're horny. How many of your contemporaries would allow a man to touch them between the legs so soon after meeting them. You're a bitch, Dee, a gorgeous little bitch. Aren't you?'

She shook her head, but her stocking tops and suspenders were already on view; her thighs soft and creamy above the thick dark bands of nylon. Just a millimetre short of her crotch he stopped, but when she gasped with relief, he thrust a hand into the rift between her legs and poked crudely at her vulva through the cobweb-fine veil of her panties.

'No,' she sobbed, as he rubbed her clitoris through the delicate gusset. She'd wanted to be more powerful tonight, more in control. She'd promised Delia she'd try.

'Let's have these off, shall we?' he said suddenly, in a strangely matter-of-fact voice. Pushing her skirt right up and out of the way, he hooked his thumbs into the elastic of her fragile silk knickers. They were beautiful little pants, in a soft, sheeny peach shade that matched her suspenders, but right now they seemed simply a hindrance.

With a peculiar, almost voluptuous sense of resignation, she lifted her hips to help him make her trembling sex naked. Something of the artist in her was able to look down on what was revealed quite dispassionately. She hadn't wanted to wear stockings, because of the heat, but they, and the pastel suspenders they were hooked to, made a perfect frame for the soft honeyed curve of her belly and the warm brown mound at its base.

Perversely, he left her silky pants caught around her ankles – an adornment more lewd by far than if he'd taken them off her completely – and pushed her knees fully open with his fingertips. His touch was very light and respectful, as if he feared for her seven-denier stockings.

'Quite lovely,' he said, sliding one hand under her, between her thighs, and pulling her bottom to the edge of the seat.

It was like being displayed, exhibited; and blushing furiously, her body heat soaring, Deana let her eyelids droop closed. Her legs lolled loosely apart, still caught at the ankles, and the cool, refreshing air felt delicious. A naughty little breeze was wending its way out from a vent somewhere and playing across her plump juicy sex. The tense, puffy flesh seemed to throb and pulse as if someone had reached out and caressed it, and to her horror and shame she sensed Jake studying the phenomenon intently.

'Yes ... Oh yes,' he cooed, not touching the clitoris that begged for his finger but pressing open her labia with his thumbs.

Deana had never felt more naked; not even on the balcony, that first time, when he'd bent her over the parapet and bared her bottom. Her hands curled into fists and rose up to draw him to her, but inexplicably he batted them gently back to her sides, then settled them down on the leather banquette with all the finality of having chained them there.

'We're going to a private house I know. It will take us three-quarters of an hour,' he said, his voice suddenly very cool, very precise. 'I'd like you to stay this way until we get there, Dee. Displayed for me ... Think of it as a test you've to pass.'

The Deana of thirty-six hours ago would've protested, rebelled, asked questions. But the ensorcelled Deana of now kept her body perfectly still, her eyes shut and her painted lips closed and quiet. She moaned once when her companion inserted a finger into her burning lubricated channel, but fell silent again – even through a faint shivering orgasm – and listened to Jake's litany of eroticism.

He spoke of the sex that they'd shared at the gallery and the moments he'd particularly enjoyed. He spoke of the things he would do to her body and what he would like her to do to his. He described what he saw before him in spine-tingling detail, every tiny feature of her physical topography – how she looked, how she smelt and how she tasted, withdrawing his finger briefly to sample her, then returning it, newly wetted, to her quim.

She came several times. Once or twice spontaneously from his words, once on the reinsertion of his finger, once when with no warning at all he squashed his thumb down on her clitoris flat and hard. Deana didn't and almost couldn't open her eyes, but after they'd been travelling some time, and her sixth sense said they were nearing their destination, she felt him take a handkerchief from somewhere and very tenderly tidy up her eye make-up, where it had been disturbed by her hot tears of shame. His face came within inches of hers as he did this, and she orgasmed again from the intoxicating scent of his body and his intimate wild flower cologne.

As the car oozed to a halt, she made to move – even though he still had her speared.

'No! Be still!' He was stern now. Icy.

Deana felt her heart pound and beat as if to burst as the well-oiled mechanism of an expensive car door lock thunked open and a blast of muggy, urban air flowed in across her immolated vulva. She tried to turn away and hide her pinkened face. She scrunched her eyes even tighter shut as if the fact that she couldn't see meant others couldn't either. But Jake seemed bent on humbling her completely. With his free hand he angled her head carefully towards the open door, and with his voice he softly commanded.

'Eyes open now, Dee.'

Even as she obeyed him, he started masturbating her, the movements rough and almost violent. Beyond tears now, she stared up into the chauffeur's cool and imperturbable eyes and saw not a flicker of response in their stony, secretive depths. Not even when she came in a harsh, womb-wrenching orgasm and grunted out her pleasure while her hips wove and bounced on the leather.

She was a spectacle. A show. A helpless female thing stimulated before a servant for the master's amusement. She felt shamed in a way she'd never experienced before, and yet still she came, her pleasure huge, somehow greater *because* of the humiliation.

'That will be all, Fargo,' said the quiet, disturbing voice of the man who'd abused her. The chauffeur turned away as he was bidden, leaving Deana exposed – her flesh moist and rippling – to the hot, heavy air of the city.

'Come along, Dee,' Jake continued smoothly as Deana cringed back. She was scared that at any moment a stranger might pass along the pavement, look in, and see her soft, pink sex uncovered and still beating slightly.

Numbed, and feeling like a prisoner in a weird, pornographic half-dream, she bent down to pull up her knickers.

'No, I think not,' he said, reaching down at her side, quickly disentangling the silk garment from her ankles before sliding it off over her shoes. 'I prefer you uncovered.'

For one terrifying moment, she thought he was going to make her alight from the car with her pubis still exposed: but he made no demur as she eased down her slim leather skirt, set her bustier straight, then snatched up her bag and scrambled from the vehicle as if she had the devil on her tail. She dared not look towards the front seat where Fargo sat unmoving, but as she glanced back into the car's interior, she saw Jake drop her panties onto the middle of the black leather seat. He seemed to study them for a second, then he grinned wickedly and joined her on the pavement, stepping lightly from the car with his familiar effortless grace.

Still smiling, he took her by the arm and led her towards an elegant Mayfair town house.

The place was innocuous and mysterious and its frontage bore no label or sign. Except for the gleaming brass numeral 'Seventeen' in the middle of its dark-painted door.

4

'Seventeen'

Looking Deana straight in the eye, Jake pressed the doorbell, then spoke the words 'de Guile' into the grid of a discreet security entryphone. His eyes were smoky and shadowed in the just-softening light of evening, but nevertheless their frankness seared her. She was acutely aware of the bare flesh between her thighs, and the gooeyness of her sex as she walked, and that Jake had knowledge of these things. He was surveying what he'd so recently exposed and enjoyed, looking straight through her clothes with those erotic, electric eyes of his and revelling in what he'd done to her body. She felt intense relief that her skirt was leather and substantial, because anything flimsy would've been soaked with her juices the minute she sat down again.

The door swung soundlessly open and a man in a dinner suit let them in; greeting Jake with quiet obsequiousness and totally ignoring Deana. She felt as if the flunky had seen what'd happened in the car as surely as the silent Fargo had. Jake escorted her inside with exquisite politeness and solicitude, but it was obvious that to the *maître d'* – or whoever he was – she was purely her master's sex toy.

Inside, the house was an elegant neutral no-place. There was no way to tell if it was a private home, a club of some kind, or even a high-class brothel. Without knowing why, Deana had a feeling it could well be all three at once, but as they were ushered into a long, spacious, dimly lit room, the impression of a club was uppermost.

There was a cleared, slightly raised area at one end of the room, which – covered in polished boards – was obviously an impromptu stage. A number of white clothed tables were scattered in the gloomy foreground, and at them, groups of people sat laughing and chatting in hushed but expectant tones. Some of them turned and stared when she and Jake passed by, and for one hideous moment, Deana wondered if *she* might be the show!

They were led to one of the tables, however, and after she'd almost fallen into her seat with relief, she relaxed and looked around. In wonder.

'Seventeen' was no ordinary house, and certainly no ordinary club. She and Jake were perhaps the most conservatively-dressed of its patrons, and if she hadn't been wearing a leather skirt and high heels, she would've felt even more of an alien.

An elegantly made-up black woman at the next table appeared to be dressed completely in leather. Skin-tight patent encased all that could be seen of her body above the table, and even as Deana watched her, she peeled open a zippered aperture in her bodice, exposed one huge chocolate coloured, cherry-tipped breast, and offered it to the man at her side to suck. He seemed almost ecstatic to do this; mainly because there was no way he could touch her. His hands lay awkwardly on the white cloth in front of him, manacled in heavy steel handcuffs. As far as Deana could tell, these shackles were all that he wore.

Astounded, she turned away and looked across the expanse of their own table to the one beyond, at Jake's side.

Its sole occupant – a distinguishedly handsome grey-haired man in evening dress – seemed, at first glance, to be having a heart attack. On the point of alerting Jake, Deana abruptly stopped short and caught her breath.

Suddenly, she recognised the distinctive way in which the man was grunting and jerking. Enlightened and excited, she heard him groan eloquently, then watched as he threw back his head, clawed at the white napery before him, and nearly knocked over his glass of champagne.

For a few moments, the man sat perfectly still – only to stir and smile indulgently when a slim young woman with straight dark hair wriggled out from beneath the table-cloth and sat down meekly at his side. She wasn't as naked as the pleasure giver at the other table, but her clothing was more erotic than nudity could ever be. Narrow black leather straps encased the whole of her body like a tailored-to-fit cage. Her exposed white breasts were especially constricted, bulging out painfully as if they'd been stuffed through a pair of matching steel rings which were rather too small for their mass. Rousing from his post-orgasmic stupor, her grey-haired companion reached out and pinched one of her nipples. The girl sobbed.

'What is this place?' hissed Deana, breaking out of her shock and torpor.

'This is "Seventeen", Dee,' Jake whispered back to her, patting her hand, his soft white shirt like a cool fire brushing her arm. 'Now shush, will you? There's a show about to begin.'

Too thunderstruck to argue, Deana obeyed. Good grief, we're in a madhouse, she thought as a woman dressed as a French maid brought champagne and glasses to their table. What sort of show does an audience like this expect?

After a couple of seconds the lighting began to dim even further and concealed spotlights swung around on to the raised stage area. Jake and Deana were sitting quite close to whatever was going to happen, and it occurred to her then that they'd been given the best table in the house. Jake put a glass of champagne into her hand, and when she took a grateful sip, she realised that the wine too was probably amongst the finest available.

He's perfectly at home here, she observed to herself as some softly weaving and vaguely eastern music started playing. This is a fetish club and he's an honoured guest. What the hell have I got myself involved in?

Got *us* involved in, she amended, remembering the deception and wondering what oh-so-straight Delia would think of 'Seventeen' and its patrons. Shifting uneasily on her seat, which was covered – surprise surprise – in fine soft leather, Deana cringed as her naked sex seemed to squelch and suck like a mouth. Unlike Jake, she *wasn't* at home here, but there was no doubt that the place did excite her.

With no advance warning, two figures suddenly appeared in the bright, white circle of light. Two men. One was slight, long haired and blond; the other huge, black and almost grotesquely muscled. Both were artfully made up, far more so than Deana herself, and both were completely naked, their glossy, depilated bodies enhanced by a bright film of oil.

As the music grew louder and more complex, the men began to move to its rhythms, coiling their limbs around each other and writhing in a slow sensual ballet. Their hands roved over one another's body and, as they worked and wriggled and fondled, within seconds they both had erections. Secret signals seemed to pass between them, and turning to face one another, they each put their hands on their hips, bent their knees lewdly and began to duel with their stiff gleaming organs. First the blond, then the black man, each dancer would smear the tip of his penis against the belly and sex of his partner...

Deana found it so entrancing it was painful. Her own body ached with an echo of their lust and she knew exactly what she wanted them to do to each other. Like lovers in reality, though, they were teasing and playing. Jousting, it seemed, with their intimate and mutual stiffness.

What's all this doing to the rest of the audience? she wondered. Her own sex, primed by Jake in the car, was simmering and bursting with need. She felt heavily engorged. It was uncomfortable just to sit, and surreptitiously – as the two men's hips bounced and jerked – she eased her warm legs slightly apart. The urge to slide her fingers down beneath the table was overwhelming, and she knew that if she did so, she wouldn't be the only masturbatrix in the room. She was probably in the minority now in *not* touching herself, but the scene was too new for her to succumb. Without thinking, she tore her eyes away from the gyrating bodies on the stage and turned in the darkness towards Jake.

Her nemesis was smiling and relaxed. And looking straight at her. As their eyes met, he slowly licked his lips, then slid one hand beneath the table-cloth. When he had obviously found his target, his body bumped slightly as a signal... To her.

What is it with you? she demanded – in silence because she dared not speak. This was a gay scene being enacted, yet plainly Jake found it arousing. And that fact only aggravated *her* arousal. There was no doubt now that he was stroking himself and Deana nearly whimpered aloud at the thought. She remembered the one time she'd seen his penis – in the afterglow, on that blessed white balcony. And she thought of it now, how it must be and feel, its rampant thickness compressed beneath the leather of his trousers. He gasped very softly and she wondered if he'd unzipped himself to give ease to his pain-tinged pleasure... But then a louder more universal gasp returned her fevered attention to the stage. To the light and the sleekly oiled men.

They were combined in a new way now, the blond sprawled

across the other's back; not quite the arrangement Deana had expected. She'd assumed that the bigger man would be dominant in the final, inevitable act; but no, it was the smaller male, the blond. He was biting the sheened ebony shoulders of his partner, and pushing his stiff red sex into the groove of his dark bottom. They were almost there now, almost copulating, and the audience was gasping again. Some did more than gasp when the black man leaned over, set his legs strongly wide, then reached back to open the way for his partner. With a cool, impassive care, he held open his own buttocks with his fingers. The blond then surged forward, his penis stabbing like a weapon, and jammed himself into his target.

As the black man groaned loud and joyously and began working himself back on the invasion, Deana too had to bow to the sexual imperative. Blushing and sweating freely, she became aware of Jake's hard scrutiny. But it changed nothing . . . Working her skirt upwards under cover of the table-cloth, she set her thighs wide apart on the chair.

'Yes!' she heard softly from nearby, while everyone else was cheering the sodomites. 'Do it, Dee,' he purred. 'Lift your skirt up and touch yourself. I want to see you come . . . Now!'

'I can't!' she protested. If she pulled her skirt up far enough to masturbate, her stockinged thighs and naked bottom would be on clear view through the open back of the chair.

'Don't disappoint me, Dee.' The threat was whispered but clear, and driven by its power, she shifted her rump on the seat and pulled clumsily at her slim leather skirt. As she eased it upwards, she shuddered, knowing what was now quite revealed. Her only comfort was a peripheral awareness of similar things happening all around her.

Her vulva was awash when she touched it, the lips enormously swollen and her clitoris pushed out and irritated. The tiny bud had been aroused too much already tonight and when she touched it herself, it was tenderly painful. Sharp discomfort sliced through her, but even so she flicked it and rubbed. Her juices flowed faster than ever, and she cried out softly as an orgasm rushed in and engulfed her.

The pleasure was sudden and unexpected. It seemed to drag her deep inside herself and away from her shadowed surroundings. Detachedly, she wondered how such an intimate, almost religious experience could occur amongst a throng of perfect strangers. How something so personal could be shown in public. Shown by herself, and by the men on the platform.

In spite of her soreness, she began caressing herself again as she watched them. The blond was obviously climaxing now, his tight buttocks tensing as he rose on his toes and rammed. Deana half expected him to reach around and bring ease to his huge dark partner, but he didn't. He clung tightly to the black man's narrow hips; selfishly increasing his own leverage with no thought for the other man's erection. His partner's penis seemed to quiver in mid-air, then leapt like a stranded fish and disgorged his white semen from its tip. Deana had never seen such a sight – great long creamy strings, jetting out and landing on the stage. She could even hear the impact of the droplets as they fell on the hard polished boards.

As the last spurt flew in an arc, and the two men seemed to crumple in ecstasy, both the stage and the house lights were killed. In total, velvet blackness, Deana could almost taste the sex in the air, feel it vibrating around her in a multitude of strange, hidden ways.

It was like being in limbo, but as her eyes began to adjust she saw evocative movement all around her. She heard hushed sighs and groans. She half expected Jake to reach for her, but when he didn't she resumed her self-fondling – overcome by the warm, sexy darkness.

The tenderness of her clitoris made her sob, but she could

no more stop touching it than stop breathing. She felt her consciousness ascend again, soaring up on a steep curve of pleasure. And as she handled her own sticky body, she sensed Jake, nearby, attending to his. She imagined his penis released from its leather confinement as he stroked it to fulfilment and relief. Her memory displayed her the balcony scene, and she saw *him* climbing over *her* back as the blond pederast had mounted his black victim. Bizarrely, she also seemed to 'remember' her sister's experiences. Being licked and touched. The tantalising 'did he, didn't he' of wondering whether he'd really been inside her.

Then it was back to being herself again, and being fingered and displayed in the limousine. She whimpered at the enormity of it, and the shaming. And how much that shame had intensified her climax. Her finger rode hard on her painful bud and she came again in a long wet burst – just as the house lights started phasing back on again. Deana's vision was blurred with pleasure, but it didn't stop her seeing quite a sight . . . Her so-called 'lover' being kissed by another woman!

The embrace was something of a shock, and even more shocking was the sensation that came along with it. The long brown curve of Jake's bare throat – as he craned backwards in his seat to be kissed upside down – was as erotic in its own way as anything that had happened on the stage. Intellect told Deana she should be jealous, but instead she felt only titillation. The kisser was stunning; an elegant, pale-skinned woman dressed in a shirt and jeans of silk-smooth black latex rubber. Her hair was a brilliant zinging red, and styled in a long thick plait, a great living hank that hung forward over her shoulder, trailed down across Jake, and lay on his heaving chest like a shimmering rope of blood.

Good God, she's almost raping him! thought Deana, aroused anew – and against her will – by the sheer animality of Jake being kissed and taken by force. The woman had complete, albeit temporary control of him and her long white hands, bejewelled with many rings, were a frame for his dark face and jaw. Her bold pink tongue was clearly visible as it darted its way deep into his mouth.

At length the clinch dissolved, and the woman straightened up like a flower uncurling to the sun. Her lips were moist, Deana noted. And naturally, deeply, and flawlessly red. There was no lipstick there to be spoiled by kisses because this strange, gorgeous woman didn't need it.

'Good evening, Vida,' said Jake lazily, swivelling in his chair to greet the newcomer less intimately.

'And good evening to you, Kazuto, my Japanese jewel,' replied Vida zestily, reaching out to touch his high slanted cheek-bone. 'I've been wondering how long I had to wait for you.'

'Business, my dear,' he shot back at her, grabbing her wrist and kissing its inner surface. 'Some of us have to do a lot of tedious wheeling and dealing to earn our crust. We can't all live the life of the creative elite.'

She's been his lover! thought Deana, her instincts clanging. She felt suddenly excluded. What if she still *is* his lover? What does that make me?

And yet when the mysterious Vida turned towards her, Deana felt bathed in a warm glow of interest. The red-headed woman smiled, deep in her eyes as well as with her soft crimson mouth, and with a playful pinch of Jake's dark cheek, she abandoned him and refocused her attentions.

'Hello, I'm Vida Mistry. Who the devil are you?' Eyes like chips of emerald bored deep into Deana's embarrassment, reminding her where her fingers still were. The name was familiar now too. The woman was a writer, quite a notorious one. Deana even had some of her books!

'Paws off, Mistry!' said Jake easily. 'Dee's my protégée tonight. Go find some prey of your own!'

Wriggling anxiously, Deana had managed to ease her skirt at least partially down over her thighs and bottom. The movement, however, was uncouth and graceless and seemed to amuse the watching Vida enormously.

'Oh yes, Dee,' she said creamily, pulling up a chair and sinking down onto it, 'he gets to me like that sometimes too.'

Before Deana could speak or even move, the other woman had reached for her hand and was kissing the sex-scent on her fingers.

'Delicious,' she whispered, her green eyes blazing. 'Why not forget this loser and come home with me?' She made an affectionate yet dismissive gesture towards Jake – who seemed as entertained as the rubber-clad authoress by Deana's pink-stained cheeks.

'Not tonight, Mistry,' he said, rising suddenly and gracefully to his feet. 'It's getting late and I haven't had Dee yet.' His narrow hand dropped casually to his leather-covered crotch and the swell of his obvious erection.

Deana was burning up now, and trembling. She felt helpless, as Jake reached out with a deft, almost magician-like precision, and managed to urge her to her feet and straighten her skirt in one smooth unnoticeable action. Both he and the preposterous Vida were treating her like an object or a possession – and against her will she was loving it. It was insane, but at the moment he'd casually remarked he hadn't 'had' her, she'd suddenly wanted *him* quite desperately. Her bare sex rippled as her skirt skated down on its lining and covered her; and she had a sudden, mindless urge to throw herself down across the table before them. She wanted Jake to caress her and take her, and she even wanted Vida to watch him.

'Come along, my dear,' he whispered in her ear as she

considered her lunatic fancy. 'We have very little time and I don't think I can wait much longer to be inside you.' He slid alongside her and discreetly pressed his loins to her hip. The bulge beneath the leather was no illusion; he was as hard as stone. As hard as he'd been in the gallery, and if it were possible, more so.

'Goodbye, Dee,' said Vida Mistry gaily as they drew away from her. 'We'll meet again soon.' There was a glint in her eyes that rayed out in the room's sultry gloom. A sharp, spiky shine that was both frightening and thrilling. Deana felt a lovely softness between her legs that shouldn't have happened for a woman, and she was almost relieved when Jake propelled her firmly ahead of him with a hand on her leather-covered buttock. She sensed him turn and make some gesture or other to Vida, but she didn't dare look around again herself.

As they left the house, the limousine slunk up to the kerb in front of them, even though Deana had seen no call of any kind made to summon it. Was Fargo a mind reader? Was Jake himself telepathic? Oh God, the prospect of *that* was terrifying!

'What do you think of Mistry?' he asked when they were sealed into the car and gliding away. It seemed he was a telepath. He'd read not only her confused feelings about the eccentric author, but the way his hands were already sliding up her thighs said he'd also perceived her desire. Her hot new yearning for *him*.

This time he was not so solicitous of her stockings, and she felt a volley of fine tickling runs, the sheer mesh popping as he grabbed her.

The slim leather skirt went back up.

'I . . . I think she's very . . . um . . . impressive,' she stuttered, her words broken up by the rough way he opened her thighs then rummaged through the curls of her sex.

'She wants you, that's obvious!' he said, taking her clitoris in his fingers just as Vida herself might've done.

'No!'

It was a squeal, a panicked squeak of denial, but denial of what, she wasn't sure. The pain in her over-pleasured clitoris? The gorgeous rush in spite of that pain? The fact that a dominant lesbian wanted her and she wanted that woman in return?

'Yes, pretty Dee.' There was a laugh in his voice as well as desire. He was playing with her love-lips now, pulling and stretching at them, creating more small pains which only made her nectar run thicker.

'I'd like to see you with a woman,' he said almost absently as he rubbed and dabbled and worked, jiggling at the soft, rude place between her legs.

'I wonder what you'd do,' he whispered. 'How you'd go about it . . . Christ, this is no good!'

Jerkily, without any of his customary smoothness and finesse, he rolled back to sit on the seat and opened his leather-clad thighs. 'It's going to be another quickie, my sweet. Duty calls. I'm flying to Zurich tonight, but I want to come in you before I go.' He grinned at his own small joke, his hooded eyes narrowing sensually as his hands went to down his belt. Without looking, he flipped open the buckle, whizzed down the slick expensive zipper, then eased out his naked, swollen penis. It stood in the close, expectant air like a tower. A fat red tower rising between twin rows of shiny vicious teeth. Deana saw no evidence of any kind of underwear, but the potential hazard to his manhood seemed to trouble him not one bit. In fact, as he began to rub himself, it almost seemed as if he enjoyed the danger, and that the threat from the zip had made his erection grow harder than ever.

'Get astride,' he said bluntly, abandoning his masturbation

to jerk up her skirt even higher. Then, taking her firmly by the hips, he helped her lever herself into position.

At last! At last! At last! she screamed inside as his glans pushed up into her haven. Rocking to and fro, she powered down onto it. She closed her eyes as she sank, and the length and girth of him seemed to go up and infinitely into her. She felt the exposed zip dig into her labia as she settled right down, but she no longer felt pain in the face of such overwhelming fullness. It seemed as if she'd never had a man so deep inside her. He was pushing against her womb with his cock-head, and the stretch of her inner flesh around him felt like silk cords pulling tautly on her clitoris. She didn't want to move. She didn't want him to move. She just wanted to be there, astride, with her hot female centre impaled on him.

When she felt his hands on her bodice, her eyes flew open, and she witnessed a scene of destruction. Oh no, not her pretty, sparkly top! Sequins popped and flew as he wrenched it roughly down to her waist and exposed her berry-nippled breasts.

'Hey, you bastard! Look what you've done!' she shouted, angry in spite of their joining.

'I'll buy you a hundred tops,' he snarled, gripping a breast in each hand and squeezing. 'God, lady, you're so beautiful!' He twisted each soft, aching mound and she screamed, her stretched quim convulsing and fluttering. The silver-silk cords had tightened now, as if connected by magic to the flesh he was mauling.

As she orgasmed, Deana looked out over Jake's shoulder into a dark void of physical ecstasy. The night streets were flowing by her as normal, yet she watched them with a goddess-like detachment.

A middle-aged woman tried to stare into the car as it passed, then appeared to frown at Deana's half-naked body. Further on, a young boy waved and whistled as if he really could see what was happening ... and the flesh of Deana's sex seemed to answer with a ripple that made love to the man lodged inside it.

When the car pulled to a halt at a set of red traffic-lights, Jake groaned, kissed Deana passionately, then jerked like a puppet gone crazy as his warm seed pulsed out against her womb.

Some time later, in another world, the traffic-lights changed back to green again. But as the black car fired up and moved forward, the couple on its back seat didn't notice ...

5

Home Comforts

It was madness to look out of the window, but Delia couldn't help herself. She had to see Jake, she just had to. Even if it meant the game was up before it had properly begun.

'What's going on, Delia? What the hell's going on? Why don't you want to meet this man?'

Peter's voice, just behind her, made Delia nearly jump out of her skin. She'd been expecting him to ask questions, but this vehemence was a total surprise. To hear his usually mild and husky tones made sharp and clipped by anger was a shock, but indefinably and inexplicably a pleasant one. It was like seeing a fat pet cat grow sleek and mean and beautiful when it put back its ears and snarled.

Slightly shaken, she dropped the curtain back into place and turned away from the window. She'd probably missed Jake and Deana anyway.

Peter. Bless him. He was always around when they needed him: with the metaphorical cupful of sugar and any other favour they might ask for.

'It's a long story, Peter,' she said, still puzzled by his unexpected anger. 'But if you've got an hour or two, I can tell you the gory details.'

Even as she watched, his irritation faded. The frown left his thin but quietly handsome face and made way for his usual amenable expression.

'Even better, Delia.' He grinned and he was good, kind 'Pete' again. 'I've got a whole evening, a flat that needs some female company to brighten it up, and a batch of my gooseberry rocket-fuel that's just perfectly aged for drinking!'

Delia shuddered. Peter's home-made plonk was sinfully delicious, but it reamed out the inside of your head the next morning.

'You're on!' she said boldly, the prospect of drinking to forget Jake de Guile being suddenly irresistibly tempting. Especially in this neat, pleasantly decorated flat – one floor above her own – which felt exquisitely cool on a night that was otherwise unbearably oppressive. By the time she'd had enough wine to forget what was happening, she'd be beyond the thrall of temperature anyway. And then she could just crawl downstairs, summon Jake the Prince into her drunken dreams and masturbate herself to oblivion.

Feeling cheered by that prospect, she watched Peter fuss with glasses and bottles and ice, and once again felt that strange surge of interest.

Gentle Peter, their upstairs neighbour, with his soft brown hair, his skinny pale-skinned body and his large hazel eyes behind owlish horn-rimmed glasses. He was no de Guile, no fantasy sex-god, but tonight he had a surprising allure to him. And he certainly had a massive edge over Russell, she thought guiltily, realising how little she'd thought about the man who was supposed to be her boyfriend. It had been a turbulent day, admittedly, but after she'd left his flat, she'd almost forgotten he existed. She'd have to do something about *that* soon too.

'OK then, let's hear it,' said Peter folding his lean frame into the seat opposite hers, then taking a deep, and plainly much needed, swallow of his ice-cooled home-made wine.

'Well, I told you about the "big boss of all big bosses", didn't I?' She paused to take a sip of her own wine, and was silenced for a full thirty seconds. Its high-octane, fruit-loaded flavour exploded on her tongue – then seemed to descale the inside of her throat. 'Good grief, Pete, this stuff is lethal!' she croaked, taking another, more cautious sip.

'The boss of all bosses,' he prompted, making Delia look up sharply. That sexy, angry edge was back again, and behind the thick glass lenses that helped him to see, his puppy-dog eyes looked suddenly and dangerously hard.

Slowly, she began. Slowly, because the tale seemed sordid told from the outside and needed conveying with care. She hid nothing though, because this was Pete, her mate and Deana's, the one with whom they'd always shared their troubles.

Sexual honesty got easier as the wine bottle emptied. As the heavy fruit nectar slid more comfortably down her throat, it seemed natural to describe Jake more fully. Without thinking, she waxed lyrical about his lips, his hands and his cock. Then moved on drunkenly to the case of mistaken identity, and the Gemini Game. Which suddenly seemed a perfectly logical and acceptable way to conduct oneself. Oneselves . . .

And as the wine warmed her belly and loins she felt no shame in describing how she wished that tonight was 'her' night with her Prince, de Guile. How she craved again what she'd had that morning. And more. How she wanted to *know* she'd been taken this time, to feel it. Feel that big, smooth penis sliding into *her* and filling her as it had filled Deana at the exhibition. As it was probably filling her now – in some luxurious bed in some exclusive hotel or apartment.

''Tisn't fair, Pete!' she said, aware that she was slurring and that she was lolling ungracefully in her armchair. Her legs were splayed akimbo in a fair approximation of how they'd been on Jake's black leather couch. She was drunk, but it didn't seem to matter. Nothing mattered but not having Jake inside her. She'd lost the toss and now her burning female furrow was making her suffer for it.

'It isn't fair at all,' she enunciated carefully, tugging at her shorts which were suddenly uncomfortable and clinging. Tight between her slim, hot legs. 'He thinks he's got "Delia" but he hasn't. He's got "Deana"!' She took another pull at her drink, surprised to find it brimming again. There was already an 'empty' on the table. 'I love her, Pete, I really do! But I wish to hell that she could've sprained her ankle or something.'

'I do too.'

The dead, blank seriousness in Peter's quiet voice was a new shock. It jerked her back to sobriety. He did what? Wish Deana had a sprained ankle? Or was it something else?

Looking up from her glass with new clarity, she saw a very different man to the Peter she knew and was fond of. This was an angry man. An aroused man. A man full of passion and fire, not the mild-mannered almost genderless friend that she always took for granted.

'You're in love with Deana, aren't you?' she asked – the illuminations coming to her in droves.

'Yes,' he said crossly. As if the heat were suddenly too much for him too, he tugged off his baggy white T-shirt, tousling his hair in the process. Somewhere along the line, he'd removed his 'mad professor' glasses, and his eyes seemed ten times as bright without them. Or was it thwarted lust that was doing that? In a relapse into bleary tipsiness, Delia couldn't work out which.

'This must seem pretty weird to you,' he went on, before pausing to swig down more wine. 'I'm telling you that I'm in love with a woman who looks just like you.'

'Not as weird as you think,' Delia answered. She took another drink of her own wine as an unthinkable idea occurred to her.

With the slow, simple rationality of the far from sober, she saw an elegant solution to their problems. To her sexual dilemma and Peter's.

'Do you want to make love to her?' she asked bluntly, as fire built low in her belly. She could see pictures in her head now. Pictures of Deana, her legs wide open, being possessed by the dark, ruthless Jake.

But no, it wasn't Deana! It was herself. Delia. Her face! Her body! If she closed her eyes she could slip into the scene: live it, make it happen. All she needed was a hard, male penis inside her.

And what if she could make an illusion for the man who provided that penis?

Draining her glass yet again, she rose to her feet and walked carefully across the room. Extremely carefully, because it seemed – very slightly – to sway ... Pulling off her own T-shirt, she dropped down onto the sofa next to Peter, then cupped her bare breasts in her hands, offering them to him as if they were a pair of softly ripe fruits.

'Make love to me, Peter,' she said, her voice faint. She flicked her nipples lewdly, to make them stiffen up and grow hard. For him.

'Delia ... I don't—'

'It's "Dee",' she corrected him, 'Dee Ferraro. I play games, remember?' The wine made her powerful and she reached for his narrow hand with its square, neatly trimmed nails. He shook, visibly, when she placed it on the slope of her breast.

'Just for tonight, Pete. Please?' It seemed strangely apt to be pleading. She would've grovelled to de Guile, wouldn't she?

'But I know the difference,' replied Peter, his voice cracking. He was protesting but his hand was already moulding her flesh. It was clear he was enjoying it.

'For comfort then ... If you can't pretend.'

'Oh Dee,' he sighed, moving in on her, even though she'd no idea whether it *was* for comfort. Maybe it was for fantasy's sake, after all?

For a moment, she drew back within herself. Calm and centred, she looked at the real man with her, not the sex-fiend who'd hijacked her body this morning. Peter wasn't Jake. He wasn't dark, or mysterious, or an insatiable creature of wealth and power. But his smooth, pale body was hard and wiry – and far from unpleasant to her eyes.

His thin arms were strong as they pulled her to him and crushed her in a tight, shocking grip. Her nipples and his were pressed up against each other. And as his mouth met hers, he moaned into it, shimmying his body as if his small brown teats felt all the pleasure that her larger, rose red ones did.

His tongue was bold too. Probing and tasting as their wine-scented saliva mingled. It seemed a prelude to a far greater blending, a bolder probing. She sighed and sucked at his mouth.

'You're so good to me, Dee,' he murmured, then sucked hard on her tongue in return. He savoured the muscular flexible organ as if it were a sweetmeat or a lollipop. A nipple or a clitoris. Delia moaned, her hips lifting and beating against him with a life that was all of their own.

There was a pressure and a heat down there now, a pulsating, tingling discomfort that wasn't unpleasant at all. The mouth between her legs seemed to whimper and beg and cry out. She was hungry. Hungry for maleness. For flesh. To be filled . . . Perversely, she still knew that Jake de Guile would be perfection inside her. Even though it was Peter who was actually here with her. Here with his available penis. A penis that was hard against her body and pressing towards her sex like a missile homing blindly in on its target. Even several layers of cloth could do nothing to deflect it.

Suddenly she wanted to be naked on a mattress with her legs open wide to receive him.

'Come on, Pete, let's do it!' she purred, aware of her own unsubtlety, but helpless to do anything about it. Scrabbling at his shorts, she tried to free his cock and get her hands on it. The button on his waistband slipped easily through the worn button-hole, but as she started to unzip him, she felt her fingers grasped firmly in his.

'Slow down, Dee,' he whispered, taking her busy hands off him and holding them still in her lap. 'I've waited too long for—' He paused and smiled boyishly. 'For something like this . . . I want it to last. I want to savour it. Just the way I've always imagined I would.'

This was a deviation from the fantasy pattern. Both with her, and by all accounts, with Deana, Jake had been swift in the taking and the pleasuring of his woman. In each case, of course, circumstances had dictated there be haste, but somehow slow leisurely sex was not what she associated with Jackson Kazuto de Guile.

Even as she thought this, she made a decision. She was with Peter now and it was Peter she'd have inside her. Jake would be hers – or she his – some other night.

'Let's go to bed, shall we?' she said, rising shakily to her feet. After unfastening her cool linen shorts, she pushed them down her legs with her panties tangled inside them. Naked, she took Peter's hand and urged him to his feet too. 'I've had enough of quickies on settees. I fancy some of that "savouring" of yours!'

A new Peter stood before her now, a tempting Peter whose worn old shorts were tented with magnificent promise. There was pleasure in sight, and Delia was ready.

'You're right. Let's do this properly.' He took her by the hand and escorted her decorously across the room. 'Let's go to bed, shall we . . . Delia?'

Somehow even Peter's bedsheets were cool. Delia sighed happily as she lay down on them and stretched out her limbs luxuriously. Reaching behind her head, she pulled out her hair-ribbon and let the whole brown glossy mass of waves fan out across the crisp white pillow. 'Come on, Pete. Join me,' she encouraged.

But for a full minute he just stood still, admiring her naked and honey coloured body.

'You're beautiful,' he whispered, sliding out of his shorts and underpants and lying down on the sheet beside her.

Who's beautiful? she wondered as he started to touch her. She felt spaced out from the wine and languid from heat and arousal. It didn't seem to matter whether it was Deana he wanted, or herself, or even this peculiar amalgamated creature called 'Dee'. Nor did it matter – at this precise moment – that the fingers at her breasts were Peter's. They were cool and gentle and skilled. It might matter later who he was, when Deana came back all aglow from Jake. But now it seemed perfectly wonderful to be with this thoughtful, less demanding lover. This lean, diffident man with his tentative sexual style and his surprisingly imposing penis.

His caresses were slow but extraordinarily sensuous – as if he were trying to imprint the entire shape of her body in his memory. The pads of his fingers rode her smoothly but comprehensively, but didn't dive for the obvious zones. He seemed content to dally in less likely latitudes. A shoulder-blade. The inside of a forearm. The arch of a foot.

She wondered if he would want to lick her sex, and she parted her legs in readiness, trying to consciously forget that only this morning Jake had licked her there.

But Peter seemed happy enough with touching. Touching her belly, the edge of her pubic hair, the long inner slope of her thigh where it was beginning to get sticky with her juices.

And as he touched, he kissed her mouth; pressing in but only lightly this time. He stroked the inside of her lips with his tongue then dabbed it delicately to hers.

The slowness, the circumspection, were unbearably tantalising and delicious. Did he know how hot it was making her? She supposed he did. For him this was a remarkable and special occasion. A fantasy come true. Even if he had called her 'Delia' out of courtesy. The gradual build-up was what he needed to make the moment fabulous and who was she to argue. 'Perfect' for him would surely mean 'marvellous' for her, and there might never be another night when wine would so blur the barriers.

When he finally touched her clitoris, she cried out hoarsely and orgasmed straight away. The intensity was incredible, and when she could quantify again, she was astounded that she'd felt so much sensation and ecstasy with not a single scrap of fantasy to help her. As she opened her thighs wider, and leaned into his slow rubbing hand, she was fully aware he was Peter and that her pleasure was complete because of him. She moaned his name spontaneously, and when she opened her eyes, and looked up into his dear, but rather short-sighted gaze, she could've sworn she saw the glitter of tears.

'Are you all right?' She reached up to touch his mouth, then felt a spark of unlooked-for excitement. He'd sucked in her fingertip quite naturally and started nibbling it. His lips felt cool, and his tongue was moist and caressing.

'Yes,' he answered muffledly, then continued his tasting by biting each digit in turn. 'I'm very all right... How about you?'

'Yes ... You've got the most wonderful hands, do you know that?' she burst out, without thinking.

'So have you,' he said, nipping at the cushioning flesh at the base of her thumb and causing a ripple of response in her quim. Suddenly she was desperate to have him in her. She wriggled her sweaty body against him, blatantly inviting him to penetrate her.

'Oh Dee,' he sighed, moving over her. His body felt unexpectedly large and strong for a man so slender and whippy. As his penis nudged its way into her damp eager furrow, she looked down the length of his narrow white back and for a second imagined it brown and exotic.

But as Peter the living man slid into her, Jake the fantasy slid away, forgotten. She still didn't know who *she* was to the man inside her, but he was just Peter, and wonderful. His cock was solid and satisfying, his thrusts long and even. There was a wonderful quality of stability about him.

He'll last, she thought happily. She'd have all the orgasms she needed and there wouldn't be that embarrassing far-too-soon finish that she sometimes experienced with Russell.

Her tender, loving Peter might look like a skinny sprinter, but as he settled into a smooth easy rhythm, she realised to her joy he was a stayer. A long-distance man.

And *that* thought was enough to make it all happen again. She orgasmed deep and hard and sweetly from simply the prospect of rapture. The knowing, the certainty of pleasure...

Panting and squirming, she angled her hips and coiled her legs round his back to intensify the glorious sensation. Her clitoris knocked hard against his pubic bone and the stiff sliding root of his penis. And as she moaned under the mind-bending impacts, she felt him shifting his body above her. Moving his weight with a neat sure grace to make their contact even closer and better...

He was asleep when she left, and she wondered fleetingly which twin it was he was dreaming of. Whichever, she'd made him smile.

Padding soundlessly down the stairs, Delia realised that she too was smiling.

Who'd have thought it? Peter! A soft-spoken superlover right on her doorstep. For several delicious, orgasmic hours he'd almost driven Jake from her mind. Almost . . .

As she let herself into her own flat, the gloomy brooding warmth brought thoughts of Jake flooding back in. Thoughts, and speculations.

What had he done with Deana tonight? Or done to her? What wild new pleasures would they have tasted together? What positions? What perversions?

Delia was tempted to go straight to bed and try and forget everybody. Jake. Peter. Russell. Deana. Life and sex were suddenly so complicated, and it'd be oh-so-much easier just to cover her head with her pillow and temporarily ignore the lot of it. But common sense and the beginnings of a headache said otherwise. If she didn't take in fluid now, and lots of it, she'd be digging her grave for the morning. She'd had a gooseberry wine hangover once . . . and there was no way she could bear having another!

After two glasses of water, the character of her thirst seemed to change. She got a sudden sharp yen for herbal tea, but when she came to switch on the kettle she found it already filled and the water not far from boiling.

After dunking her tea-bag quickly, she took her mug and padded towards the lounge, in search of her sister.

Deana was sitting in the dark.

A cold hand clutched Delia's belly. What was wrong? Deana loved brilliance and light, why was she skulking in shadows?

Delia's fears turned to anger, furious white anger, when she turned on the lamp and saw the state of her twin's face and body.

Deana looked as if she'd been dragged sideways through

a hurricane! The pretty coiled hair-do they'd worked on so carefully was a tangled tumbling mess. Her lipstick was smeared across her face like cherry juice. And strands of half-detached sequins were dripping from her glamorous bustier. Her sheer dark stocking a striped mass of creamy creeping ladders.

'The bastard! He's raped you! The absolute, shitty bastard!'

Delia was wracked by a sudden almost painful guilt. This was *her* fault. She'd let her foolhardy, sexually brave sister get hurt and degraded. The turn of a coin was pure chance, she knew it, but somehow she still felt that she was to blame. That she was the one who should be sitting there battered and dishevelled . . . and perhaps hiding worse beneath her skirt.

'He didn't actually.'

Something in her sister's voice made Delia look more closely.

Deana was cradling a cup of tea of her own, but over the top of it she was smiling. A smile that Delia had often seen before. A slow, silky, sexy, self-satisfied grin that she'd never been able to replicate – even though she had the exact same face to do it with.

'Oh . . .'

'Yes . . . Oh.'

'So, what happened?' she quizzed. 'Something must've . . . You look as if you've been molested by a gang of sex-starved navvies!'

'Well, I suppose he was hungry.'

Deana's words were dreamy and cryptic, a match for the smile itself. She ran a fingernail down one of her ladders, and the pale streak widened and lengthened. 'But he made himself that way.'

'What do you mean?'

'Brace yourself, Sis.' The smile was naughty now. And it got naughtier and naughtier as softly, calmly and in very great detail, Deana described her evening.

Delia went hot, cold, and then hot again. Very hot. She thought she'd experienced wildness with Jake, but what Deana described was insane. A deranged dark dream that turned on both teller and listener.

Masturbation. Exposure. Fetish clubs. Lesbians. Being made to come in public. Being shown, intimately, to servants. It was all so extreme. So much heavier, deeper and more deviant than her own slight thrills. What had happened in Jake's office was tame to him. Almost a norm...

Suddenly, a stark fact surfaced. She too was 'Dee'.

'But I can't do all that!' she cried, her panic rising.

'Yes, you can, love,' said Deana softly. 'In a way, you already have. It isn't just a face we share. You know that, don't you? Deep down...'

Delia had a great yearning for a glass of Peter's wine. Herbal tea couldn't settle all this... Because Deana was right.

Their pleasures had been different tonight but the craving for sex was the same. Deana had found what she wanted elsewhere. Out on the sharp edge of daring. But she, Delia, had found an equal comfort at home. The colours of experience were different but the conclusion was ultimately the same.

'And anyway –' Deana was studying her intently now '– what have *you* been up to while I've been out?' Her artist's all-seeing eyes had obviously noticed something. Some change that Delia wasn't aware of. 'You've got a look you never get with Russell. You look as if you've had quite a seeing to.'

Oh no, if she told Deana about Peter, she'd also have to tell her who he loved!

'You sly witch,' said Deana, her face wreathed in smiles. 'You and Peter. Well well well, I never would've guessed. Does Russ the Wuss know?' Her eyes narrowed, turned ever-so-slightly calculating. 'Does this mean I've got Jake to myself?'

'No, it doesn't!' Delia felt wild and panicky, her body and her senses rebelling. It was crazy. Not like her at all. But what her sister had just recounted had made her want Jake more than ever.

'There is no "me and Peter",' she went on, trying hard to sound reasonable and calm. 'And there's no "me and Russell" any more either.'

Deana looked genuinely delighted and opened her mouth to speak. But before the inevitable questions, Delia cut in again.

'The Gemini Game's still on, Deana,' she said, her voice soft but steely, 'and it's my turn next. So you'd better let me know when that is . . .'

6

One Man's Geisha

Deana hadn't known when or where. It was Delia who found out herself, two days later, when she walked into her office and sat down. There was a blue envelope in the exact centre of her blotter, and beneath it lay a slim leather folder, also blue. Frowning, she slit open the envelope with her fingernail and eased out its meagre contents. A single sheet of very fine grade sky-blue writing paper.

Dee, began the message in a firm black script, *I'm back. I'll send the car tonight at eight. Be ready, the way you were last time, but dress casually. Dress to be undressed.* It was unsigned.

When she'd read the note, an impulse made her lift it to her face and sniff. It was usually only women who scented their letters, but this particular correspondent was a blatant and unashamed rule-breaker.

Delia smiled. She'd been right, that lovely floral smell of his *was* there, the paper was heavy with it. As she inhaled deeply to draw in the fragrance, a bouquet of lush memories assailed her. Her own and Deana's ... A tell-tale heat rose spontaneously to her face as she thought of what her sister had told her.

It had been a lurid account, but lyrical. And those graphic details, plus sex in general, had been occupying most of Delia's mind-space for the last two boiling hot days.

And it wasn't just 'Jake and sex' either. There was Peter too.

It still seemed something of a marvel to her that their mild-mannered neighbour could turn into a sexual Superman. She wondered how much the wine had to do with it. Would he be just as dynamic sober? Would she, for that matter?

Well done, Delia, she congratulated herself, sighing. Now you've got another 'situation' on your hands. Not content with having to break – gracefully – with Russell whilst playing this mad game with Jake and Deana ... you've now managed to get yourself involved with *another* man!

But would it stop at three?

Since that first morning in Jake's office, she'd found herself checking out all sorts of men. Male colleagues she'd never looked twice at. The boy who brought in the sandwiches. Stray men in the street and in shops. Almost before she realised what she was doing, she'd assess their faces and bodies, then wonder what they'd look like naked. Within seconds she'd have them mentally in bed. Her body would rouse as she imagined each man's performance. It was shocking and right out of character, but she had a distinct feeling that her sex drive had changed forever. A valve in her body had opened and her hormones were pouring out unchecked. She felt flooded with a wild erotic input, her libido limitless and surging.

And now this!

Putting aside the letter, she flipped open the leather folder. Ranged in two neat ranks were a dozen or so credit cards, all made out in her name. A set of computer-printed slips informed her that she now had unlimited credit in places she'd only ever dreamed of shopping. Another of Jake's notes said why.

For your hundred tops.

It puzzled her at first, but then she remembered Deana and the shredded bustier.

The swine! He thinks he can buy us!

Delia felt dizzy with a mix of emotions. Outrage vied with

arousal. Insulted proprieties were undermined by a luscious sense of decadence. She had a sudden, thrilling awareness of how it would feel to be a courtesan. A kept woman showered with exclusive gifts in return for the use of her body. She slid out a card and eyed a world famous logo, then unfolded the letter again.

Dress to be undressed it said.

As she studied the stark, black symbols, Delia felt that sly dark pull again. The lure of immorality. Suddenly it all seemed so logical . . .

If Jake was the one who took the clothes off, he was the one who should pay for them. Why not?

In the end, she wore her own clothes. Or more correctly, hers and Deana's.

The soft, loose shirt in wild pink silk was one of her favourites; and the skin-tight black lycra leggings were Deana's. Delia had originally picked out a pair of dark, tailored trousers, but Deana had discarded them. Everything about this escapade was both sexy and daring, she'd pointed out. It was up to them to dress the part. *Both* of them.

Out in the drive, at eight o'clock, the car cruised its way to a halt. Inside their flat, the sisters kissed and hugged, then one stepped out onto the porch while the other slid back into the shadows.

Delia found the blond chauffeur chilling. His face was a blank, handsome mask and his haircut shaved and brutal. So this was the infamous Fargo, she thought. The hard man. She watched his approach warily, then pictured him toting a sub-machine gun in a mercenary army. It was difficult to imagine him being interested in sex at all. He seemed too ascetic for arousal.

'Good evening, ma'am.' Fargo's voice was as gravelly as his

face suggested, but his demeanour was exquisitely respectful. As he helped her into the limousine, Delia found herself wondering what *he* looked like naked.

The cool, leather-covered seat was strangely affecting. It felt familiar to her. Dangerously evocative. Inextricably linked with sex. Deana had sat in this very same place with her pubis uncovered. She'd ridden Jake's cock here, her warm thighs astride him. She'd come in this car. Come and come. And Delia could feel the echoes ... Hear the shrill cries of pleasure. She could almost feel Jake inside her, feel her body grip his with its tight inner muscles. Running her fingertips over the leather, she gasped when her flesh roused and fluttered. Soft, moist heat seemed to flow inside her close-fitting panties.

What lay ahead, she hardly dare contemplate. What did an 'at home' with Jackson de Guile amount to? There'd been no mention of dinner, but she wasn't hungry anyway. Not for food. It seemed appalling that a man should invite a woman to his home purely for sex, but Jake was a sensualist. And direct. He seemed not to need the games that other men played.

She had a sudden vision of herself on a couch before him. Her body spreadeagled, her sex open. She was pinned. Fettered even. Her vulva exposed to his perusal.

Other sights followed on ...

She was kneeling at his feet with his penis in her mouth; his erection was huge and dark. She was drooling and her lips were stretched around him. She remembered the taste of the Prince – as vivid as life – and knew without question that Jake would taste the same. Or better.

The journey took nowhere near as long as she'd expected and she was still lewdly dreaming when she realised it was over. The powerful, almost noiseless car had drawn to a silent full stop. At a loss, she stayed where she was until the door swung open beside her.

'We've arrived, ma'am,' Fargo said neutrally, offering his arm to assist her from the car.

Arrived. But where?

Delia didn't know what she'd been expecting, but they had drawn up before a large, immaculately kept Regency town house. One of those terrifyingly expensive residences which were so beautifully situated that only the most wealthy could afford them. But then again, Jake *was* wealthy. Unimaginably rich and powerful. He was only a prince in her dream-world, but he probably had more money than most real royalty did. This blue-doored house certainly seemed to suggest so.

On the front step, a young woman stood waiting. An ebony-haired sylph of a girl in a crisp white dress and shiny black high-heeled shoes. Her face was indistinct from where Delia stood on the pavement, but her slender form was silhouetted dramatically by the soft, golden toned light flowing out from the hall behind her. She was of medium height, and as she moved forward in greeting, Delia saw a most unusual and delicate face. Perfect cameo features, long dark uptilted eyes, and a smile like the rising of the sun. Given Jake's own eastern heritage it seemed obvious that she came from Japan.

'Hello, Dee. I'm Elf. Jake will be busy for an hour or two, so he's asked me to take care of you.'

The voice was husky, and as harmonious as the lovely, porcelain face. Delia felt a worrying surge of excitement.

'Do come in,' Elf went on. As soon as they were close enough, she slid her arm around Delia's waist in a gesture of intimacy. 'Don't be shy, Dee. There's nothing to be scared of here.'

Not so sure that was true, Delia let herself be led inside, dimly aware of the car gliding off behind her.

Who the hell are you? She wanted to ask her elegant new companion, but the sheer surprise of Elf's presence, and the perfect assurance of her touch, seemed to disperse Delia's questions like mist.

The entrance hall was spacious, and its decor so subduedly luxurious it was almost bland. Delia remembered something Deana had said, and wondered if this was the same strange featurelessness that had prevailed at Club 'Seventeen' – a calm plain backdrop for all that was weird and outlandish.

When she caught sight of a large glowing painting that hung on the far wall of the hall, her first impressions were drastically altered.

Within the bounds of a heavy rococo frame, a naked couple were entwined and screwing, their bodies meticulously defined. No detail was skimped, no genital nuance skimmed over, yet the image was tasteful and beautiful. Delia knew that Deana would most certainly have commented on it, but she herself dared not. Her artistic sister would see subtleties of tone and brushwork that she couldn't. To Delia the painting was just sex.

Welcome to the Pleasuredome, she thought bemusedly. Yet as they ascended a wide, lushly carpeted stairway, she was already starting to feel more at home. And unbearably curious about Elf.

'Who are you?' she asked as they reached the landing and crossed towards an open, beige-painted door. 'I...um...Jake never mentioned...'

'I suppose you could call me his valet.' The oriental woman smiled, her face open and pleasant. 'I care for him. Look after his needs and his welfare...' She paused and when she turned to face Delia, the smile was more oblique and seductive. 'And I care for his guests too. Please come this way, Dee. Jake has instructed me to pamper you.'

Delia's confusion returned, more strongly this time. If he's got a beautiful woman like you, she said silently as Elf led the way, what on earth does he want me for?

The room they entered was the hugest bathing and dressing area that Delia had ever seen. A great, softly glowing cavern of peaches, creams and apricots, it was complete with every imaginable facility for luxurious personal grooming. The bath itself was bigger than her living room.

'Please ... May I help you take off your clothes?' Elf asked politely, as if it were the most normal thing in the world to visit a man for the evening and have his servant undress you.

'Er ... Yes,' Delia replied, sliding rapidly out of her depth. She allowed Elf to take her bag from her, then gently start unbuttoning the flowing silk shirt. The oriental girl seemed quite happy to perform her sensuous duties in silence, but nerves made Delia want to chatter.

'Is "Elf" your real name?' she asked, her voice wavering. Having removed and neatly folded the shirt, Elf next slid her hands around Delia's back and unclipped her bra. As she drew away the soft lacy scrap, her fingers brushed the skin she'd exposed. Delia shuddered wildly, then blushed. Her nipples were hard and puckered. Seconds later she moaned, because having put aside the bra, Elf calmly cupped the flesh it had cradled. Squeezing gently, she stroked her thumbs across the stiff protruding peaks.

'No, just a pet name,' the dark-haired girl whispered. 'My real name is—' It was a series of animated sing-song syllables and the answer to a question Delia couldn't properly remember. Struggling to concentrate, she registered that it was, of course, a Japanese name.

But the girl could've been a Martian for all Delia cared. So tenderly and so skilfully did Elf's fingers work that their nationality, and even their gender didn't matter. The touch was pure pleasure, a pure, sexually arousing sensation that made Delia weave her hips in mid-air.

'You're so sensitive,' murmured Elf, clasping together the

tips of her first fingers and her thumbs and tugging lightly on Delia's teats. 'Jake told me how beautifully you reacted.'

She should've been outraged that Jake had discussed her body and its functions with a servant, but she wasn't. Elf was caressing her so beautifully that nothing seemed to matter. Those slender golden hands were moving and flicking and pinching with all the skill and perfection that her master had employed just days ago. It was a bizarre kind of surrogacy. Jake was otherwise occupied – so he'd deputised his female valet to give pleasure to the latest of his mistresses.

Pleasure ... and an orgasm. Delia sobbed loudly, fighting her own buckling legs as a hot rush of love-juice slid out of her. She felt it trickling like silk between her swollen labia and dousing the soft gusset of her panties.

'Oh! Oh God,' she whimpered, grabbing at Elf's shoulders for support, then swaying against her body like a reed against a wall while her vulva still beat like a heart.

'Easy. It's all right. I've got you,' said Elf, abandoning her fondling now its purpose was served. She held Delia firmly, supporting her as she stumbled, then led her to a white leather couch which stood close by. Settling her on it, she soothed and cajoled her like a child who'd had a sudden fright.

'Come on, Dee. let's get these off.' She dipped down to slip off Delia's soft black flatties, then gliding smoothly upwards, she hooked her thumbs into the waistband of the borrowed black leggings. 'Help me now, sweetheart,' she whispered.

Delia obeyed like an android, lifting her bottom and letting Elf peel away the snug garment.

All that was left now was a pair of plain but pretty white knickers – chosen specially for their smooth neat cut that wouldn't show through clinging lycra. These too were pulled off with no further ado, leaving Delia embarrassed by their wetness. There was a dark, sticky mark on the gusset, but Elf hardly even seemed to notice . . .

Women probably cream themselves all the time here, thought Delia. She was beginning to feel manic now, hysterical. She laughed nervously as Elf urged her up onto the couch.

'Relax, Dee. Let your body go loose. I'm going to give you a massage now and I think you'll enjoy it. Jake always does.'

Delia turned meekly onto her front, imagining Jake doing the same thing and his cock pushing hard against the couch. If Elf's hands could bring a climax so easily and so quickly to a guest, it followed that she must also use them often on her master.

As if reading her mind, Elf spoke up as she prepared the soft-scented oils. 'What do you think of Jake then?' she asked, as if she were enquiring about a mutual boyfriend rather than her own employer. 'Doesn't he have a wonderful body?'

'I—' Delia bit her knuckle. She'd been on the point of saying 'I haven't seen it yet!' but at the last moment she remembered that Deana *had* seen it. If not all, at least some . . . She'd certainly seen Jake's cock!

'Yes,' she muttered, then purred spontaneously as strong Japanese hands ran all down the length of her leg. 'He's beautiful,' she added dreamily, knowing it must be true. If she'd seen the Prince in her fantasies, she'd inexplicably seen Jake naked too. 'I've never seen a man with such perfect, unblemished skin.'

'Thank you,' said Elf with pride in her voice. 'I'm the one who cares for his skin. I spend many hours conditioning it. I use oils like this . . .' She poured a pool of the stuff onto Delia's right buttock then spread it across her left one too. 'Massage. Deep cleansing. Exfoliation. He loves to feel sleek and smooth.'

'Oh yes,' mouthed Delia again, imagining what all that sleekness and smoothness would feel like pressed against *her*.

Imagining that Elf's clever hands were those of her master. Making it Jake that massaged, moulded and sought out all the tiny pains and tensions. They were his fingers now that delved into folds and furrows; as soft as a dragonfly in some places, and strong, almost cruel in others. It was Jake who had the rounds of her buttocks in his palms, pulling and manipulating. Jake who dipped his fingertips insolently into her; testing her abundant wetness, pressing down lightly but doing nothing to relieve her arousal.

'Not yet,' said Elf quietly, confirming that the massage was now sexual, if indeed it had ever been otherwise, 'not too soon. You've got to save something for Jake.'

'Yes. All right.' It was difficult to agree. She'd come once already, but the craving for pleasure was strong. She needed fingers between her legs. Fingers or a tongue or a cock. A man or a woman – the difference was arbitrary. She wriggled slowly, her sensuous movements making a lie of her muttered acceptance.

Sex was new to her. Real sex, that was. The hot, simmering eroticism that this silly seasonal weather had brought out in her. She was aware that her experience so far was limited – but her capacity, she suspected, was not. She felt hungry. Voracious. Insatiable.

Where would it all end? she wondered. Could she be as sexy as Deana? Her body tingled again as she imagined out-performing her sister. Winning the game. Getting Jake as the prize, all to herself. She didn't know if she wanted that, but the idea of being *able* to was electrifying . . . Like a jolt of raw power to her nipples and clitoris. With a moan, she turned over and offered her breasts, her belly, and her naked sex to Elf.

'Touch me again,' she ordered, excited by the imperious new note in her own voice. The throaty sensuality she'd never heard before. 'There'll be plenty left for him.'

'Of course,' replied Elf, returning to her duties, a paragon of geisha submissiveness.

'And you can talk to me too,' Delia continued, in love with her sense of power. 'Tell me about him. About his body. What he likes and what you have to do for him.'

'I do everything for him.' Elf's voice went low and suddenly very tender. Did she love Jake, as well as work for him? It seemed probable ... 'I serve him from the moment he rises until the moment he dismisses me for the night.'

As she spoke, Elf began unfastening first the belt then the buttons of her dress. In seconds she was stepping out of the crisp white tube, and in contrast to her care with Delia's clothing, she kicked it carelessly aside.

Delia had half expected the beautiful girl to be nude beneath her dress, but instead she wore a tiny, unstructured bra in pale pink silk with a matching pair of loose French knickers. Her body was slight but strong-looking and though her breasts were small, her nipples were large and very dark. They showed clearly through her filmy pink bra. Her pubis was almost visible too; silky tufts of straight black hair peeked endearingly from the drifting crotch of her panties. Even more showed as she reached across to the marble counter for her bottle of sweet-scented massage oil.

'How do you serve him?' Delia persisted, her voice breaking slightly as Elf began anointing her body. Starting with the twin hollows of Delia's groin, she slid the oil around in tiny circular movements, the action precise and tantalising. She went nowhere near Delia's labia or clitoris, but the sensations were already unbearable. Delia bucked her hips and whimpered.

'I rise at five-thirty and take my master a glass of hot water with his favourite herbal infusion. As he drinks this, I lay out his exercise clothing. He either runs, or trains with light weights.' Her fingertips dove in harder then and made Delia's vulva pout open and her clitoris lift at its centre. 'But before he dresses, I relieve his erection with my fingers or lips so he can exercise without distraction or discomfort.'

It was said with perfect, quiet calm, but its effect on Delia was immediate. Her clitoris shuddered with pleasure, then seemed to pump waves of it out through her body. She cried out, clawing at the leather of the couch and kicking her heels; orgasming in her fingers and toes as well as her genitals. The ecstasy was total and all the more wonderful for its cause . . . the thought of Elf with Jake's penis in her mouth; his flesh between her soft red lips.

As the moment enveloped her, Delia grabbed roughly at Elf's slim hand and jammed it between her own legs. In heaven, she rocked her fluidised sex against it, and rode out the deep-seated spasms on the vee of Elf's fingers and thumb. Her love-dew ran everywhere, its flow thick and slippy as it mixed with the warm scented oil.

The room was air-conditioned, but as she lay still, getting her breath back, Delia felt her limbs had melted. She listened intently to Elf's spicy description of her master's most intimate toilette. She moved slightly, from time to time, to facilitate the continuing massage, but apart from this she was just a floating, nerveless blob of oil and blissful secretions. A most pungent prize indeed, she thought wryly, wondering how Jake would react if he came in now and smelt her . . .

'I'd like to have a bath, please, before I see Jake . . .'

Elf looked up from her work on Delia's left ankle, her smile inscrutable. 'Of course. I'll see to it.' She pummelled out a last kink of tension, then set the finished leg down on the couch. 'Why not just relax here for a few minutes? And I'll prepare a tub.'

'Yes, that'd be lovely,' Delia answered with gratitude, then let her eyelids flutter closed. She needed time to herself now. To think, undistracted.

I must be a bisexual then...

Her sex shivered at the word. Tempted to touch herself, she posed several other pertinent questions to herself.

What about Deana? Was she the same? She'd always been bolder where sex was concerned. Maybe she'd been with a woman already? It'd be typical of her, she liked to try new things. And she *had* been a bit cagey about her meeting with Vida Mistry. Was this something that even Deana was embarrassed to admit to? The yearning for female flesh...

But what about me? Delia pondered, aware she'd been evading the main issue. She sneaked a long, admiring glance at the calm and self-possessed Elf.

The Japanese woman was so elegant and deft in her movements. Swishing precious essences into the swirling, pond-sized bath, then laying out stacks of fluffy towels. With grace and care, she set out porcelain bowls full of fruit-shaped soaps, and lotions and talcs in beautiful cut-glass containers. Elf was lithe and sleek and slender, her gilded skin superb. Beneath the thin silk of her bra and pants her body seemed to radiate perfection.

But is it Elf I actually want? thought Delia, still confused. Or is she just a surrogate ... a replacement for Jake?

Delia sat up on the couch. She felt restless and sexually needy in spite of her climaxes, but suddenly that made her smile. There *was* plenty left ... Her labia were still puffy and sensitised. She was engorged and ready to be touched again. Or sucked. Or buffeted by a strong man's body as his penis drove into her channel.

She put her hand down and stroked herself, knowing that for all the pleasure she'd taken from Elf, it was something less refined she wanted now. Something crude. And though she'd always flinched from saying it, just one word could express the craving.

She wanted to be fucked. She wanted Jake's cock inside her, and this time she wanted all her wits about her too. Eyes wide open. No grey areas. She wanted to know what he felt like inside her, and to see his reactions to being there.

No fantasies, no dreams, just Jake de Guile shafting her to glory and beyond. Ready for him now, she leapt lightly from the couch and smiled at Elf. The delicate Japanese had turned towards her, as if uncannily sensing her awakeness.

'How's my bath coming along?' Delia enquired, feeling a *frisson* of pleasure at the confidence that rang in her voice.

Elf made a gracious, bowing gesture towards the pool, then stepped forward with a thin strip of ribbon. To tie up her honoured charge's hair before guiding her into the water.

How beautiful they look, thought the man studying the monitor.

His irreplaceable Elf – and now this new one. This brown-haired Italianate Ferraro with her lovely confusion, her unnaturally hot body, and her volatile responses. What would she say if she knew he was watching her? That there was a tiny but all-seeing camera concealed in the bathing room's fanciful cornicing? He imagined the indignation, the right-eous female wrath she'd feign. And it would be feigned, because he already sensed that exposure both thrilled and aroused her.

These girls were superb, he decided, well satisfied with such an apposite pairing. Slender geisha-like Elf, so dark, graceful and precise; Dee, also dark, also slim, but earthier and fruitier somehow. She was wild and steaming, an animal for all her pretentions of refinement. He blessed his luck – and his judge-ment – in selecting her. When she cried out in pleasure he flipped open the wings of his robe and played his fingers down the length of his cock.

As his hand moved in a familiar rhythm, he watched the strong slender line of Elf's hand, wedged against Dee's open crotch. It excited him even more that the new girl had put it there herself.

His guest was the one who was working, that was clear. She was jerking herself off, riding the vee between Elf's fingers and thumb, actively creating her own stimulation instead of lying back and letting it happen. The way she writhed made his balls twitch and ache.

She was just what he needed right now. His optimum woman. And as he observed her rocking and whimpering, he searched through his own pleasure zones. There was a uniquely sensitive area beneath the mushroom-shaped head of his penis ... Yes! He found it – purely by touch – and groaned out loud, his eyes locked on the screen and the image of the climaxing Dee.

He felt elated that she was so new and unjaded. She was a nymph, and perfect for games. Familiar well-used scenes would be fresh with her, revived. She was canny yet innocent, and so delicious and adorable that he wanted to lick her breasts this instant and put his fingers inside her vagina. He wanted to stroke her and touch her, play in her soft sexy furrow and fondle her dark anal cleft. He wanted to molest her tight little bottom, even though he knew it would initially disgust her. She'd hate it and she'd fight, but then she'd be hotter than ever. Squeezing his glans, he wished he had a covert radio link as well as closed circuit TV. That way, he could relay his instructions to Elf, direct the action, and make Dee take the caresses he ordered.

Uncannily, as if she seemed to hear him, Dee rolled over. Her firm breasts bulged out from beneath her as Elf began working her shoulders. Jake knew that strong firm stroke himself, and it didn't surprise him when Dee responded. The prone woman bore down against the couch and with a faint, broken sob – so clear through the hi-tech speaker – she eased apart her legs and wriggled.

Jake moaned too, his penis huge and throbbing. With his free hand, he thumbed the zoom button and the camera seemed to close in tight on the deep, shadowy chasm between Dee's round buttocks. His balls jumped dangerously and he knew he was right on the edge, imagining the hot, tight grip of that silky, split-peach bottom.

She'd protest, of course. She'd complain and try and squirm out from under him. He pictured her thrashing, twisting, trying to protect that forbidden and vulnerable entrance from the push of his violating organ.

But he'd get his way. Either through force of will or by far more gentle means. He'd finger her sex until her anus pulsed and opened. As it fluttered on the screen, he mentally put Dee in restraint.

They were in a feather bed together, he fantasised, and she was face down, her narrow wrists handcuffed to the headrail. Her bottom was raised and ready for him, lifted by a thick silk bolster beneath her pelvis. Enhancing the fantasy, he decided that she wasn't naked. Instead she was almost prudishly clothed in a Victorian winceyette night-gown, and this angelic, voluminous garment made her situation ten times as lewd. Her arms and shoulders were enveloped in the soft, chaste fabric, but the long creamy skirt was folded up, neatly, and pinned at the small of her back.

She was perfectly covered and modest from the waist up, but with her pale twitching rump all displayed like two perfectly sculpted orbs. Spheres of unsullied woman-flesh on which to gorge his perverted appetites. She could struggle all she liked, but if he took hold of her thighs, positioned himself between her cheeks, and just leaned forwards, he could take her virgin bottom with ease.

Lost in his obscene, dark dreams, he fell back, ignoring the TV monitor, and paraded other visions through his mind. As his engulfing hand dashed to and fro, he imagined Dee in a dozen grossly ravished poses.

He saw Elf holding Dee's hands while he inserted objects in her body. Vibrators in her vagina and her bottom, and his penis in her willing open mouth. He almost felt her gurgling around him as the relentless, infernal technology played havoc with her sex and her rectum.

He saw her strapped in a frame, bent at the waist, being buggered by Fargo as Mistry applied a black crop – with chilling accuracy – across her churning, uptilted backside.

He saw himself, taking her gently and with consent, pushing his shaft tenderly and carefully into her well-greased bottom. They were lying on a soft, plush rug, rocking together, joined. The rug was by a window that looked out onto a garden. She'd cry with pleasure as he moved in her anus and reached around her to titillate her clitoris. He heard her call out his name in gratitude as an orgasm gripped her and her bottom rippled gorgeously around him.

'Dee,' he moaned softly, then came in a warm, thick surge that splashed semen across his open brown thighs.

Delia was a connoisseur of baths. A lingerer, a soaker, she wallowed for hours at weekends when time wasn't pressing.

But she'd never had a bath as sybaritic and luxurious as this one. Elf conducted the proceedings in the traditional Japanese style, and Delia just went with the long flow of pampering. She was washed – everywhere – whilst sitting on a little wooden stool set on the tiles beside the bath-pool. She was even led to the lavatory, her performance there supervised in a way that was both unnerving and erotic. Finally, she was allowed to submerge slowly and blissfully into water of just the right temperature. Not red hot, like a real Japanese bath, because that would've made her sweaty and flustered. This pool was just delicately and silkily tepid, and perfumed with roses and jasmine.

She was dozing when a soft hand touched her on the shoulder. 'OK, Dee?' enquired Elf gently, crouching at the side of the bath, her loose bra hanging free of her body. Her breasts were completely visible.

Her beauty made Delia wakeful. She sat up in the water, showing her fuller, plumper breasts in return. Elf smiled, her dark eyes gleaming, but her actions and demeanour were quiet and completely asexual. She helped Delia out of the water and towelled her dry. With neatness and delicacy, she smoothed Delia's body with a perfumed lotion and her face with an expensive French moisturiser. She gave her a new and subtly sensual make-up and brushed her hair into a lush, gleaming fall.

The final touch was a pearl necklace which she clasped around Delia's throat. A single, heavy, breath-catching row of perfect satin-pink spheres. The jewels were obviously and frighteningly real, and as Delia stood before a long portrait mirror, she fingered them in awe and wonder. A matched string like this must be worth thousands. It made her nervous to wear them. They were probably the most rare and costly thing she'd ever had next to her skin. Except Jake himself, of course.

'It's time now, Dee,' said Elf from just behind her, smiling at their reflections in the mirror.

'But what about clothes?'

'He wants you naked,' the Japanese woman said simply, taking Delia's hand and already urging her to follow.

'But I can't—' Delia protested. The words were negative but she was already moving forward . . .

'You can!' Elf laughed softly, opening the door to the passage and pushing Delia gently outside. 'You're beautiful, Dee. Your body is perfect. It's too gorgeous to hide. Come on.'

Strolling bare-arsed through the corridors of Jake's wonderful house was a strangely sensual experience. The decor was rich, layered and opulent; and she was nude. Her surroundings were formal and classical; and she was a naked offering, ready only to be screwed and enjoyed. She was in a palace, her Prince's palace; and she was his undraped possession.

On this upper floor, the works of art were blatantly sexual. She remembered Deana's description of the exhibition and wondered now if the best and most pornographic pieces were here. Elf didn't chivvie or hurry her, so there was plenty of time to study the pictures and photographs as they passed. Plenty of time for her eyes to widen, her mouth to drop open, and her sex to grow hot again, and moist.

The most explicit pieces were representations of Jake himself. Photographs and drawings of him as naked as she was and involved in various esoteric sex acts. There were scenes of him alone, with a woman, and with several women. There were even some pictures of him with men.

Delia wondered what her sister would think of these most private of private exhibits. With her pure, vibrant talent, and her openly sex-loving nature, Deana could probably have created work of at least the same quality or even better. With either paintbrush or pencil or camera. Or maybe even her own living body?

They were standing before a door now: a plane of smoothly painted panels, quite neutrally featureless and menacing. As

Delia hesitated, Elf said, 'Don't be frightened,' and reached forward to twist the handle.

Delia's heart started pounding and leaping as the door swung open in front of her...

7

The Throne Room

The room Delia entered made her think of Jake's office at the de Guile Tower. He seemed to have a penchant for these long spacious areas, and what stretched out before her was more like an eastern potentate's throne room than a bedroom in a London town house.

The decor was unconventional too. Each wall was hung with a translucent Japanese-style screen or *shoji*, although instead of being the traditional pale fawn shade, the hangings here were fiery and vivid. Shades of orange, sand red, cerise and ochre. They were painted too, the designs like swirling nebulae, lit from behind by cleverly recessed lamps.

It was an odd place, womb-like and moody for all its spacious dimensions. The atmosphere was sultry and mysterious, the ruddy light menstrual with its reds and rich venous pinks. It felt like being inside a woman – which was probably what Jake had intended.

Scattered around on the deep piled, almost purple carpet were a series of low backless couches and huge squashy bean-bag style cushions. There were other items of furniture around the periphery, but with the light so diffuse and angled they were difficult to properly identify. The only true, visible focus of the room was the largest couch, which was set on a kind of platform, one step up.

This couch was strewn with soft, fat cushions and was the

only one possessing a back – a high, almost kitschy shell-shape of buttoned scarlet velvet. Lounging against it was Jake himself, a cool blue poem on a hot red page; his lean brown body enswathed in a thin azure silk robe. The pose was so clichéd and improbable that he looked like the hero of some cheap, erotic novelette. If Delia hadn't wanted him so much she might have laughed.

Yet even in repose, he had power. He looked more like her Prince than ever, but as she moved closer, she felt a sudden, intense, and annoyingly sexual irritation . . .

The swine was asleep in his splendour!

Creeping silently forward, Delia could hardly believe what she was doing. According to Elf, Jake was supposed to be 'busy'. What she ought to do was storm straight up to him and raise hell. Deana would've done . . . but she was Delia, the diplomat, and not as feisty as her freewheeling sister.

And anyway, he looked too beautiful.

Delia found it hard to believe that this was only the second time *she'd* met this man. Standing just inches away, it felt as if she'd been obsessed with him forever. Her dreams and fantasies, and Deana's fulsome descriptions, made her feel as if she knew him completely. Mind, body and soul.

It was probably all false, she realised, but one thing was obvious and true. Sex was the key to him, the secret. He was the most erotic being she'd ever met; and right now, in his utter, cat-like relaxation, he was a far more stirring and sensuous sight than anything in his outrageous art collection.

He was stretched out full-length on his soft red throne, his bare feet peeping from beneath the embroidered hem of his robe. She could see now that it was cut as a real Japanese kimono, with the distinctive square-cut sleeves, but she doubted if any samurai warlord had ever worn anything so flimsy. The silk itself was indecently thin and left nothing to the imagination. She could see not only the firm clean lines of his limbs and torso through it, but also the shape of his penis, his testicles and the mat of his black pubic hair.

Poseur! she thought, angry but already falling deep into lust. Wearing blue in a red room was pure drama, and could only be pre-meditated. That the damned thing was also virtually transparent was skirting dangerously close to being camp – but she didn't think that would bother Jake at all ...

He stirred then, and Delia gasped when she noticed his hair. It was unbound tonight and looked longer than ever as his slight, uneasy movement made it ripple like a wave across the cushions. Some strands were clinging to his face and throat and shoulders, sliding across his skin as he turned unconsciously in sleep. The effect was pure seduction and Delia felt weak as she stared at him. She sensed Elf standing close by her side.

'Glorious, isn't he?' the Japanese girl whispered, and in spite of her sexual confusion, Delia was forced to agree.

'Yes, he is,' she answered, half under her breath.

A tenth of a second later, it dawned on her that Jake was faking. He was a consummate manipulator. How could he *not* be awake, *not* be listening, and *not* be playing his games with her?

'Why thank you, Mizz Ferraro,' purred a familiar whipped-chocolate voice, and stretching languorously, Jake sat up. As he did so, his robe gaped open and his eyes – which she realised were the same shade of blue – flared hot and bright with mischief.

'You look rather glorious yourself, might I add,' he continued, rubbing his hand idly across his body, then reaching out to touch her before she could protest, respond or even blush. His fingertips brushed her jaw, her pearl-encircled throat, then slid on and down to cup her left breast. He flicked the erected nipple with his thumbnail, then leant across to kiss her on it. By the time he'd licked, then sucked, then bit her slightly – and straightened up again – her skin was pink all over and her sex was swollen and dripping.

As he settled back, the filmy floating robe billowed open to his groin and Delia saw wisps of dark hair. His penis was still shaded by several layers of overfolded silk, but the sight of its furry black accompaniment made her quiver. It looked flossy and vital, and quite at odds with his sleek chest and limbs. She remembered Elf's mention of shaving him . . . and she imagined a glittering cut throat razor being drawn across his face. Then across his legs, his arms and his pectorals too.

With her head full of bizarre thoughts and visions, Delia couldn't shape conversation. She was stark naked, shaking with desire. Her verbal powers were gone. 'Good evening, Jake,' she said at last. 'Elf said you were busy.'

'Well, I have been, in a way,' he replied, reaching up to sweep a thick black tress of hair from where it had fallen across the side of his face. There was an impish quirk to his lips and something in the sly, sideways flick of his slanted eyes made Delia catch his look and follow it.

On a low hardwood table with legs carved in the shape of dragons, stood a small, flat-screen TV set. The image it showed was static and empty. And familiar. It was the luxurious but now abandoned bathing room, and the white leather massage couch was standing at exact centre stage.

'You shit! You pervert!' she shrieked, aware with a peculiar detachment that she sounded more like Deana than she'd ever done. 'You've been watching us, you creep!'

'Yes, of course I have,' he said, swivelling on the couch to sit cross-legged and flashing them not only a grin, but also another glimpse of his sooty-black pubis. 'Women are always more natural when they believe they're unobserved.'

She could've exploded with fury. He was such a chauvinist, such a pig! She wanted to either punch him right in his truly gorgeous face . . . or have him take her and ravish her immediately. The urges were exactly equal, and her anger and indignation were exceeded only by her boiling embarrassment. She'd responded like a maenad to Elf, hadn't she? She'd shouted. She'd climaxed. She'd cried.

'What's the matter, Dee?' he asked gently, taking hold of her and pulling her down onto the cushions beside him. 'It was nice with Elf, wasn't it? You can't say you didn't enjoy it.' He was snuggling her against him now, as if she were a recalcitrant child. Cradling her to his body, he touched her breasts exquisitely, then slid his fingertips down across her belly.

'Now come on, sweet Dee,' he cajoled, tilting her face towards him. One hand held the back of her neck, while the other was already at her furrow. 'You don't want Elf to be upset, do you?' His finger danced insultingly on her clitoris. 'If you carry on complaining, she'll think that you don't like her.' His wide blue eyes were absolutely steady and absolutely serious. It seemed impossible that below he was caressing her. Slowly. Remorselessly. Irresistibly.

Delia's hips began to move. She hated herself for it, but she couldn't stop herself. He was treating her like a toy; a rub-me-and-I-wriggle doll. But it was the very demeaningness, and his quiet little pep-talk, that made her body burn and ache beneath his fingers.

As her bare bottom squirmed on the cushion beneath her, she was humiliatingly conscious of her juices. Slippery wetness was flowing out of her, over Jake's fingertips, and soiling the luxurious fabric. She could feel her pleasure building quickly and solidly, sensations zinging wildly through her body. It stormed through her nerves, limbs and glands, then returned redoubled to her vulva – and the slim brown hand that possessed her.

'Dee, oh Dee,' he murmured. 'D for "delight". I don't think I've ever had a woman so responsive.'

'But you aren't having me!' she gasped, her hips bucking upwards as he taunted her by withdrawing for a second.

'Ah, but I shall,' he whispered, his mouth against her ear as his finger resumed its torment. Pressuring her so delicately that her thighs opened wide to encourage him. 'When Elf's had you, my darling, and you've had her.'

'I don't understand! I . . . Oh God! No! Ungh! Ungh! Ungh!'

It was happening again. The heavy pulsations. The wrenching pulls at her womb. The pleasure so great it seemed painful. The impossible abandonment of dignity . . .

I'm not like this, she thought blearily. This isn't me! As the feelings faded and tempered, she lay back in Jake's arms, a floppy burnt out husk.

I'm not an orgasm machine. It's hard for me to come. How the hell can he do this to me? Can *they* do it, she thought confusedly, opening her heavy eyelids to look at Elf, who was kneeling on the carpet next to the couch and watching the proceedings intently.

And then she remembered Peter.

I came easily for him too, didn't I? No problems, no struggling and straining. I never even worried about it. What's happening to me? She looked up at Jake and wondered if he had infernal powers. Had he affected the weather? Done something to the ozone layer that meant the whole city was swathed in a seething erotic mist? Was he the Devil – who changed everyone he met into a sex-fiend?

It seemed so, because as Delia's body still twittered and jumped, Elf rose to her feet to undress. At Jake's slight nod, she reached around behind her back and unfastened her tiny pink bra. As the clip was freed, she caught the flimsy scrap in her fingers and held it against herself, the very picture of virgin modesty. The look she gave Jake was pure seduction, straight from the 'floating world' of the geisha trained to please, and its answer was a haughty flick of the fingers. Continue . . .

Obedient, yet strangely unbowed, Elf let the pink silk drop to the carpet. Her breasts were small but beautifully shaped, slightly pointed and with the darkest nipples Delia had ever seen. Broad, plump buds of deep marooney brown that looked lovely with her slightly olive skin. They were erect too, and Elf drew her fingertips across both of them, to emphasise their exotic perfection.

'And the rest, please, Elf,' said Jake huskily. He licked his lips, clearly affected, even though the woman was his constant companion and her body must surely be familiar.

'Of course,' Elf said softly, sliding her dainty hands to her waist and hooking down the elastic of her knickers. Slowly, teasingly, she slid them down and stepped free of them, this time showing no trace of shyness.

Delia envied her. Not only for her grace and composure, but also for her sweet, tight body. There was no flaw whatsoever in Elf's trim figure: her waist was narrow, her hips gently swelling, and her deep-navelled belly was completely and uncompromisingly flat. Unconsciously, Delia adjusted the way she was lying, trying to hide her bigger curves. She wasn't fat, but she had a definite belly, where the other girl was virtually concave.

'Don't worry, pretty Dee,' Jake said quietly in her ear. His fingers slid up from her vulva and cupped the slight bulge of her belly, 'I rather like this.' He moved her flesh in a slow, subtle circling movement and Delia moaned. She could feel it pulling on her sex-lips, aggravating her still-tender clitoris. When his thumb slid into her navel, she pushed herself upwards to meet it.

Jake had long hands, and as he made a span across her, his middle finger reached down between her labia. He touched it to the tip of her sensitive bud, then squeezed the whole clasped area with his palm. Delia moaned again, momentarily imagining that her bladder was full and how excruciating this pressure would feel then.

Delia's thoughts began to whirl. Jake was still gently fondling her, and Elf – his Japanese handmaiden – was on her knees again, obeisant. Her fingers slid up Delia's warm thighs. Reaching for her wide-open readiness . . .

'She's all yours, Elf,' whispered Jake.

Confused, Delia felt his hand withdraw and her body being arranged on the cushions. When he seemed satisfied with her, he moved to the far side of the couch and started stacking more cushions behind his back . . . to watch her in comfort, she realised.

She turned her eyes to him, imploring silently, befuddled by what he expected of her yet intensely excited too. It would be Elf's hands and mouth that did the deed, but it was Jake who controlled them. He was their puppet-master, relaxed and sprawled beside them, directing their most sensual actions with virtually no effort on his part. He seemed happy to do little else but watch.

'Rest easy, sweet Dee.' He smiled quite kindly. 'She's the best. I promise you.'

Still not sure, Delia shuddered violently, and bit her lip. Jake noticed this, and as if to reassure her, he leant forward again, kissed her cheek and touched her breast, then returned to his post of observer. Flipping open his opulent kimono, he set free the stiff flesh of his erection – which sprang up and slapped loudly on his belly.

Torn between surrender to Elf and the ultimate fascination of Jake, Delia whimpered softly, her eyes on his swaying, red shaft. She'd felt it in her, she knew that now, but this was the first time she'd seen it.

Like the rest of him, his cock was a cliché. Everything about Jake de Guile was superior, unique, or the best, and his penis was no exception.

Delia hadn't seen a lot of nude men in her life, but Jake put her others in the shade. His cock was long, but not only that, it was broad too. Vital and succulent with beautifully defined veins that bulged along its elegant length. She watched with awe as it pulsed between his fingers; a gorged and circumcised crown atop a shaft that was thick, hard and tempting.

He was rubbing unashamedly now, his hips lifting high off the couch. The strokes were long and his joy in his own penis uninhibited. As he tilted back his head, and purred low in his throat like a cat, his long-lashed eyes closed ecstatically.

Elf had paused in her efforts and she too was watching her master. She caught Delia's eye and smiled complicitly, passing her small pointed tongue across her lips as if relishing Jake's savoury flesh.

All art and delicacy were forgotten now. The man before them was just bringing himself off like the healthy male animal he was. Going straight for pure release. As Elf and Delia looked on, he drew back one leg crabwise, tensioned the other one straight, and pumped his pelvis to and fro in the air. It was an act of naked, erotic athleticism and his red sex waved crazily in their faces ...

As his crisis approached, they saw the eye at the tip of his penis pout open. The tiny little orifice seemed to pulse at them, and wink, then dilate again and spurt out its tribute.

'Yes! Yes!' he cried, his semen flying freely and high. Some of it landed on the couch and some on Jake's own body. Several droplets spattered onto Delia; on her pale curving belly just inches from Elf's golden fingers.

Jake slumped back against the cushions, panting, but all eyes were on the silky white stuff that had shot out so gloriously from his body. It lay on Delia's skin like a string of living pearls, and without thinking, she touched the gems around her throat.

After a moment, Elf surged forward, bent over, and started licking. Her pink tongue lapped neatly at Jake's semen, cleaning it off Delia's skin, then swallowing it down as if it were ice-cream or some other rich pudding.

Delia was astounded. And jealous. She had a powerful urge to dash Elf away and bend double to lick her own belly. She stared downwards, perplexed, then started wildly when she heard soft laughter. Male laughter, low and satisfied.

'Don't worry . . . You'll get your chance.'

To her astonishment, Jake was already at work on his cock again, pulling slowly at its sticky sated length.

'If there's anything left!' she countered. He was good, he was wonderfully potent, but even so he was still only human!

Jake laughed again, reading her perfectly. 'Don't worry, sweet Dee,' he said, his light voice rich with humour, 'the well's not dry. There's plenty more where that came from.'

'You conceited bastard!'

Enraged, she tried to throw herself across the couch and hit him, but Elf was far too quick for her.

Delia yelped in protest and struggled, but without knowing quite how it had happened, she found herself lying sideways on the couch. Immobilised. Elf was stretched taut across her, holding her arms – and Jake, the smug devil, was still laughing.

'Most people think *Fargo* is my chief "minder",' he said silkily, leaning alongside so he could look into Delia's eyes, 'but in that they're quite quite wrong.' He touched his fingers tenderly to his servant's soft black hair. 'Let her up, love,' he whispered.

The Japanese woman complied instantly. She smiled fondly

at Delia, almost as if she'd just caressed her rather than flung her flat on her back in a martial arts death grip. 'Forgive me,' she said, helping Delia to sit up, 'it was a reflex. We've had some strange people here in the past, and I can't take a chance with Jake's safety.'

'It's all right.' Delia touched her fingers to her hair in a tidying gesture, and wondered what Elf meant by strange. Everybody was strange here... Then she rounded on the still smirking Jake, 'But you, you make me so angry!'

The trouble was – he was smiling at her, his blue eyes twinkling – that he also made her desire him.

You really are the Devil, Jake! she thought, not doubting for a moment that he could more than fulfil his claims. He'd probably have another rampaging erection within minutes. And have her begging him to put it inside her.

She'd never met a man like him, and she didn't really want to meet another. That he should have this kind of power was too frightening, and she wondered how her sister had coped with it.

Deana would be at home here, she decided. Deana was audacious and experienced. She enjoyed the spice of strangeness and conflict.

'What're you thinking about, Dee?' asked Jake lazily, lying back and stretching, his fingers still moving on his penis. 'One minute you're giving me hell, and the next you're miles away! What is it, my sweet? Am I getting to you?'

Of course you are, you swine! she fumed, but contained herself.

'I was just thinking about my—' She stopped short. She'd been right on the point of saying 'sister'. 'About my boyfriend... After all this –' she gestured around the exotic room, and at Elf, and at Jake himself '– he seems so boring. I think we'll have to finish...'

'Yes, do that,' said Jake matter-of-factly. He was stroking his cock in a slow luxuriant fashion as he appeared to consider her dilemma. 'You're too bright to be dragged down by a dullard, Dee. You need partners who will fuel you. Someone to stoke your heat, not dampen it.' He flashed a quick bright glance at Elf. 'Someone like Elf. Now kiss her and make up after your fight.'

Not knowing why she kept kow-towing so helplessly, Delia leaned across and pressed her lips against Elf's. The Japanese girl's mouth was as soft as petals, and the kiss as complete and perfect as any ever shared with a man.

For a few seconds they stayed perfectly still. Then everything happened at once. Not overtly, but within and far more momentously. Up until now, Delia had been passive, and had gone with the flow. Suddenly she felt both active and wanting. She wanted to kiss Elf, and she wanted her to know it was a willing and consensual kiss. She wanted Jake to know that too, even though she sensed he was aware of it already.

There wasn't so much difference between a man's kiss and a woman's, she decided, falling back against the cushions beneath Elf. The Japanese girl's mouth was as strong as a man's and her tongue was as muscular. She forced Delia's lips open effortlessly and stabbed at her soft inner moistness.

Delia had always loved kissing, sometimes even preferred it to sex, but being kissed by a woman before a watching man was a thrilling and novel development. As her own tongue swirled around Elf's stiff, darting one, Delia was acutely conscious of Jake. His intent, dark presence was an aura around them; a second mouth exploring and tasting; a second body, superimposed on Elf's as the slim girl lay full-length on top of Delia.

Their bodies were touching at all points now, and Elf was stretching and shimmying. The slow sinuous movement was like a caress in itself, while dainty but karate-honed fingers travelled up and down Delia's flanks and thighs. Breasts rubbed against breasts, nipples against nipples. Their navels seemed to kiss as lubriciously as their mouths, and the fine dark hairs of Elf's silky pubis were twining with Delia's more wiry ones.

Are our juices blending too? Delia wondered dreamily. Within the vessel of their still-joined mouths she imagined a strong sexual nectar, a mix of Elf's moisture and hers. Her saliva gushed freely at the thought, shocking her. She'd never even tasted herself, let alone another woman. She felt Elf become more excited above her, as if she too could taste their cocktail. The other girl was moaning too, a low incoherent mumble – in her own language – which sent vibrations humming right through the kiss.

The circuit was complete now, and still deeply aware of Jake – more than ever in fact – Delia passed her fingers over Elf's slim back. It was so cool and inviting, a long firm sweep that ended in her small rounded bottom.

Elf had a lovely rump, superbly tight and muscular yet fruity and easy to get hold of. Her buttocks were like a pair of nectarines in Delia's fingers and she squeezed them as if testing their ripeness. Elf squirmed in her grip, chuntering inanely into the wetness of the kiss, and Delia realised the caress had special power ...

The rougher the handling, the more Elf seemed to respond. Her pubis worked hungrily against Delia's, and she churned furiously when Delia pummelled her bottom cheeks.

Delia felt a great rush of confidence, a sense of strength and control. She could make Elf writhe and dance against her, simply by playing with her buttocks. Intoxicated, she pushed her bare thigh in between Elf's legs and held it there, jammed tight against her stickiness.

Delia could feel everything. Every bit of it. The sacred female shape: soft, spongy folds, nut-hard clitoris, warm seeping fluid that wet them both. She gripped Elf's rear firmly and rocked their bodies together, and even as she did so, she felt other hands moving to caress them both.

Jake was lying alongside now, his heat a part of their maelstrom. He was chanting too, encouraging them, his husky voice blending with their moans. And when Delia's fingers strayed down into Elf's anal cleft, she found *his* there too, stroking rhythmically at the tiny tight rose.

Elf was thrashing now, struggling between them. 'So warm, so sweet . . .' she whimpered, trailing her lips across Delia's face, then nuzzling her way down to her shoulder. She let out another wild Japanese cry, then started bouncing her sex against Delia's thigh, and clawing with sharp nails at her bottom.

As the dark girl almost flew into her orgasm, Delia turned her head to one side and met Jake's blue eyes. They were like slitted chips of fire, burning with lust. He was still stroking Elf, his rhythm sure and steady, but as his servant shivered and climaxed, he leaned deep into the tangle of bodies and kissed Delia full and hard on the lips. She felt his tongue push inside her mouth, just as Elf's had done, and she shuddered in response.

Soon, she thought, deliriously, soon it'll be his cock pushing in. That lovely hot bar, moving, plunging and stretching. Possessing her famished vagina as surely as his tongue took her mouth.

Unexpectedly for a woman so disciplined, Elf suddenly seemed completely overcome. She went limp between them, her slight body inert as if she'd passed out from the sheer weight of pleasure. Delia held her tight and still, loving her smooth-skinned lightness and the way she smelt strongly of sex.

Delia could have lain like that for hours, entwined, but plainly Jake had other ideas. He climbed gracefully off the couch, then lifted Elf up bodily and laid her down gently on the carpet. Taking a cushion, he plumped it vigorously, then tucked it beneath Elf's cheek, sliding back her silky black hair and arranging it in a curtain across her shoulder. The action was so achingly tender that Delia felt a hard pang of envy. She watched him kiss the girl reverently on the forehead, and that done, resume his place on the couch, sitting cross-legged in a supple-limbed half lotus squat.

'Just me and you now, sweet Dee.' His eyes were unblinking. Unnerving.

'But won't she wake up? If she's your bodyguard, won't she hear the slightest sound?'

'Not if she wills herself *not* to.' He smiled. 'Elf has many special powers and this is just one of them. We're alone now, Dee. What do you want?'

'I want you to fuck me.'

It was as if she'd escaped reason and was functioning purely on sex. An eye's-blink after she'd said the words, she still couldn't believe them. She was Delia Ferraro, super-cool and circumspect; she rarely swore, and until now had hated crudeness. In spite of everything that had happened, she blushed.

'Wonderful,' he murmured, his cock rising hypnotically as he spoke, stiffening and straightening between the pressed-back spread of his thighs. 'You're beautiful, Dee. So pink. So warm.' He touched his fingers to his hardness, rubbing himself slowly, making its tiny love-eye open and weep. 'You want this then, do you?' He squeezed the crown of his sex and a jewel of clear fluid popped out.

'Yes.'

Why deny it? It was true. And there was no way to keep it

from him anyway. 'And *how* do you want it?' His eyes closed briefly, as if his own hand was infinitely delightful to him. He stirred slightly, adjusting his elegant eastern pose, and the drop of pre-ejaculate shimmered. Delia would've given anything for the confidence just to lean over and take it from the tip of his cock with her tongue.

'Go on,' he coaxed, jiggling himself so the droplet quivered precariously.

'I . . .' It looked so tempting, so tantalising. What would it taste like?

'Do it, and I'll love you in any way you choose. Any way at all. Even if it means—' He shrugged. 'Well, even if it means I don't come myself.'

What kind of infernal game was this? Surely one single lick of his cock wasn't enough for him? It was only a few millilitres of moisture . . .

She hesitated, then just as Jake's hand reached towards her, she inclined herself down towards his penis. As her lips touched him, she felt his fingers settle on the side of her head, riffle quickly through her unbound hair, then delicately caress her cheek.

His flavour was strangely bland. There was a trace of saltiness, but not much more. Even so she relished him, and lapped greedily at the tiny winking hole. When she'd cleaned him of that first fat droplet, she curled her tongue around his sensitive cock-head, then flicked boldly at the vee-ed groove beneath.

'You angel,' he gasped, his fingers sliding through her hair to control her, his touch still gentle and light. 'You clever, clever angel . . .'

Even as he spoke, she felt more slipperiness in her mouth, and tasted more salt. She wondered if he would come then, lose his grip, become over-excited and ejaculate. The thought of that excited *her*. Set her own juices flowing. She hollowed her cheeks and sucked, determined to best him.

'Oh no you don't, you minx!'

He laughed, as if to let her know he'd rumbled her intention. Sliding in his thumb beneath his own stiff flesh, he pressed down on her lip and forced her to release him.

The temptation to bite his thumb was nearly as strong as the craving to lick his cock had been, but this time Delia refrained, reaching up to prise his hand from her face.

'Why not?'

'Because I want to make love to you, Dee. Do something plain and simple with no tricks. We could even try the "missionary", if you like?' His grin was wicked and sparkling. She'd have done anything for it, and for him.

Even so, she sensed he was still playing with her. For a man like Jake, the 'missionary' position could well be a novelty. Should she indulge him? she wondered. Or be contrary, just for the sake of it?

But in the end, old habits died hard ...

'I'd like that,' she said, looking up at him, 'And at least this time, I'll see your face while we're ... we're together.'

As he swept his thick hair back from his face, he frowned. Delia felt a cold rush of panic, and ran furiously through recent memories. Specifically her sister's.

Deana had sat astride Jake in his limousine, and Deana was no shrinking violet. She'd always said she liked to 'look' ...

'I ...' Delia hesitated, then took a chance. 'It was dark in the car, Jake,' she said, 'and in the gallery you were behind me,' His eyes narrowed. 'And when we were in your office ... Well, I was in shock at finding out who you were. I was "out of it" most of the time.'

He gave her a thin studying smile, then leaned over and touched his mouth against hers.

'True,' he murmured, 'all true. So this time we'd better make up for it. I'll keep my eyes wide open. But only if you do. Deal?'

She nodded. She'd no idea if she could comply though. It was hard to meet his eyes already. They were cool sapphire stars in a hot red night, brilliant with sex. When he came they'd probably blind her. 'In that case, sweet Dee—' He was uncoiling himself. 'Let's make love.'

Jake was a strong, fit man who concealed his physical power. Before Delia properly knew how he'd done it, she was on her back and stretched out. He wasn't on top of her yet, but his thigh was across her belly, holding her down. On his side, beside her, he slid a cradling arm beneath her and held the other one poised and ready. He was choosing his first target, she sensed, and his cock was like a steel prod against her.

She had a great sense of being his toy again. Of waiting for her buttons to be pushed... And this time, she liked it. Jake seemed to deliberate for a long long time, holding her tight and quivering with need, while he made his choice from her body. How could he do this? she wondered. How could any man as ready as he was be so precise and so surgically cool?

Would he touch her breast or her belly first? The skin in each place seemed to tighten and sensitise in readiness. Her thigh, perhaps? Her nipples? Her navel? Would he touch her first on her sex? Push his finger straight into her channel?

In the end it was her face.

'You're not scared of me, are you?' he asked, brushing aside a few strands of her hair.

She was scared. Scared of the game being revealed. Scared of his anger. And yes, scared of just *him*.

But those were wimpish fears and she could handle them.

What really frightened her was herself. Herself and the way Jake would change her. The way he'd already changed her. In the few days she'd known him she'd done some unthinkable things, and he was bound to push her still further . . .

'No!' she lied bravely, summoning the family guts and boldness. Deana's fighting spirit. Mirroring Jake's own action, she reached up to touch his face, then shivered as she smelt his scent. The blended male odours of cologne and sweat and semen.

Suddenly, touching wasn't enough. She slid her fingers round the back of his neck, then dug them into his thick, straight hair as she pulled down his face for a kiss.

He met her strongly, but yieldingly too. His lips were firm and cool, and they opened when she pressed in her tongue. She felt empowered and dizzy as if his mouth were filled with a drug.

His body tilted as they kissed, moving over hers, and his free hand slid down towards her breast. He cupped her quite naturally and easily, his fingers curving inwards around her. With his thumb centred firmly on her nipple, he pressed in, then flicked to and fro. He was gentle but forceful, and for a second she was reminded of Peter. It was the same kind of cautious hunger . . . But when she opened her eyes and looked into Jake's dark blue ones – as she'd promised – she knew there was no real comparison.

Peter was a nice man who genuinely cared for her. Jake was an unprincipled sexual predator. Glorious, but ready to play out any role or ruse in pursuit of what he wanted from a woman. And the worst of it was, even though she understood his self-serving nature, she couldn't combat it.

Jake's slow, light handling of her breast produced a predictable reflex reaction. Her pelvis rose beneath his restraining thigh, and fresh juice ran from her sex. She wanted him to press his thigh in between her legs, but he held his position. Not quite touching her pubis.

She felt like screaming with frustration. Her vulva was aching for strong hard action. She wanted his cock inside her. Opening her body, forcing it wide, and laying waste to her hot wet vagina. She wanted him to take her and screw her without mercy or pause.

But he was playing with her again, suppressing his own power to break her.

I won't beg, thought Delia grimly, gritting her teeth. I want him. I need him. I'd dying for him. But I won't whine like a bitch for his cock.

Her body thought otherwise, though, and as her pelvis rose hungrily against him, he pulled himself up and away.

'Stop teasing me, you bastard! Get on with it!' she hissed. She was angry, furiously angry – a hot rage that boiled in her sex and ate at her body like acid . . . She could almost feel it sizzling.

'With pleasure,' he whispered, eyes bright blue as he manoeuvred his body to comply. Taking his weight on his elbows in the classic manner, he moved himself across her, and his prick bobbed insistently at her thighs. She could feel its blind clubbed head pushing gently, and she drew up her knees to receive him; angling her body so he slipped in like silk between her labia. His glans seemed to skate around her sticky-wet folds for a moment, then lodge fairly and squarely at her entrance.

Delia bucked up fiercely, trying to work him deeper, but Jake held steady. His cock-tip was only just inside her, nudging at her warm, tight snugness.

'Hold still! Don't be so impatient . . . There's plenty of time.'

Enraged, she redoubled her efforts, grabbing and mangling at his bottom just as she'd already grabbed at Elf's. Delaying penetration was hard work for him, and she knew it. His thighs and buttocks were twitching with effort and she considered stroking his anus to force the issue.

But even as the thought crossed her mind, he started powering downwards and inwards.

'Slowly, slowly, slowly,' he cooed, still holding her gaze. Millimetre by millimetre he eased his gorged flesh inside her, stretching the natural resilience of her portal and triggering a whole new bundle of nerve-ends which had always been passed by too quickly.

The sensations made her heart race. She was being held open by the bulk of his penis, her vagina tickled and titillated in a way that was fabulous and for her, unprecedented. Above her face, Jake's eyes were like navigational beacons; steering her flesh towards the secrets of knowledge.

As he pushed in a tiny bit further, and his cock-head was trapped by her muscles, Delia spasmed around him – and at the same time felt a cool plume of fear.

What if this was a test? A measurement of some kind? It had never occurred to her before, it had never mattered, but what if she and Deana weren't actually the same down there?

Panic made her hotter than ever, and sweaty. What if she was tighter than Deana? Or looser? And their folds might be differently arranged ... She could be coarser, wetter, slicker, more or less clinging. The variables were infinite.

The moment seemed infinite too. She waited for a query. For angry words and withdrawal. She waited for Jake to say, 'I know ...'

But there was nothing.

Instead, he sighed heavily, then put his lips to hers. His tongue plunged into her waiting mouth at the very instant his cock took her sex.

The sense of possession was so complete it almost denied

her of breath. He was in, deep in, and quite still. In stasis. It was as if he were imprinting himself on his territory, matching their codes, marking her forever as his.

Movement, when it did come, was a shock. Jake's lunges were long and smooth – and on each out-stroke he held himself above her and looked straight down into her eyes, his cock-head throbbing tensely just inside her.

He didn't speak or cry out or even grunt, but his whole body said 'This is me. What you wanted. Watch my eyes.'

Delia was gone now, lost in it, only a fragment of her mind still working. She had no conscious thoughts, only prayers that his eyes wouldn't change. And start asking, 'Which one are you?'

But it was hard to remember who he was now. She could only think of him as flesh. Living bulk inside her. A huge male presence in her body. She felt stretched around him, battered by his hardness, her delicate interior fluttering and melting as her perceptions of space-time distorted. She could *hear* her own orgasm, see her collapsing waves of pleasure as fluttering silvery ghosts. She could taste light, and watch her own scream of ecstasy as it came barrelling towards her and smashed in through the membrane of reality.

The last thing she registered was warm, hot redness. Then blue in the redness. Jake's eyes as he thrust into her ...

8

Samurai Dreams

It was the first time Deana had ever truly envied her sister, and she didn't like the feeling.

Throwing off the single sheet from her naked, perspiring body, she gave up on sleep, slid her legs out of bed and stood up. Whether getting up would make things any better was debatable, but she'd always preferred action to inaction. She snatched up her thin cotton robe, she shrugged it on and padded her way to the kitchen.

Deana loved this little flat of theirs, and she'd invested a lot of her flair in it, but suddenly it looked drab and uninteresting. Because of where Delia was. And who she was with ... Taking a sip from her glass of fizzy water, Deana switched off the light again. The dark was far easier to brood in.

It was a better environment for imaging too, although that maybe wasn't such a good thing to be doing right now. It would be better to keep fantasy to a minimum tonight. To resist dreams. Because they'd probably hurt like hell.

When she closed her eyes, though, it seemed that the damage was done. The pictures had already arrived ...

You're mad, she told herself, stroking her thighs through her robe as Jake appeared in her mind. Cool, dark Jake and her sister Delia, nude in an acre-sized bed, screwing like animals and screaming with pleasure ...

Oh well done, Deana, anyone would think you were a masochist!

She found it difficult to believe how badly she was reacting. In this same position, Delia had shown far more sense. When it was her night 'off', she'd found another man to keep her company.

For half a second, Deana considered turning the game back in on itself. She could sneak upstairs and pass herself off as Delia... It could work if she was sharp, but Peter would be trickier to fool than Jake. He'd been around her and Delia for years and years and might notice the differences. They were almost indiscernible, but they *did* exist.

There was one big flaw in this plan however, and in her heart of hearts, Deana was glad of it. Peter *knew* that it was Delia who was out tonight, because she'd told him herself. Damn!

She considered her options with little enthusiasm. Maybe I should just get a proper drink and watch TV on the all-night channel? Or I could try sketching, perhaps, or read a good book...

Hold that thought!

On the word 'book' another vision had formed. A quite different one this time. The dim and decadent interior of the so-called club 'Seventeen'... And in it a certain beautiful authoress with a long, fire-red plait and a distinctive taste in clothes.

Vida Mistry.

Who wrote books.

Ignoring her flapping robe and the loss of its flimsy tie, Deana ran through into the living room. She stubbed her toe on the way and swore, then shrugged philosophically. It was that kind of night.

Down beside the window was an over-filled bookcase which

threatened to collapse any second. Snapping on a reading lamp, Deana scanned the shelves with purpose.

What she was seeking was secreted on the bottom shelf. Hidden there by Delia no doubt, who, up until a few days ago, had always worried about 'appearances'. The works of Vida Mistry would never win any top literary prizes, but that didn't make them any less notable. What Deana now pulled from the shelves was some of the most salacious modern erotica available.

She thumbed quickly through several of the volumes, searching for something that she'd only just realised was plaguing her. A connection. A name. It had been in her mind since the day after the art exhibition, but unsurprisingly her thinking had been muddled.

Flicking and flicking the pages she smiled when certain ones fell open quite naturally. These books were so sexy. And some bits were sexier than others ...

The Pleasure Palace. Return to the Pleasure Palace. In Love with the Boy. They were all hot 'reads', but what she was looking for was not in a novel.

At the bottom of the heap she found it. *Seven Mistry Tales*, a collection of short, sensual stories which had appeared in the sex magazine *Encounters*.

The cover of the *Mistry Tales* was crinkled at the edges, as were many of the pages themselves. This particular book had spent quite some time in the bathroom, getting dangerously damp and curly while Deana tried to read it and caress her own body at the same time. Sometimes, it had been simple touches with her fingers, inspired by the blood-stirring prose; at other times, she'd have to run the shower or the bath taps to hide her vibrator's loud buzz. It was silly really, there was nothing to be ashamed of. And she knew that Delia knew anyway.

There was no shower now, and she didn't need it. She didn't even need the vibrator. She was burning up already, just from envy. Because her sister was getting what *she* wanted.

But jealousy was a self-defeating route. The game was the game, and Delia was just taking her turn. Her fairly allotted slice of heaven... Deana knew she would have to make her own amusement, create her own pleasure. And this much-read book could help her. Slowly, with ceremony, she sat down on the sofa, flicked aside the wings of her robe and eased open her thighs. Opening the book too, she closed her eyes and ran her finger down the page of contents.

When she looked down again, the connection snapped shut. She'd found what she was looking for. And she couldn't understand why she hadn't looked sooner.

The story was called, rather fancifully, *The Face of Lord Kazuto.*

Why on earth didn't it click right away? Deana wondered. It had been obvious at 'Seventeen' that Jake and Mistry had once been lovers, and maybe even still were. But it wasn't until now that Deana realised how significant that relationship had been. Vida had written about her lover in a story – about Kazuto, her Japanese jewel.

Excited, and with her body softly trembling, Deana turned to the page. She'd read the story plenty of times, but never with eyes that had seen its hero in real life. Its beautiful samurai hero with his long black hair, his strong brown body and his magnificent woman-slaying weapon.

The Face of Lord Kazuto wasn't Vida Mistry at her wildest by a long shot, but in its own way it was quietly powerful. It was mannered, lyrical almost, and more gentle in character than she would've expected now she *knew* the characters.

Now she was ready, Deana paused and wondered if she really wanted to masturbate. Moments ago she'd been desperate for it, her body all primed for her fingers. But now she almost didn't want to do it. Didn't need to. The story, the night, and her own imagination would do it all for her, be all the stimulation she needed. Breathing deeply, centring her mind, she began to read ...

It was a humid night, such as many in this season were. Keiko looked down at the face of the sleeping man before her, and she prayed to her gods that he dreamed of her.

It's me, Lord Kazuto, Your Keiko-chan. Your wife. Do you remember what we used to share here? Here on your futon ... Before you went to war, then came back with your eyes dead from killing?

With a rustle of embroidered silk, she knelt down beside the low, flat bed, touching the corner of its quilted mattress with her fingertips, because she hardly dare touch the man himself. It pained her deeply that she felt this fear, that things were so changed between them, when months ago they'd been so close it had been almost unseemly.

His new young wife, she'd been prepared for this bed by maids who were equally new to her. They'd bathed and perfumed her, brushed her long black hair until it gleamed. Then, ignoring her naive cries of protest, they'd opened her virgin thighs and stroked the sensitive portal of her womanhood to prepare her for the touch of her newly wed Lord. At the same time, they'd opened the books her mother had given her, the Shunga pillow-books, and made her look closely at the lewd but exquisite drawings of lovers in heavenly congress. By the time she'd studied each image, her belly had been aching for the things that she'd seen, and her loins were on fire for her Lord.

Then, in accordance with his wishes, her path of love had been opened for him. Her maids, between them, had deflowered her with a slender ivory rod. One swift stroke of pain, and she'd been ready for him, and she'd asked the kami of fleshly conflict to make her brave. If Lord Kazuto were to be as hard as the harigata, she must learn to bear him with grace.

How ignorant I was, she thought now. The harigata had been beautifully crafted, and she was grateful to this day for its carved likeness to her husband's mighty member. But that was all the ivory rod was. A likeness. A cold, hard thing with no spirit or animation. Lord Kazuto himself, when he'd finally possessed her, had been just as stiff and unyielding as the harigata, but so warm inside her body, and so silken, that her unrestrained cries had beat against the shoji and threatened to alert the whole household to her ecstasy.

'Kazuto-chan,' she mouthed now, moderating her words out of respect while her womanhood flowed like a river.

Each night while he'd been away, she'd shed this same lotus dew, remembering the pleasures of their pillowing. She'd woken from demon haunted dreams, her body wet and aching, and been forced to seek out the harigata to calm her longing for her Lord. With its cool hard comfort inside her, she'd let her fingers play amongst her petals as her husband's had done. Then, when the moment came, she'd soar like a spirit to paradise with his beloved face clear in her mind and his pure noble name on her lips ...

It was wonderful stuff, and it was working, Deana realised. Almost without thinking, she'd been slowly rocking her pelvis, and flexing her hot inner muscles in a subtle, automatic caress. She wasn't crying, but when she reached between her thighs and touched herself, she found her flesh just as sticky as Keiko's. Stroking her vulva thoughtfully, she returned her attention to the narrative ...

In the early days of their marriage, whilst replete with the pleasures gained on this very futon, Keiko had had no need of the cold harigata. With gracious courtesy, her Lord had requested her company each night: sometimes wooing her with a slow, almost respectful ritual, at other times taking her brutally. He was just as much a warrior in love as he was on the field of battle. But in the pillow world there was no shame in surrender. At least not for Keiko, as she revelled in the slight sweet pain of his member surging in her channel.

Sadly, though, this sojourn in heaven had been brief.

'I entrust you with the management of my affairs, Lady Keiko,' he'd said on that last morning, bowing deeply and respectfully before swinging astride his war-horse. The leave taking was formal, and though Keiko was sad, she bore it with all composure, buoyed up by memories of his true farewell to her, in the scented shadows of the bedchamber.

The months of conflict had been long and dour, but to honour him as he'd honoured her, their reunion before the household had been as controlled and calm as their parting before his troops. But what troubled Keiko now, and hurt her so deeply it was hard to conceal, was that their private dealings were consistently as distant as their public ones.

Unlike many ladies of the Shogun's court, Keiko had been fortunate enough to receive her husband back from the war in one piece. At least his physical wounds were slight. She sensed however, to her sorrow, that his psyche had suffered far more than his body – and that the horrors of conflict, no matter how noble and justified the cause, had damaged him profoundly as a man.

He no longer summoned her to his chamber at night, even though sometimes she still caught the black fire burning in his eyes.

Not a word was exchanged between them on the matter, but some sad, internal wisdom told Keiko that her husband had a great fear of impotence. And that his pride, and his horror at the thought of losing face, meant there was no way to put such fears to the test.

Would they ever be lovers again?

Stop it, Keiko! she told herself sternly, looking down at his dear sleeping countenance. You are as much a samurai as he is, and as such, defeat does not exist! Her pale features set in determined lines, she turned to the small lacquered chest she'd brought with her.

'Kazuto,' she mimed again, wanting to touch him but knowing the moment was not yet at hand. She knew that he'd been taking a sleeping potion prescribed by his physician, but by now its effects should be lessening.

She wondered for a moment if he were pretending to sleep. Was he assuming a mask of oblivion to save them both from embarrassment? Lord Kazuto the fearless, the Shogun's right hand, he was the last one to admit to a failing.

At the thought of masks, she smiled and brushed her fingers across the black box, then returned her attention to the deeply sleeping man. It would be a shame to cover up such beauty.

It had been Kazuto-chan's face that had first enslaved her. His features were so fine, so pure, and so exquisite that they could have been a woman's. It was true that he had a perfectly barbered moustache and beard, and a striking scar from an earlier battle. But even so, his face was as symmetrical and harmonious as the most delicate of woodcuts. Without his hairy, masculine attributes, Lord Kazuto would have been as beautiful as the most sought-after courtesan. This beauty, combined with his wit and intelligence, his strong athletic body, and his many skills and achievements, were what made Keiko love and adore him. Chief amongst these talents, she'd loved his awesome performance at the pillow, and it was this gift she sought to restore . . .

But the man before her was the proudest of warriors and a master strategist; she'd have to use the wiliest of subterfuge to preserve his samurai honour.

In this heavy humid heat, Lord Kazuto slept with no quilt or coverlet, his long muscular body clad only in a thin cotton yukata. And his troubled thrashings, beset no doubt by dreams as bad as Keiko's, had left even this only barely fastened. It was a simple matter to slide her slim fingers under its edge and render his sprawled body all but naked ...

This picture was easy for a visualist like Deana. She'd not yet seen Jake naked, but she could more than imagine him so ...

Other things were a little trickier though. Mr Sleek 'n Cool with a beard and moustache? She was intrigued. After a few seconds' thought, she added it into the vision and agreed with Keiko. He still looked beautiful hirsute! Smiling, she read on ...

Keiko sighed.

Even at rest he excited her. Silken juice was flowing between her thighs, soiling her fragile kimono where she knelt with her legs folded under her. Her small shapely breasts ached and hungered, famished for the gracious touch of her dear Lord husband's fingers.

He was unroused, but even so his quiescent member was imposing. She remembered it bold like a sword inside her, and her resolve strengthened. She would have him again, and soon. Stiff as a wooden pole, yet sliding like a breeze through reeds in the silken dew of her channel. She would feel his seed gushing inside her before long, and she said a silent prayer that the gods might guide her efforts.

Tearing her eyes from the beauty of her noble husband's

nakedness, she turned to her lacquered box and opened it to reveal some strangely varied contents.

On top were two moulded paper masks, polished, white and painted, and crafted with holes for eyes, nose, and mouth. In design they were much like traditional masks of the Noh theatre, but being only paper, and not cedarwood, they were much lighter and more comfortable on the face. One depicted a powerful but anonymous lord; the other a peasant girl, of lowly rank but beautiful and intelligent. Keiko smiled fondly, remembering more tranquil times before the war, when the whole household had taken pleasure in performing simple but elegant dramas.

Beneath the masks were a number of stoppered ceramic flasks, and as she lifted them out, Keiko's nostrils flickered at the delightful rush of odours.

The lovely smells must have filtered into her Lord's consciousness too, because suddenly he began to stir and his lush black eyelashes fluttered.

Moving purely on instinct, and as deftly as she could, Keiko leaned across him and fastened the lordly paper mask across his face. For an instant, she thought his finely honed senses might be her undoing, and that he might attack her or summon his bodyguards. But then his night-black eyes flared and glittered through the twin slits in the paper and as he watched her don her own thin mask, she knew that he'd effortlessly divined her purpose. That he understood how she sought to revive their intimacy without compromising the integrity of his 'face'.

'Rest easy, noble stranger,' she said, adopting a slightly sing-song tone to reinforce the illusion of a play. 'I regret the imposition on your valued time, but may I ask your Lordship a favour?'

He nodded slightly and Keiko's heart sang. 'Esteemed Lord,' she went on, bowing low, 'I am a humble student of the arts of medicine and it would honour me greatly if you would allow me to examine your fine and honourable body in the pursuit of my scientific studies.'

There was a long pause in which Keiko hardly dared draw breath.

'Proceed, scholar,' he said at last, his voice low and carefully controlled. 'I too revere the sciences. I am pleased to assist you.'

'I thank you. You are most gracious.' More bows now, so low that her mask almost grazed the tatami. 'Please do not trouble yourself to move, my Lord,' she murmured, straightening up as she sensed him stirring again. 'You are most conveniently placed for my studies.'

Removing the stopper from one of the flasks, she poured a little of its contents into a delicate porcelain bowl, sniffing appreciatively as an intoxicating aroma rose up. She repeated the process with a second flask, then a third, then another, almost swaying as the blended perfumes engulfed her. Using a small whisk she ensured the mixture was perfectly combined, and smiled at the power of its ingredients.

The apothecary had vouched for this combination, although the scarf that Keiko had worn across her face meant that the man had no knowledge of the person to whom he was recommending it.

Oil of ylang-ylang for sexual stimulation; vanilla with similar qualities; and geranium for harmony and for soothing. But it was the very final element that was the most potent – pure, refined oil of lotus of the highest quality, reputedly the most irresistible aphrodisiac ever discovered.

On the pretext of protecting her costly kimono, Keiko made herself naked, noting the increased brightness of her loved one's dark eyes and praying it was a favourable omen. She hardly dare look at his genitals.

Coating her fingers in the oily elixir, she began a slow smooth massage of his chest and made a point of working carefully at each group of muscles as if she truly were examining his anatomy. Her wild, rash urge was to fondle his male member directly, but with great difficulty she governed her passion. She dare not hope too hard what the oil might do to Lord Kazuto, but she could feel its strong effects on her. The lotus oil was making her own flower pout and ache and swell, its petals almost painful in their craving for her dear love's touch.

For several almost endless minutes, she worked dutifully on his upper body, grateful in a way that the slits of her mask did not permit her gaze to go astray. It was only when a small grunting cry issued urgently from behind the mask of her 'subject', and his body began to shift and sway beneath her flexing fingers, that she permitted herself a glance towards his groin.

Lord Buddha be praised! Her lover's mighty staff was rising before her very eyes, its bold head swelling and weeping in a joyful resurrection. A true samurai weapon now, it reared up from its master's slim, manly loins and invited the hand or body of a woman to embrace it. Keiko curbed her immediate instinct to engulf him, sensing that matters were as yet still critical. If this new vigour should fail him now, his loss of face would be even greater than before. With a control that defied all her previous limits, she continued her exploration of his torso.

'Gentle student,' gasped the man behind the mask, his authoritative voice suddenly gruff and broken, 'pray extend the scope of your examination a little . . . I fear you are neglecting certain areas.'

'Why thank you for your consideration, my Lord,' Keiko answered humbly, masking her delirious joy. 'It is not every day that a lowly scholar meets someone so concerned with the advancement of science.'

Still hesitant, she let her hand travel downwards then skirt the base of his stiff swaying wand. She marvelled at the soft silkiness of his intimate male hair, then admired the increased gloss of each strand as she combed him with her warmly oiled fingers. Almost with fear, she touched his noble upthrust flesh, then sighed with relief and happiness when, instead of collapsing, it grew harder and prouder and stronger in her hand. She fondled him gently, her lightness of touch for his pleasure now rather than from caution. This was a veritable battle-lance she had in her grasp, and she knew with a happy woman's certainty that it would not now lose its rigidity – except under the most blissful of circumstances.

She let her fingers play coquettishly over him, savouring the deep pulse of blood in his veins and the fat, moist stretching of his sovereign helmet as it throbbed out its demand for her body and for the haven of her thickly dewed channel. In her other hand, she fondled his twin ripe fruits, so heavy in their warm, crinkled sac.

'My Keiko-chan,' he crooned, his hips lifting her prize towards her. 'My gentle wife ... Relieve me from this torment ... Let me in at your heavenly gate!' With one impatient hand he tore off his mask as the other reached hungrily for her body.

'But, my Lord,' she said coyly, simpering behind her paper face, 'I am but a simple medical student, bent on the furtherance of science ...'

'You're a minx and a goddess, my Keiko-chan!' he cried, his voice rich with lust and contentment. 'Now straddle my weapon or I will rise up and throw you flat on your smooth white back!'

'As you wish, my Lord,' she whispered, moving with all the grace she possessed onto the futon ... and then onto the body of her husband.

Her portal seemed to laugh with pleasure as he breached it, and as he filled her, she ripped aside her mask so that her long cry of fulfilment might not be in the slightest way stifled.

'My love! Oh, my love!' she screamed, as the kami bore her soul up to heaven . . . and she looked down with the happiest of eyes at the face of her Lord Kazuto.

Deana let the book drop, her fingers tingling, her imagination whirling, and her sex more hungry than ever. It was hard to detach herself from Keiko, but fiction and truth were quite different. Mistry's samurai lady was satisfied now, and content. And she, Deana, was neither.

Was the story based on reality? she wondered. Had Jake doubted his virility, and Vida reassured him? It was an unlikely but intriguing idea.

But how could Jake not be strong? There seemed to be no chink whatsoever in his power or confidence. His sense of total control. And yet unlikely as it seemed, the concept of a less than omnipotent Jake was bizarrely appealing. Deana was used to being the boss in her relationships, particularly where sex was concerned; but with Jake, she'd never even been given the chance to take charge.

What would it be like? she mused. To make him bow. Bring him to heel? Should she go in hard, as Vida probably did? Or wield a gentle dominance, like clever old Keiko with her samurai? Either way, she could barely sit still at the thought.

She'd touched herself only briefly so far, yet she felt unbearably excited and randy. Desire nagged her, heavy and pitiless, and her sex-folds were swollen and puffy.

It was as if Vida Mistry had reached inside her head and used the subversive power of words to stir her. It was mental masturbation, a sweet, sly, sinuous magic that had worked on the principal human sex organ – the mind. Deana's visual and spatial imagination had made her uniquely susceptible, and now she was hot and wet, her labia unfurled and engorged like the petals of a succulent flower. She hardly dared touch her clitoris. Making a fork of two of her fingers, she slid them down either side of it, making the tension itself a caress. The tiny bead leapt and pulsed, then seemed to swell to twice its size.

And in her mind, Deana saw a wealth of curious visions. Illusions from a dark, deep pit. She saw herself, in leather, tying straps around a taut, cringing Jake. She was holding his cock, squeezing it and making him cry, while Vida Mistry did unspeakable things to his hind parts. She heard him whimper and sob, saw him spurt, and felt her hot sex ripple in the grip of a fiendish harness . . .

In the real world, it was she who sobbed. Writhing on the couch with her hands between her thighs, she moaned as her vagina convulsed and her clitoris quivered and leapt.

'Oh Jake, oh Jake,' she whispered, wishing him with her, 'why in God's name aren't there two of *you* too?'

Delia didn't come home that night, and Deana was more scared now than jealous.

Under normal circumstances she wouldn't have worried. For her own part, she stayed out often enough, and Delia herself spent the odd night with Russell. Personally, Deana wouldn't have spent an hour with him, but there was no accounting for taste . . .

But that was beside the point. This stop-out was different. Jake wasn't Russell. Their worlds and preferences were light-years apart, and Jake in himself was infinitely dangerous.

As she decided she couldn't eat her breakfast, Deana felt a hard squeeze of hatred. Not at her sister, because what had happened was chance. Or fate. Or luck. It had been that initial flip of a coin that had set up the sequence, and she could so easily have been the one herself.

Her anger was directed at Jake, and she felt protective of

her sister. Delia had been the one to spend a whole licentious night with him, and she was the twin least fit to deal with him, if his demands became excessive. He'd been inventive enough in brief encounters, what on earth would he get up to with a whole night to play in? Deana's skin started to goose pimple at the thought, and her sex became hotter. She felt more scared than ever for Delia.

And she was powerless to help her. There was nothing she could do. She didn't know where he lived, and even if she did, making contact was risky. Delia might still be with him now. In his bed.

Tense and uneasy, Deana made ready to go into her agency. It was completely unlike her, but she found herself constantly listening for the door, for the phone, for anything. She went to and fro to the window a score of times. Later, and ridiculously irrationally, she even caught herself scanning the crowds on the Tube in search of a face like her own.

As a freelance, Deana's hours were fairly relaxed and she could come and go as she pleased. She took advantage of this, and often worked from home; but every so often, Robin – who ran the collective – insisted she come in, show her face to clients, and prioritise her work. Today was a day he'd insisted.

It was also an unbearably slow, dragging day. Her fund of inspiration was arid and what she did produce was wooden and characterless. Everything about work and the hot city was drab and oppressive. She tried to call Delia several times at de Guile International, but each time she was either 'in conference', 'at lunch' or just plain 'unavailable'.

'Unavailable.' What did that mean exactly? Was she with Jake? Being wooed or tormented. Or both, perhaps? Deana threw her pencil down, her head full of Jake, resplendent in some kind of executive's chair and with Delia sitting astride him as she herself had done in the car. She shook her head to clear it and the image changed. There was no relief though ... This time she saw herself – or was it Delia? – spread across the surface of a long oak desk, with Jake thrusting hard between her legs.

When she arrived home, grubby and weary, Deana could hear the TV in the flat. Delia was back, it seemed. But was she safe and sound? That was the question. Deana hardly dare call out and ask.

The first thing she saw when she walked into the living room was a large, rectangular, white card box. It was the sort of packaging an exclusive dress store might use, the sort that Delia often turned up with but which Deana never did. Her clothes came wrapped in plastic carriers ... if that.

The store logo was unfamiliar. She'd half expected it to be 'Janet Reger', 'La Perla' or some sort of designer ready-to-wear, but instead there was just the word 'Circe'. Deana recognised the Palatino Italic script, 36 point. Very plain, very classy ... but why a witch who'd turned men into swine? Jake was a chauvinist, but no pig. Far from it. He was dissolute, decadent and a pervert extraordinaire; but he was the most refined man she'd ever met. No woman – not even herself in her wildest moments – could ever rob Jake of his elegance.

She was assuming the box came from him, but it could always just be Delia treating herself. She might've been high on fabulous lovemaking and dying to spend some money. Deana often had that urge herself but she usually bought a painting or some books. Or those huge, hand-made Belgian chocolates which were the foodie equivalent of orgasms.

When she opened the box, all doubts about its origins dissolved. There was only one person in their lives at the moment who would purchase such a thing ... Deana touched leather and her stomach quivered. She lifted out the contents of the box and felt sick with excitement. How typical of Jake to buy this.

'This' was the most remarkable piece of lingerie that Deana had ever seen – a boned and laced basque made from flawless, pure white leather. It was fine and sleek, and fragrantly erotic, and her fingers shook as she stroked it.

Wear it for me, she imagined him saying. She could hear him, see him, feel him, as automatically she clasped the basque to her. It wasn't her usual style, but she'd no doubt it was exactly her size; a minor masterpiece in leather, so thin it felt fluid. Its texture was like cream to her exploring fingertips, and both virginal and deviant, it menaced her. Smooth and strange, it was a pleasure to hold against her body. But could she ever put on such a miracle? It was just 'not her'.

'It fits,' said Delia calmly. 'I've tried it.'

Deana almost dropped her find when her sister walked into the room, soundless in her stockinged, shoeless feet.

'God, you made me jump!' Deana dropped the basque back into its wrappings, and then, when she looked at her sister more closely, she frowned.

She'd expected Delia to look different somehow. Radiant. Beatific. Completely suffused with sex . . . But Delia just seemed her usual cool efficient self. There were no visible signs of debauchery either. No love-bites. No bags under the eyes. No pasty face or stifled yawns.

Deana stared hard, but Delia didn't waver or seem fazed. 'You haven't got long, Deana,' she said briskly, lifting the corset back out of its box. 'You're being picked up at half past seven, and he wants you in *this*.' She shook the strange garment chiv-vyingly, and its suspenders danced and bobbed. 'So you'd better get a move on and get into it.'

Deana took the basque back from her sister and fingered its sensuous surface. 'Never mind "get a move on",' she shot back with some spirit, 'hadn't you better tell me how you came to be out all night? I've been worried.' She paused, guiltily. It was true, she *had* been worried, but her jealousy had bothered her more. 'I'll start getting ready if you'll get us some wine then tell me everything that's happened.'

'You'll have tea,' replied Delia firmly, 'and I'll brief you while you dress.'

She was already on her way to the kitchen.

Will my sweat stain the leather? Deana wondered, hoping it wouldn't.

Waiting in the corset, she felt hot and uneasy. She was uncomfortable in the bloody thing, but more uncomfortable by far with the twists and turns of life. The disquieting parallels. The weird coincidences . . . it was like being in the Twilight Zone. Having fantasies about geishas and samurai while your sister was making love with a Japanese bath girl.

But when Deana rationalised events, they didn't seem quite so unlikely. Jake was half-Japanese himself so why shouldn't he have Japanese staff working for him?

Similarly, why shouldn't Vida Mistry pick up on Jake's exotic heritage and use it in her stories? The black hair, the oriental eyes – they were perfect for a glamorous fictional hero. Especially if you'd had an affair with that hero. And the fact that things were happening contiguously wasn't so strange either. Everything seemed to be happening at once since that night at the gallery.

So Jake has a female valet? So what? It was Delia's description of her responses that was the bigger shock. Deana had been astounded by her sister's matter-of-fact account of her first brush with lesbianism. She was still astounded. But more by Delia's unruffled sang-froid than by the physical blow-by-blow details. She seemed so calm describing another woman's hands on her body and sex. Deana doubted if she herself could act so coolly . . . She certainly wasn't cool now at the thought of the night ahead.

At the end of her account, Delia had at least had the grace to blush. But Deana wondered now if she and her sister's sexualities might not be all that different.

Delia had taken pleasure with Elf, and she, Deana, was attracted to the weird and wonderful Vida. There was nothing to choose between them except that Delia had put inclination into action. They were both latent bi-sexuals who'd found their true selves at last.

Deana shifted position on the sofa. The basque was harassing her, its tightness on her body so different to her usual minimal underwear. She liked featherweight cottons and silks: pants she could hardly feel, bras that were really just wisps. Unstructured camisoles and G-strings. All these bones and hooks and laces were purgatory. She knew it was more imagination than anything, but she was finding it difficult to breathe.

Constrained in the basque, she felt as if her whole body and mind were controlled by it. The thing had a form and character all of its own. It moulded her flesh to its shape rather than adapting itself to hers. It made her submit, but it also made her beautiful.

Taming her near-perfect figure, the pale fetishistic corset imbued her with an elegance and mannequin-like deportment that she'd never before possessed. Her nature was always to stroll, skip, bop along. But the basque allowed none of these. In it, she was forced to stand up straight and glide. Be stately . . . She felt like a brand new woman, and the experience was deeply disquieting.

A cocktail dress borrowed from Delia didn't help matters either. It was as completely unfamiliar as the basque was, but Deana had nothing in her wardrobe that was meant to be worn with a corset. She slid her fingers across the ruched magenta silk, and imagined the tight white hide beneath, ensheathing her. Sweat popped out afresh and she felt a murderous urge to panic. To rip everything off and say 'to hell with it'. But she didn't. Because rising at last through the layers of discomfort came a new and strangely genital excitement. Constriction forced her blood and organs downwards, building tension and pressure in her sex.

In a sudden illuminating moment, Deana's feelings about the white basque changed. Completely. As the pressure in her vulva mounted, she understood the dark lure of containment, the magic of being bound in and laced. Her clitoris felt lively, and exquisitely tender. She wanted to reach down and touch it, to put her hand between her legs, but the vivid pink dress was too slim.

'You bastard!' she hissed, not sure if it was the garment or its giver that she cursed. He was controlling her with it, dominating her. He'd wrapped her in snow-white leather and enslaved her. And he wasn't even here yet!

But even as the thought coalesced, a coolness trickled right down her spine. The ghost of a long, elegant finger ... A man's slender, narrow-tipped, perfectly manicured finger.

And when she slid to her feet and went to the window, the limousine was purring outside ...

9

Comings and Goings

What a strange way to end a relationship, thought Delia, almost skipping up the steps after paying off her taxi.

She felt light, free, exhilarated. She felt wicked, outrageous, almost giddy. And very, very sexy. Laughing softly as she opened the door to the flat, she realised that she'd never really enjoyed herself all that much with Russell anyway. It was so ironical that tonight, in the course of their furious parting row, she'd finally got sexual pleasure from him!

Deana would be proud of me, she observed, throwing down her bag of belongings on the settee and marching into the kitchen in search of something to drink. An achievement like this deserved a special treat, and with a heavier hand than usual, she mixed herself a large gin and tonic and sank half of it in one long swallow.

She still couldn't quite remember how she and Russell had managed it, but somehow they'd ended up screwing out their fury on his immaculate off-white lounge carpet. And – for the first time ever without recourse to fantasy – she'd had an orgasm with him inside her.

For about half a minute afterwards, while he huffed and puffed on top of her, she'd wondered whether to back-track and suggest they try again. But sweet reason, common sense, and the pervasive guiding spirits of both Deana and Jake had swayed her. This 'jackpot' with Russell had been a fluke, a one-off fuelled by their mutual antagonism. If they stayed together they'd slide straight back to the way they were. A going-through-the-motions, low-grade boredom that had a killing effect on the sex drive.

'No way, my man. It's over,' she whispered, then sipped at her drink. 'Here's to you, Russ. It was tedious . . . but at least I've learned something. Second best isn't worth it!' It was a philosophical, turned about salute, but it seemed to set the final seal on things. She glugged down the rest of her gin, then set about mixing another.

I'm turning into an alcoholic, she decided, still feeling buoyed up and wicked. It was true, she'd drunk more than usual in the last few days, but the days themselves had been far from usual. She'd been through a wild, erotic upheaval, but delicious as the process was, she couldn't see it lasting forever. Well, not for her at least. Deana maybe, but not her, Delia, whose sense of equilibrium had always been strong. Except, perhaps, when she was worrying about her sister, and feeling just a little bit jealous.

This must be how Deana felt last night, she supposed, sitting down on the settee and kicking off her shoes. As she swung her legs up onto the seat, settled back and took a pull of her new drink, she felt a sticky trickle between her legs, the last remnants of Russell sliding out of her body and her life. The sensation was startlingly pleasant, and it took her back to that first morning at the office, when Jake's flowing essence had shocked her too. It'd been that cool, silky flow that had made her realise what she'd done. What he'd done . . . That he'd had her within minutes of meeting her.

But what was Jake doing now? Holding court in his fancy-dancy throne room with a leather-clad Deana at his mercy? Delia grinned into her drink, remembering her sister's surprise at being told that female overnight guests did *not* share the de Guile master bedroom.

She'd been surprised herself. She could've slept on a rail when she'd fallen into a sex-dazed stupor on Jake's luxurious couch, but she hadn't expected to sleep so deeply that she'd wake up somewhere else. Alone.

The room she'd ended up in was one of the most beautiful she'd ever seen – a designer decorated courtesan's boudoir complete with an antique four-poster bed. She hadn't been alone for long in it, though. She'd just been wondering whether it had been Jake himself, the faithful Fargo, or even the remarkable Elf who had carried her there, when the Japanese girl had brought in breakfast. More pampering ... Fresh hand-baked croissants with butter and preserves. Plus sublimely strong coffee. While Delia had devoured and drunk, Elf had run a bath for her. And afterwards, when she'd soaked for ages in aromatic, muscle-soothing bubbles, Delia had emerged to find all her clothes laid out and waiting for her, newly laundered and pressed. Even down to her panties.

Jake – Mr Busy – had already left for the day, it seemed, but his household ran efficiently in his absence. When Delia was ready to leave, Elf had handed her the box containing the leather basque, and the note containing Jake's precise instructions for its wearing.

Instructions that Deana had laughed at on reading, and that Delia knew for a fact her rebellious sister was not quite following.

It was typical of Deana. She'd always bucked any kind of authority, especially male. Delia had always found that for her own part, success came with going with the flow ... Which was what she'd been doing with Jake. If Deana let her tearaway tendencies get the better of her, their game would surely falter.

Delia didn't like to think about the consequences of that just now; and happily a knock at the door meant she didn't have to. With a grunt of equal parts irritation and relief, she swung her legs off the couch and went to meet her caller.

On the doorstep stood Peter, his faintly gawky frame ridiculous in voluminous surf shorts and an overgrown T-shirt. But it wasn't his unfortunate dress sense that really caught her attention. It was the red hot look in his eyes.

He was eating her up, gobbling her with his gaze. They'd talked calmly together on the day after their night of wine-soaked sex and as far as Delia knew the air between them was clear.

But Peter's eyes now said otherwise; they were dark and stormy, the pupils huge and black with arousal. The strangest thing was that his stare seemed as much for her clothes as the body inside them. For several seconds Delia was puzzled by this, then the truth dawned.

Tonight was a sultry night in a silly season, and when she'd been preparing to go out, Delia had felt especially oppressed by it. She'd abandoned the chic two piece she'd picked out initially, and raided Deana's wardrobe instead. Amongst the haphazard jumble of garments, she'd found a nice, floaty T-shirt styled top and matching skirt which was surprisingly elegant for Deana. Its 'floppiness' had felt quite odd to Delia at first, but the fact it was so cool and light had made up for everything. As had the fact that Russell had hated it at first sight. He'd often criticised Deana for her vagabond, thrown-on look, and it had given Delia a special, spiteful buzz to turn up looking just like her sibling.

The trouble was she now looked far too much like her sister. The woman that poor Peter loved!

He flinched when she reached out to touch his arm and guide him into the flat. 'Whoah! It's me, Pete...Delia. I only wore Deana's frock because it's cooler.'

In the living room, he simply stood and stared at her, an

expression of confusion and frustration on his quietly handsome face. After a minute, he shook his head, then took off his glasses and polished them nervously on the corner of his T-shirt.

'That's the first time in years I've got you mixed up,' he said quietly, settling his specs back on the bridge of his nose, and staring at her wanly through their lenses.

'Wishful thinking?' she enquired, trying not to sound tart. Nobody was with quite who they wanted to be tonight... except Deana.

'I'm not sure...I don't know,' he answered uncertainly, shifting his weight from one foot to the other. 'I don't really know what I think since the other night.'

Lord have mercy, thought Delia despairingly. As if things aren't complicated enough!

Even so, she felt a small smug spark of pleasure. There'd never really been much in the way of rivalry between her and Deana up until now because they'd always gone for entirely dissimilar men. But Jake had changed all that. They were in competition now, and though she loved her sister not one bit less, Delia felt at a distinct disadvantage. Deana was wild, flamboyant and earthy, a far more obvious sex object than she was. So it was nice to know that Peter – suddenly so decidedly fanciable – liked *her* as much as he did Deana.

And more than 'liked'.

As discreetly as she could, Delia let her gaze drift lower and settle momentarily on his technicolour shorts. The eye-searing cloth was pushed out quite clearly at his groin...

Catching her look, Peter blushed, and it was a curiously touching sight. He coloured beautifully. 'Sorry,' he muttered, his fists flexing at his side as if he longed to clasp his hands to his crotch and hide the bulging evidence of his urges.

'There's no need to be.'

Delia felt an exhilarating wash of power. She was in control here; she could grant or deny this nice man's pleasure. She'd had her own sexual release tonight already, and now it was down to her entirely whether Peter – poor rampant Peter – got his.

Yet she didn't want to cheat him. Offer him a body which had already been 'used' somehow. In spite of his protestations about respecting her freedom and her choice of relationships, she sensed he'd be deeply offended to find her wet with another man's semen.

I suppose I could get a quick shower, she thought, then decided against it. With Peter the moment had to be grasped immediately. His natural caution and politeness would make him back off if there was the slightest hesitation on her part. She felt a sudden strong yen for that drink she'd been having and as her mouth watered for it, an answer to the dilemma appeared.

Feeling deeply female, she smiled at him. 'How about a drink?'

'Yes. Yes, please!' He smiled back at her, looking grateful and slightly less nervous.

'Right then, you sit down while I fetch you one. I'm on G and T, is that OK?'

'Wonderful! Fine!' He flopped awkwardly down, and as she picked up her own glass and slid from the room, hiding what she knew was a truly wicked grin, she heard him flicking through one of Deana's many magazines.

She was still grinning as she swigged down the last of her gin, then took a large mouthful of tonic, swooshed it around and swallowed. She'd no real personal experience of such matters – yet – but common sense told her that alcohol could well have a startling effect on the most sensitive areas of the human body. Particularly the male human body . . .

For a moment, she wished she could talk to Deana. Deana who had experience and daring. Deana who never had qualms or doubts about her sexual performance. Deana who'd probably done most things and all of them far more often than Delia had.

Hard on the heels of the wish came a curious, almost tingling revelation about its nature. Right now, with what she had in mind for Peter, she yearned for her sister's sexual skill. But only that. She wanted to be able to do what Deana could do, but not to *be* her. It was suddenly just fine to be Delia Ferraro about to make love to Peter; and not Deana Ferraro in the dark and deviant clutches of Jake de Guile. And that thought made her happy. She didn't have to strive and she didn't have to worry, she could just be herself and enjoy it. Smiling, she poured herself a fresh glass of tonic and made Peter a fierce G and T, then strode back boldly to the living room.

Peter had abandoned his magazine and was lying half slumped in his seat, his glasses off and his eyes closed as if weary.

Was he tired? Delia knew only too well how emotional upheavals could wear a person out. Her own sleep patterns were crazy now, when before, she'd always slept soundly for a consistent eight hours. Padding softly on her still-bare feet, she put the glasses silently down, and crept towards the drowsy man on her sofa. She fanned her skirts out as she sank down and knelt at his feet, and as the soft silk fell across his ankle, his eyes flew open in alarm.

He was short-sighted, she knew, but in that moment their gazes locked in a perfect incontestable communication. She made an offer and he acknowledged and accepted it.

'You don't have to do this,' he whispered, as if raised voices could fracture the spell.

'But I want to.' She laid her hands lightly on his exposed lower thighs and felt him tremble.

'Well, in that case ... Oh God—' His voice faltered as she slid the fingertips of both hands up the loose legs of his shorts and reached for the treasures at his groin. 'Oh yes! Please! Do it!'

Deliberate and teasing, she withdrew her searching fingers and let them rest on his bare knees as if she were deciding what her next act should be. She could feel moisture on his skin, and goose flesh, the sort that came from great excitement, not fear. Strength and exultation washed through her and she reached for the draw-string of his shorts.

The knot was slack and easily dealt with and in seconds she was grasping at his waistband and easing it downwards. Foraging beneath the gathered band, she hooked her fingers into his underpants too, then eased down both shorts and pants in a single crumpled bunch.

'Hup!' she urged softly, and like an obedient child, he lifted his bottom. With his hips still raised, she pulled his clothes right down to his ankles in a long bold yank, then suppressed a giggle at the stomach-slapping bounce of his cock as it swung and swayed like a jack-in-a-box. Its tip was wet and shiny and on the upswing it seemed to cling slightly to the gloss of sweat on his belly.

Sitting back onto her heels, she beheld a simple but magnificent sight. A naked penis, erect in its blind-eyed glory as it pointed its way to the stars ...

It was funny how an act that had never been her favourite was suddenly a bewitching obsession. She'd never wanted to suck Russell's unimpressive and forgettable instrument, but the idea of man-meat in her mouth was now delectable.

Peter didn't have quite the elegant weapon that Jake did – the hard, pure blade of a twentieth-century samurai – but what he did have was no mean shaft. It was fine and sturdy, fat, and a good, long length, its moist rounded head a delicious temptation to the mouth. Even as she watched, another drop of pre-come oozed out.

Will he taste like Jake, she wondered, her attention winging back to the hot red room and the man who'd lain on the couch. Would Peter be neutral and salty too, or would he have an individual flavour of his own? There was only one way to find out.

Almost cross-eyed with concentration, Delia touched the thick veiny shank and made it wave to and fro. Peter gasped and gritted his teeth, his eyes shut tight again now, his lean face a mask of submission. Submission to her will . . .

Delia felt wild and unstoppable, crazy for experience and pleasure, but completely in control. Shuffling closer, she tugged away the constricting clothes from around his ankles, then edged apart his feet and eased them forward. Pressing down on his splayed-open knees, she brought his pelvis sliding towards her so that his cock reared up, perfectly presented to her mouth. He cried out like a child when she leaned in towards his body and took the tip of him in between her lips.

She was vaguely aware of him collapsing backwards, his head twisting this way and that, his throat bared and vulnerable. She imagined the sight to be fabulous – but her primary attention was lower. On the pale naked plains of his loins and thighs, and at the heart of the matter, his cock . . .

When she sucked him experimentally, he jerked in her mouth and squirmed his hips on the seat. It was almost as if the sensations were too much for him and he was trying to get away, but Delia refused to let go. He was her prize, her treat, her living lollipop and she was determined to have him. She curled the fingers of one hand around his shaft, and with the other hand she cradled his balls.

This cock was hers now, and she would have everything

about it. She would take its heat and its hardness and she would drain it of its strength and sap. Every silk-smooth drop.

But not straight away, and not simply. This was a learning experience for her, an act to be taken slowly. She would savour it and memorise his every reaction. His every taste and texture. And even though she was only a student at this, she had no doubt in her mind that she already knew enough to enslave him. She could make this man, Peter, her creature with perfect ease. He'd be her grateful slave when she'd finished, to do with whatever she pleased.

It was an exquisite thought, as seductive and delightful as the taste of the flesh in her mouth. Salty stuff was flowing freely from the tiny little orifice in his glans, and as Delia sucked hard and instinctively to draw it out faster, Peter moaned like a man under torture. She felt his hands close around her head, his wrists and arms tense and shivering. He was fighting a driving urge, a need to grab at her hair for leverage and drive his cock into the depths of her throat. With her mouth chock-full of him, and her saliva flowing down across her chin, her mind seemed to be working with extra-ordinary clarity. She could feel the fight in him, feel him dying to thrust and pump and come, yet resisting it in case he made her choke.

He was sobbing now, crying and mewling out her name. *Her* name. 'Delia,' not 'Deana' or even 'Dee'. If she could've laughed with triumph, she would have done, but as it was she just swirled her tongue around his glans, tautened the fine skin of his cock with her fingers, then sucked at him till her ears popped and her eyes started watering with the effort.

Her reward was a long, broken shout that echoed eerily around the small room. He was one of the gentlest men she'd ever met but as he came, he gouged her tender scalp with his nails and filled her mouth with great bouts of his thick, hot semen. Spurt after spurt of it flooded her throat and within seconds she was struggling to swallow. Gulping, she tried hard to listen as well. And to understand the demented ramblings of a lover she'd driven crazy with her lips.

His chest was heaving, he was panting and gasping, but somewhere in the raving babble of his orgasm, Delia could've sworn she'd heard him tell her he loved her...

Men will say anything when they're coming, she thought as she let him slip out. Any old rubbish at all, she observed fondly as she kissed his red shiny tip.

She kissed his thighs, she kissed the dark, fuzzy floss at his groin, then unable to resist, she pressed another kiss to his soft, sticky penis.

But when she started to lick it, she felt his hand come alive amongst her hair. Moving more gently this time, he caressed her scalp, each tender stroke an echo of the flickings of her tongue.

'I love you, Delia,' he murmured as she adjusted her position and closed her fingertips very lightly on his balls.

Any old rubbish, she thought dreamily...then sucked.

'You look superb, Dee,' observed Jake laconically as Deana settled down in the limousine beside him. Her heart was pounding so hard she was surprised he didn't tell her he could see it. She was trying to project an attitude of cool, but she didn't think much of her chances...Inside she'd never felt hotter.

She was hot in Delia's stupid dress. Hot, in Jake's ridiculous perverted idea of underwear. Hot, because the man himself was just inches away, and all she wanted to do was close the distance and get him inside her.

Half-dizzy with it all, she had the weirdest idea. Had he

impregnated the leather of the basque somehow? Steeped it in an aphrodisiac potion that was passing through her skin into her bloodstream? Each time she'd met him she'd wanted him, but tonight it was out of all proportion...

Jake wore very little leather tonight, which Deana thought strange given his usual, almost fetishistic fondness for it. His shirt was made of heavy black silk, and he wore it tieless but primly buttoned up. His trousers were Italian, also black, and cut with a gorgeous fluid bagginess that was breathtakingly sensual. As a kind of afterthought, the whole lot was topped off with a natty figured satin waistcoat in a black on black shadow print. The only leather item he was wearing was a narrow belt with a discreet silver and black enamel buckle.

'You're rather quiet, my sweet,' he whispered, leaning close and kissing her throat. The gesture was surprisingly affectionate, and as he made it, Deana breathed in his fragrance. It was heavy and sweet and spicy, drifting out from his sleekly bound hair in a wave so potent it stunned her. To her chagrin, she swayed against him, her giddiness doubling and redoubling at the unyielding strength of his body.

'You're not feeling uncomfortable, are you?' he enquired, his long eyes narrowing but in no way diminishing in radiance.

She thought 'Bastard!' but she said, 'No, not in the slightest,' and had another stab at cool, unruffled airiness. 'Why on earth should you think that?' She even managed a small insouciant smile.

'You just won't be "easy", will you?' he replied, moving infinitesimally closer, parting his moulded lips and running his tongue across the upper one. He looked as if he were a wolf about to savour his dinner... or the feeding of some other strong appetite.

'Easy for who?' Deana felt the hair on the back of her neck prickle, like a sensor scanning for danger. He was testing her somehow, she realised, but her natural urge was to rise up, challenge him, and try some subtle tests of her own.

'Easy for us,' he said, still closing, still insolent and still resolute.

'And who might "us" be?' she persisted, her heart revving up in a deep adrenalin produced pound that seemed to bounce it up and down in her chest.

He was within millimetres now, though she couldn't have said how he'd got there.

'Dee . . .'

'What?'

'Shut up!'

And then there was no gap between them. No gap between their pressing, sucking lips; no gap between their bodies as he forced her back against the seat and explored her. His hands moved quickly and roughly, travelling across her body in a grope that was almost adolescent. He was checking for the presence of the corset, she realised, his fingers pressing at her whaleboned waist and her securely cupped breasts – squeezing and testing the elasticity of both flesh and the constraints he'd put upon it.

She wanted to say 'Yes, you swine I'm wearing your sodding corset!' but she couldn't because he wouldn't let her. He was filling her mouth with a tongue that seemed twice its normal size, and that stifled any last shred of protest.

Almost flat on her back on the lushly upholstered seat, she felt his fingers sliding beneath her, then grabbing at her buttocks where they jutted beneath the edge of the corset. She gasped when he took a round of flesh in each hand and pulled and circled it lewdly. The tension between her bottom and her sex was suddenly intimate and maddening; tiny connected muscle groups tugged furiously on her soft pulpy membranes and made her clitoris stiffen and swell. The nubby little organ came alive in an instant, grew stretched and hot and ready, rising up for the touch of its master.

But just when Deana thought she was going to scream into his mouth, Jake pulled back and away from her. His eyes were like lapis lazuli in the darkness and he stared down at her limp, sprawled body. 'Let's see if you've obeyed me . . .' His voice hoarse, his eyes bright, he pushed crudely at her pretty silk skirt.

'Bad girl,' he said, touching her pubis through the sheer white panties she'd put on in blatant defiance of his instructions. His finger burrowed in cruelly and poked at her clitoris without gentleness or finesse, punishing the most sensitive part of her body by callously stirring it to pleasure.

When her hips bucked in response, the prodding hand was snatched away, and through a haze of frustrated lust, she saw him reach across to the console beside his seat and press impatiently at one of the buttons.

'Pull over,' he rapped and immediately the car began to slow.

'No,' she moaned, anticipating Fargo's eyes again, so cold and blank and dismissive as he studied her naked genitals.

'Yes,' said Jake calmly, but when retribution came it was not in the form she'd expected.

Lying on the seat, she couldn't see out of the windows, but she sensed they were in a quiet but well-lit street. Frozen by excitement and desire, she waited for Jake to summon his robot-like servant around to the back passenger door and was surprised when instead, he wound down the dividing glass and simply said, 'Your knife, please, Fargo.'

Apprehension gripped her and her innards churned.

Then she heard the words 'drive on' and the hum of the dividing glass rising.

'I specifically asked you not to wear panties.'

Jake's voice was terrifyingly ordinary, and his free hand surprisingly gentle as he pushed her tight, ruched skirt up to her waist and lifted the elastic of her panties away from her body and the basque. There was a small ripping sound, and then another, and it was then that Deana understood the purpose of the blade.

He'd said 'no panties' and he'd meant it; so now he was slicing them clean off her body and chopping them up into ribbons. He was perfectly calm and almost unconcerned, as if he carved up lingerie on a regular basis. Maybe he did? she thought suddenly. He seemed capable of just about anything.

When her panties were destroyed, he snapped the knife-blade back into its guard, laid the weapon aside, then gathered up the scraps of white cloth. Most of these he stuffed into his waistcoat pocket, but several he continued to fidget with; absently winding and unwinding them around his left index finger as if he were thinking intently and considering his next act of outrage.

'Let's see,' he said matter-of-factly as he toyed with the ruins of her knickers. 'I shan't punish you, sweet Dee, because we're going to the house of someone who'll do it far better than I ever could.' He let the thin strips of cotton unfurl, then hang like tiny fluttering streamers in the heavy luxurious gloom. 'But we must mark the event somehow.' Another pause ... Another narrow, menacing grin. 'Take off your dress.'

'What?' Her sex throbbed again in delicious horror. 'Are you insane?'

'Not quite. Now kindly take off your dress, Dee ... Or shall I chop that up too?'

She *wanted* to take off the dress, and her mind offered a perfectly rational reason to do so. It was one of Delia's favourite party frocks and she'd be absolutely furious if it were damaged.

Proudly, Deana turned away from him, inclining herself forward as gracefully as she could and reaching around to hold her hair off her shoulders.

'My zip, please,' she said quietly. He wasn't going to get the better of her. She wasn't going to be fazed. Even though the corset reached only to her navel, and to lose the frock that covered it would be to show him her belly, her sex and her bottom – all rudely framed in suspenders and sheer, smoked-beige stockings.

Slowly and carefully, Jake complied, the deft way he unzipped her an indicator of how many dozens, nay hundreds, of other women he must also have undressed. She imagined them as she was, stripping for him in cars and being coerced into unthinkable acts. She recalled her visit to club 'Seventeen' and the men and women there who'd been little more than chained and naked slaves . . . And she knew then, with absolute certainty, that Jake had taken bound women there himself. The thought made her clitoris throb and her sex-lips pout and engorge.

But that isn't you, Deana! her mind protested as she wriggled out of the dress and tried to look coolly unconcerned.

Ah, but it is, whispered another sly, internal voice as she folded the pink silk mass and set it neatly on the seat beside her. Her thighs trembled feverishly as she fought an almost overpowering urge to cross her legs and hide her wet sex from Jake.

You want to do it, don't you? the hidden submissive persisted. To show yourself. You'd do anything for him, admit it. Walk down the Mall nude. Be smacked and fingered by strangers. Open your legs and masturbate in broad daylight in a crowded room. Doesn't just the thought of it make you cream? her devil's advocate taunted her. If Jake stopped the car again right now, and had Fargo screw you on the bonnet, you'd be coming before that icy, hard-faced bastard had even got his trousers off!

'Open your legs, please, Dee,' Jake said pleasantly, still twirling his little strips of cotton.

Deana obeyed him, acutely conscious of her own stickiness as she did so. She didn't look down, but she guessed that her dark curls were glossy with the fluid of sexual excitement and that her marshy, blood-filled folds would be standing proud and crude and announcing her condition to Jake. Even as she shifted her thighs, she felt a dangerous little twitch in her clitoris. If he touched her even once, she'd have a huge, shaming orgasm in an instant.

But he didn't go anywhere near her clitoris.

Instead he tied the ends of the strips of her torn panties into a knot and pushed that unceremoniously into her vagina, leaving the white tails dangling outside.

It was a humiliating badge of 'disobedience', and somehow the bundle of small white streamers made her crotch look ten times as bare and drew critical attention to her wetness.

'That's to show that you've been naughty,' he said, uncannily echoing her feelings. 'When I walk you into Vida's presence, she'll know straight away that you're due for a well-earned punishment.'

'Vida? We're going to see Vida Mistry?' The thought was exciting and Deana's stuffed and decorated vulva seemed to pulsate in a hot flush of yearning.

To see Vida again, be paraded before her ... Oh God, that would mean getting out of this car half naked and with the shreds of her torn-up panties hanging down between her legs.

Jake's grin was pure, beautiful evil. 'Yes ... You're going to have to walk through the foyer of Vida's building just as you are. Bare-bottomed, and showing your curls and your streamers to the world.' He leaned over and kissed the corner of her trembling mouth. His saliva was cool on her lips as he licked his way gently around them. 'You've been a bad girl, Dee. Disobedient. And now you have to be shamed for it. But don't worry, I'll cover your eyes and plug your ears. You won't see who's looking at your sex and your arse . . . and you won't hear them calling out what they think of your pussy and your bottom. And your pretty little dangling ribbons.'

'I can't,' she croaked against his skin, her body sweating heavily in the corset and the ripples of a tiny fleeting orgasm threatening to dislodge her white cloth rosette.

But the words she spoke were a lie. She could do it. She even wanted to . . . She'd passed through the barrier now, gone over the borderline between her world of the natural and normal, and his of dark sweet deviance. The two realms were as different as night from day, but suddenly she was happy in the shadows.

To walk through an apartment block foyer with her naked crotch on view was quite acceptable and expected in Jake's world. An everyday occurrence. It was up to Deana now to conduct herself accordingly.

As the car turned a corner, she wondered how many more minutes' grace she had. For the first time, almost, in the whole of this strange, lewd drive, she looked out through the tinted glass windows. They were speeding around a crescent shaped road that ran down along the riverside, but within seconds, the car turned once more, and pulled into a large spacious forecourt. Looming above them was an imposing modern apartment block – its façade unmarked, discreet and anonymously opulent. It was a place where only the very richest people lived, but then again Vida Mistry was reputed to have a substantial private income on top of her earnings from her books.

As the limousine slunk to a halt, Deana's courage faltered

and she looked pleadingly at Jake. He smiled at her and nodded, his face full of mischief and his eyes like twin blue stars. For the first time in their short but strange relationship, Deana wondered how old he was. Delia would know, from office gossip, but she'd never spoken of it and Deana herself couldn't even begin to guess.

His hair – shining softly in the light from the building's frontage – was as black as a raven's wing and showed not a single strand of grey. His body was fit and lean, superbly athletic and limber, and he moved like a man at the leading edge of his prime. His face was clear-skinned, his eyes always bright, and yet – up close, in the instant before kisses – Deana had seen that it wasn't unmarked by time. He had character-lines, crinkles at the corners of his strange eastern eyes that came only from years of smiling. The man was a beautiful enigma; and without knowing why, she knew she'd do anything he asked of her. No matter how weird or appalling it seemed, or how much it went against her nature.

Even as she thought this, he was flipping open a glove compartment and taking out some intriguing but now neces-sary items: a tiny pair of foam earplugs, a black velvet eye mask – and causing a shock of exquisite terror in Deana's pounding heart – a set of shiny, lightweight steel handcuffs.

'We must always do things properly,' he said softly, snapping them on before she could protest, securing her hands in front of her rather than behind as they did in the cop shows.

Her first urge was to pull at the cuffs and struggle, but after a couple of seconds a peculiar change took place. A shift of perception. A metamorphosis. She felt safe in her bonds, all responsibility sloughed off like a skin, and that was a condition that suited her. Suddenly her body felt soft and loose in its constraints, strangely peaceful, all the hassle of making choices beyond her. Jake was her sexual arbiter now, and even the simple act of leaning forward for her blindfold brought a fresh spark of pleasure in its wake.

'Trust me. I'll guide you,' he whispered in her ear before inserting the small sponge earplugs and creating for her a zone of dark quiet.

A breeze of slightly cooler air indicated that the car door was open, and then strong male hands and arms were assisting her out onto the pavement. The same hands led her across an expanse of several strides in length, then over a threshold and onto some hard, unyielding surface that she deduced was either marble or tiles. She could hear vague voices, and pick out Jake's distinctive tones ... but she couldn't tell whether he was conversing with the taciturn Fargo, or whether some boggle-eyed commissionaire or thunderstruck passer-by was even now staring at her naked, be-ribboned pubis.

The thought of that inflamed her, and as the guiding hands indicated she halt for a second, she instinctively parted her legs to give the unseen oglers an improved perspective on her sex. Quite wild to display herself, she flaunted her hips, then felt a pair of cool lips settle just below her ear and mouth the single word 'slut' against her neck. The sound was barely audible, but its severity cut her skin like a brand. One of the previously gentle hands grasped her naked buttock and squeezed in a long steady pinch the whole firm pad of muscle. She moaned softly, heedless of watchers and listeners, her clitoris trembling with a spasm of forbidden delight. Even his insults were gorgeous to her now.

A faint, slightly familiar vibration came up through her feet, and seconds later she was pushed into a lift car – driven on by the vicious grip on her bottom cheek, and then by an indecent swooping finger that prodded her tight anal furrow.

As the car began to rise, she tried desperately to send out feelers of sensation and divine whether they were alone or accompanied. The small space was hot and intensely claustro-phobic. She could feel only – presumably – Jake's hands on her, but that didn't mean there weren't others near by.

She imagined herself in the centre of a dozen lusting men all watching as her tormentor fingered her. He was stroking the groove of her bottom now, tickling the tiny rose-hole, and she couldn't keep her itchy hips from weaving or her thighs from flexing and splaying. A hand swept into her sex from the front, a fingertip settling on her clitoris as another pushed hard into her anus. She was speared from two directions now, and she gulped and gasped uncouthly. The two internal foci started rocking her reciprocally, prodding her back and forth in a steady but syncopated rhythm.

As she orgasmed heavily and wetly, there was a swish that said the car door was open. Still controlled by the intruding finger in her bottom she staggered out onto some landing or other, horridly suspicious that there were people all around her to witness and take pleasure from her shame.

'Please,' she begged incoherently as she was goaded down an unseen corridor, or perhaps into the foyer of a spacious penthouse flat.

After a few yards only, the quality of the atmosphere around her seemed to change and she heard a variety of faint sounds to the front of her.

Laughter and greetings. Voices. Jake's and one other, a familiar one that she'd heard only briefly, but recently . . .

10

Sweet Mistry

'How charming, Kazuto my darling,' said Vida Mistry with genuine warmth as gentle fingers prised the foam from Deana's ears. The sound was bright and exciting after the semi-silence, and she found herself anxious to be able to see again. To see the famous authoress with new eyes, and with a vivid new insight on her work. There were no good fairies here to answer Deana's prayers, only demons, but even so it seemed that *they* were listening. Within seconds the blindfold was removed. A hand remained shielding her eyes, but a moment later that went too, and she could look out into the room and see how many were observing her shame.

There were in fact only four people in what appeared to be the lounge of an extremely luxurious flat. Herself, still handcuffed. Jake, beside her and smiling. An unknown young woman dressed in a strange and stylised maid's costume. And finally the near legendary Vida Mistry, a vibrant and brightly clad figure in a room full of cream and beige furnishings.

Striding forward with graceful confidence, Vida looked every bit as beautifully weird as she had in 'Seventeen'. Her long, crimson hair was wound into a high, crown-like knot, and she was wearing high heels and an attractive, but unusual trench-style satin evening coat. Without its belt, it would have looked a bit like what used to be called a 'duster coat', but Deana doubted if Mizz Mistry had ever dusted in her life. She looked like a woman who either commanded or coaxed other people into dealing with such matters . . . while she existed only for pleasure. That and looking absolutely fabulous.

The shiny, cinch-waisted housecoat was a zingy peach-orange shade which should've clashed hideously with Vida's bright hair. In actual fact, it looked marvellous; perfectly emphasising the magnificent pallor of her skin, the glint in her large green eyes, and the wine-tinted lushness of her lips. The woman was an event, a total sexual happening from the glistening corona of her flaming red hair to the tip of her shiny black narrow-toed stilettos. Deana felt her vitals stir danger-ously, and thought of her sister's surprising new discoveries. Also with a woman . . .

It's in us both, thought Deana, quivering anew with a hard and stomach-clenching arousal. Delia succumbed to Elf, and now I'm turning on for Vida. What is it that Jake de Guile starts in us? Has it always been there? Or is it just a spell, something that'll go away when he does?

The thought of Jake leaving was a nasty one, but happily there was no time to debate it.

'How kind of you to remember my birthday, Kazuto,' purred Vida. She was kissing Jake prettily on the cheek, but somehow managing to watch Deana out of the corner of her kohl-rimmed eye. 'I didn't expect such a delicious present as *this*.' She spun away from the kiss and turned. 'A brand new toy to play with. I presume that she *is* for me?' She was touching Deana's blushing cheek now, but this time looking sidelong at Jake.

In another world, Deana would've spat defiance, rebelled, and told the pair of them to go to hell. She was a grown woman with a mind of her own and she couldn't just be 'given' to someone. But this was their world and their mindset, and all she could do was just stand there in her corset and handcuffs, her body awash with excitement.

'She's yours, my love,' replied Jake, his voice extraordinarily breathy and tender. Deana was embarrassed by her own flush of jealousy, and suppressed it. For her, now, the emotion was inappropriate. A 'thing' couldn't be jealous of its owner; a play-toy had no status and no rights. No claim on either Jake *or* his fabulous literary mistress. Deana's only role now was to serve them . . .

'Why thank you, my darling,' answered Vida, squeezing Deana's breast very gently, then abandoning her altogether and virtually wrapping her body around Jake's.

It was one of the most sensuous and showy embraces that Deana had ever seen, easily out-steaming any film or TV clinch she could remember. The mouths of Jake and Vida seemed to coalesce, their lips pressing, nuzzling and nibbling, while their tongues darted and dove and visibly duelled. Vida slid one hand up Jake's chest, shoulder and neck, then burrowed her fingers in his bound black hair, dishevelling his immaculate pony-tail and threatening to destroy it altogether. Her other hand settled comfortably on his crotch, squeezing at his fast-growing erection and massaging his sex through his trousers. Deana watched, entranced, as his slim hips did a bump and grind against Vida's circling palm. She could almost feel the sweet, rising surge of his penis. Would he come in his pants? Would he cry out and slump against Vida, his lust jetting freely yet concealed, his release inspired and provoked by those flexible red-nailed fingers?

Even as she watched them, Jake's hips bucked furiously and he detached his lips from Vida's. His head fell back, his handsome face contorted and his brown throat taut and working as he groaned out a long cry of pleasure. And as he stiffened and convulsed in her arms, Vida's red mouth fastened on his neck, sucking like a vampire, her white teeth biting his flesh.

It was this Dracula-like kiss that seemed to galvanise him. He shook Vida gently free of him, then held her at bay with a strong hand clasped lightly around her silk-clad upper arm. 'You crazy witch!' he hissed. He wasn't angry with her, that was obvious; his expression looked far more like wonder. Deana could see his whole body shaking, and his full mouth darkly bruised from Vida's kisses. On his smooth brown neck there was a small ring of deep, purple teethmarks.

'And will *you* also serve me?' enquired Vida silkily, circling her fingers around his throat, drawing her nails across the scar she'd inflicted.

'Not tonight, Vida,' he answered quietly and seriously, 'but soon . . . Soon I'll need it.'

For all her almost trance-like state, Deana was deeply intrigued, and with no warning a stark vision filled her mind. She saw Jake locked in bondage and submissive. His strong body bowed to the will of the imperious Vida, his sex humiliatingly exposed. Without thinking, Deana sobbed with dark pleasure . . .

'Methinks this little one wants some attention,' drawled Vida, turning to her. The authoress's voice was plummy and mannered, but there was a fresh leap of fire in her eyes. They glittered like emerald darts, pinning Deana against the wall of her own outlandish new desires.

'Have you had her yet tonight?' Vida continued, slinging one strong hand around Deana's waist, while her other dipped down into her sex. Deana felt her flesh being probed by knowledgeable fingers, her juices tested for quantity and consistency, then stirred and slicked and scooped.

'No . . . Not yet,' Jake answered, just at the moment that Vida brought her sticky fingers to her lips and sucked them.

'Hmmm . . .' she mused, her pale face thoughtful and concentrated like a wine connoisseur testing a vintage. 'Delightfully wet. And very savoury. Almost as delicious as you, Lord Kazuto.'

Trembling and delicately stimulated, Deana felt a small glow of real-world contentment. It *was* true then. The story in the book had once been real. If only she were in a position to ask questions . . .

Jake nodded and smiled but said nothing; and Vida continued her examination of her prize. Her birthday gift, Deana remembered, feeling faint with the effort of trying to retain just a fragment of her dignity while Vida's hands went everywhere and spared nothing.

It was eerie that their birthdays were so close. That this vibrant and sensual woman with her peculiar clothes and even stranger desires, was a Geminian like herself and Delia. Deana thought of what had happened on the night of *their* birthday. How good white wine and an attitude had got her down on her knees and begging for sex at Jake's outrageous exhibition. It seemed such a long time ago; she'd gone through almost evolutionary changes to bring her to where she was now.

'Shall we begin, Vida?' enquired Jake, moving smoothly to stand behind Deana. His hands grabbed her buttocks and jiggled them, just as his satin-clad accomplice worked her breasts free of the white hide corset, and arranged them like a pair of overripe peaches on the platform of the folded down cups.

'Yes, let's,' said Vida, running her pointed pink tongue in a slow, moist circle around her lips. 'She's so tasty, Jake. A real prize . . . I can't wait until she loses control.' Her eyes wild, she squeezed Deana's nipples in a hard pinching grip, and laughed softly when her victim groaned and fell back into Jake's vulgar hold on her bottom. 'Bentley, the door if you please?' she rapped out to the silent, unmoving maid, who Deana had forgotten existed, but whose presence now added more shame.

Her legs were barely working any more, but somehow Deana managed to move forward, propelled by Jake's strong hands on her bottom, and by Vida's guiding touch as she lifted her victim's wrists with the cuffs and led her forward as a mistress leads a slave. Which was what they now were. Dominant and plaything. Goddess and worshipper. Power and submission. But where, oh God, did Jake fit into all this? Was he an observer or a participant? A part of the scene or just a watcher?

'Welcome to my sexuarium, Dee,' announced Vida with a flourish as they entered a softly-lit, potently scented, and extremely bizarre room indeed.

Half bedroom, half boudoir and entirely outrageous, Vida's 'sexarium' was a lush tumble of several luxurious furnishing styles that blended into one harmonious whole. Deana could've spent hours just studying the individual facets of the decor, but there were certain very particular items of furniture that commanded her awestruck attention.

A beautifully crafted wall-frame could have no other purpose but to secure a human body for punishment. Red leather restraints with shiny brass fittings hung strategically at each of its four corners, and Deana immediately imagined herself in them, stretched and spreadeagled for some exquisite and long, drawn-out torment. For pleasure or pain, but which of them, she hardly seemed to care.

In the vision, she saw Jake standing behind her, fully clothed but with his flies hanging open as he levered his penis into her sex ... or maybe somewhere else? She remembered *Against the Parapet* and quivered helplessly at the awful, yet obscenely compelling idea of being buggered.

The frame was not the only *objet* that was exclusively

devoted to sex. In another corner was what looked like a perfectly restored antique dentist's chair, also fitted with restraints. The leather of the seat was a deep aubergine-plum colour, and the foot and leg rest had the curious feature of having been modified so that the sitter's lower limbs could be separately secured. Thus a tormentor – or lover – could stand directly between the recumbent's thighs with total access to the genitals. Deana shivered in the pit of her stomach, every nerve and membrane in motion. She was aroused beyond belief and all they'd done to her was make her look at the accoutrements of their pleasure.

The more normal contents of the room included a large brass-railed bed, a selection of brocaded pouffes and ottomans, and a fabulous full-sized French *chaise-longue* which was plainly a priceless antique as well as an evocative object of beauty.

Not quite so beautiful was what could only be described as a punishment bar. Fitted out in the same dark leather as the chair it was an upholstered wooden horizontal suspended between two inverted v-shaped supports. It looked like some kind of deluxe saw-horse, and fitted into the polished floorboards to the front and back of it were the inevitable leather-cuffed restraints.

'So many lovely ways to arrange you,' whispered Vida in her ear as Jake ambled over to the *chaise* and sat down, completely at ease. The maid, Bentley, went around to the various sources of light, and adjusted their brightness according to some prearranged instruction.

'What's your choice then, Lord Kazuto?' Vida was unfastening the sash of her coat as she spoke. After sliding the bright sheeny wrapper down her shoulders, she then straightened her arms to let it fall. Bentley stepped close and caught the coat before it hit the floor, and Deana just gasped . . . Vida was wearing a corset too, but it was nothing like her own white leather one.

Vida's voguish garment could easily have caused amusement – to the uninitiated. A classic 'Sixties' style fitted corselet, it had circle stitched bra-cups and a sleek, uncompromising bodice of fine elastic-mesh net. It was the colour of exaggeratedly salmon-toned 'flesh' and its heavy serviceable suspenders held up a pair of fully fashioned American tan micro-mesh stockings that looked perfect with Vida's high-gloss patent court shoes.

Deana looked from Vida's astounding corsetry, to Jake's appreciative eyes, and back again. It was obvious that the novelist aroused him because he was massaging his groin in long, slow, circular strokes.

'Your discretion, sweet Vida,' he purred, shimmying his linen-clad hips in response to his own blatant rubbing. 'It *is* your birthday ... All I ask is that you go easy on her because she's new to this. She's been disobedient and she needs to suffer, but I don't want her marked too badly. She's got a perfect, beautiful bottom, and it would be a shame to scar it.'

'Don't worry,' Vida said briskly, snapping her fingers for Bentley, 'there won't be a bruise on her tomorrow. A bit of a glow, maybe, but nothing more drastic.'

'You're on! I'll check,' said Jake with a grin.

It was as if they were discussing an inanimate object, thought Deana, her bare sex alive and excited. She was flesh for their amusement – a woman's body, but treated like a naughty child, punished for a minor wrong-doing.

'Now then, Dee, time to make yourself useful.' Vida turned towards her. 'I want you to undress your master. I want to see him naked ... Look sharp, girl. Hand the clothes to Bentley as you take them off. We don't want such lovely things creased now, do we?'

Deana looked down at her cuffed hands and Jake laughed softly. 'Don't worry, my sweet,' he said to her almost kindly. After leaping lightly off the *chaise*, he stepped up close, then took one of her wrists in his strong brown hand. With just the slightest flick of his fingers, he undid first one cuff then the other, then slid them off and handed them to the quietly waiting Bentley.

Deana felt both diminished and angry. She'd been standing around like a ninny in those cuffs and she could probably have had them off herself in seconds. They were just as much toys as she was, and Jake had tricked her.

But the anger disappeared as quickly as it had come. Fakes or real, the handcuffs were merely a symbol of restraint, one image in this elaborately constructed tapestry of images, and necessary to both her role and theirs.

And now Jake was before her, waiting for her to serve him and take off his clothes. Mercifully, it seemed he felt inclined to help her, because he sat back down on the *chaise* again and lifted his feet one by one so she could pull off his black Italian loafers.

Vida had been right, both Jake's footwear and his clothing were lovely. Deana admired his shiny hand-stitched shoes as she passed them to Bentley, and was equally impressed by the pure silk socks he wore beneath them. His feet were longish and his toes perfectly pedicured and they smelt as much of his intoxicating cologne as the rest of him.

Jake stood again for the rest of his disrobing and Deana found herself intensely aroused by the process. *She'd* never seen him anywhere near fully nude. Delia might've seen him without his clothes, but for his hurried sexual couplings with herself, he'd only ever unfastened his trousers. She'd seen his cock – and felt it inside her – but she'd never seen or touched the rest of his naked skin.

The next item off was the dandyish black brocade waistcoat. And as first it, and then the other things came off, the three of them worked well as a team. Jake inclined his graceful body whichever way was needed; Deana slid off each garment in turn; Bentley took each item from her and put it to one side over a chair, folding where necessary.

Beneath the black silk shirt was a chest and torso that made the artist in Deana draw breath and long for her pencil. He was so smooth, his muscles so firm and sheeny: strong-looking but in no way exaggerated or pronounced. She imagined him as a dancer or a runner when he exercised, doing martial arts or Tai Chi Chuan. There was no way this man pumped iron; weights, yes, she could quite see that. But wielded with surgical precision to tone and sleek and tighten, not build up gross bundles of muscle. She found herself wanting to draw him or kiss him, and the urge to press her mouth to his gleaming skin was so strong that she fumbled with his belt.

'Take care, Dee,' he threatened softly, pausing in the proceedings to lift his hand and pinch her right nipple. The pain was sharp and twin-focused, attacking her clitoris with pleasure from within as surely as Jake hurt her breast from without. She groaned, unable to help herself, aware that even though the nearby Bentley seemed totally immune to all this, Vida was sitting on the edge of the bed, stroking her pointed chin thoughtfully and watching every action with interest.

As his trousers came off, Deana faltered again. More seriously this time, her senses sent spinning into turmoil by what lay beneath the tailored black linen.

She'd wondered earlier – a lifetime ago it seemed now – why Jake hadn't worn leather tonight. But she'd been deceived . . . because he *was* wearing leather after all. Instead of the designer silk boxer shorts she'd half been expecting, her dark and beautiful master was wearing a dark, beautiful garment at his loins.

A very kinky garment. An abbreviated black leather posing pouch, a triangle held in place only by shoelace-like thongs that stretched up over his narrow male hips. When he twisted slightly in stepping out of his trousers, she saw that the whole assembly was entirely backless – apart from another fine thong that ran rudely up the chink of his bottom to tie with the others at the small of his back.

'Nice,' murmured Vida from the periphery, while Deana wanted to fall to her knees and rain kisses on such an object of glory.

The pouch was minuscule, and presumably fitted snugly around his genitals when they were soft and quiescent. The difficulty now was that Jake was far from quiescent, and the paper-thin leather was pushed out inches away from his body, tented obscenely by the force of what it failed to contain. Deana could see her own fingers shaking wildly as she reached out towards Jake's groin.

'Ooh no, keep that on!' Vida said breathily, leaving her place on the bed to join them. 'I really like that, Kazuto-san. I just knew there'd be leather on you somewhere.'

Deana wished wholeheartedly that Jake would move at that moment and give her a sideways view, so she could see the thick, silky bar of his penis where it pushed out the pouch from his groin. As it was she could see his balls hanging heavily beneath it and the lush sooty cloud of his pubic hair where it stole out from its inadequate container.

'No no no! Such pretty sights aren't for you, unworthy one! You have to be punished first.'

Vida's low, clear voice was kinder than her words suggested. And her fingers were solicitous and gentle on Deana's right arm as she led her away from Jake in his gorgeous near-nudity, and towards the menacing span of the punishment bar.

'I'm going to paddle your bottom now, Dee,' she explained

as if it were the most normal and usual thing to happen. 'It will hurt you more than you can possibly imagine, but with any luck it'll also make you unbearably horny.' She smiled then, calm and wise as if explaining an eternal verity. 'And if you're a good brave girl under the pain, we'll give you an orgasm afterwards.' She was pushing Deana against the bar now, snapping her fingers for Bentley. 'But if you perform poorly, of course, we'll have to leave you unsatisfied. And I think you can imagine how unpleasant that will be.' As Deana went slowly forward across the leather-covered beam, she felt her tormentress's soft, cool fingers rest lightly and coaxingly on her bottom.

The boned corset made her position across the bar almost painful, but Deana managed not to protest. The threat of being left randy after all this was too horrendous to contemplate, and no matter how much Vida and Jake hurt her, she was determined to bear it with stoicism and earn both her own sexual release and their respect for her fortitude and strength.

She almost fell at the first hurdle though, when Bentley shackled down her hands and feet, stretching her limbs awkwardly and making the corset press deep into her belly.

She bit her lip as unseen hands adjusted her on the bar, arranging her thighs so she was as lewdly exhibited as possible, and slyly fingering her folds and the groove of her bottom in the process.

'She looks extraordinarily good,' commented Vida conversationally. 'I think I'm really going to enjoy this.' The fingertips continued in their rude exploration, but Deana still couldn't tell whose they were.

There was a long pause then, and though Deana could no longer see her, she sensed that Vida's green eyes were wide and assessing. 'So much so in fact,' Vida continued, sounding pleased with herself, 'that I think I'll have a glass of champagne before I start. It always adds that extra little sparkle.'

After that, there was a second long, frustrating wait whilst Bentley was despatched to fetch the wine. Deana was anxious to begin now, to taste the pain and see if she could stand up to it. And more than that, Deana, muttered a subversive voice inside her, you want to find out if you'll like it!

It was shocking, but she could almost answer that already. Even the idea of being beaten across the bottom was doing diabolical things to her vulva. She could feel herself pouting open, her vagina a dripping chasm, and the tender convoluted lips above it standing swollen and proud, puffed up with the blood of arousal. Her clitoris was a solid throbbing knot, protruding as it never had before, sticking out and begging silently to be touched. The worst of it was that she knew the others could see this; see her body aching for something or anything to put it out of its misery.

The door opened and closed and after a moment or two there were the sounds of a popping cork, a busy, whooshing fizz and the soft glug-glug of fine wine being poured into glasses.

The glasses clinked.

'To excess!'

'To everything!'

To hell with it, don't keep me waiting! thought Deana, the muscles of her bottom twitching tensely. She sensed the two of them standing close behind her, watching her idly like two guests at a cocktail party, totally at ease in their bizarre fetishistic clothing – or in Jake's case, the lack of it.

'You're right, Kazuto my darling, she does have a beautiful bottom . . .' Fingers touched Deana very delicately, tracing the inslope of one buttock with a fingernail and making her automatically clench her sphincter.

'Quite lovely,' said Jake, his voice sounding strangely affectionate, 'but I think it needs a little decoration...Something here.' Another finger, a substantial and more male one, settled right into Deana's anal crease, then pushed carefully at the tightness of the hole there.

She moaned. She couldn't help it. When he touched her there, she felt a grubby but irresistible rush of pleasure. A mad craving for things that were vile but which made her poor wet quim pulse and weep. Her bonds held her tight but she tried to wriggle, tried to entice him even though she hated her miserable, slutty self for doing it.

'I've got just the thing.' Deana heard Vida move away then return. Jake laughed.

'My darling Vida, you're outrageous!' he said, but Deana sensed his almost boyish excitement and felt dread herself at the thought of what that 'thing' might be.

'Do you think it'll go in?' His finger wiggled slightly in its niche. 'She's very tight. I wouldn't want to damage her.'

'It'll go in,' said Vida confidently. 'I've had one in me before now...It's easy when you use lots of cold cream.'

Jake chuckled, and Deana sensed him shaking his dark head in disbelief at Vida's sex-crazed exploits.

What is it? Deana thought wildly. This thing they're going to put into me. It must be a dildo or something. A vibrator. But then, as she heard Jake pouring out more champagne, she *knew* what it was. The wicked naughty thing they were going to put in her body, the thing they were going to *cork* her with.

Bentley was ordered to bring cold cream and a few seconds later, Deana felt the stuff being plastered on and into her bottom, then pushed inside in dollops, its texture thick and heavy.

'Hold her open,' instructed Vida.

Deana felt fingertips settle on the inner curves of her

buttocks, pulling gently but firmly, then *it* was against her ... The thing ... The champagne cork, unbelievably fat and unyielding as they began its outrageous insertion, rocking it this way and that to gain entry to her untried opening.

'Oooh! Oh no!' she whimpered, as horrifying sensations assaulted her. She'd sworn to be brave and silent, but this was so much more than she'd expected. She keened and whimpered and shook her head, but still they persisted. After a few moments, Jake came around to the front of the beam – presumably leaving Bentley to help Vida – and crouched down, beautiful and almost naked, to comfort Deana through her trials and torments.

'Easy ... Easy, sweetheart,' he whispered, stroking her face with his fingers and lifting her hair back out of her eyes. 'Relax. It's only your mind saying it feels bad. Years and years of people telling you it's wicked and dirty to take pleasure in your bottom ...' He started kissing her then, sucking and licking delicately at her lips, nibbling and coaxing, then poking in with his tongue in the same rocking rhythm that Vida was using on her bottom.

Deana groaned into his mouth. It didn't matter what he was telling her, the sensations were too strange. Her sex was throbbing and leaping and rippling, almost climaxing with dark, forbidden pleasure. As the cork finally popped into her and lodged there, she had an orgasm of sharp and painful intensity, jerking herself viciously in her bonds and crying out like a wounded animal as Jake's mouth slid away from hers.

When she regained the use of her senses, he was standing up in front of her. The leather G-string had succumbed to the pure hard force of his erection, and his penis was pointing out above it, an obscene limb of ruddy blood-filled flesh that stood proud from his flat brown belly. In spite of her bonds and her shaming, or maybe, in a strange way, because of them, Deana felt a great longing urge to suck him. Ignoring the dangerous churn of her bowels, she strained forward as far as she could, stretching her neck and tilting her head at an awkward angle in an attempt to get his penis in her mouth.

'Just one little suck then,' intoned the smooth, arch voice of Vida, as if from a thousand miles away. And as Jake tilted his hips, flexed his thighs, and flaunted his sex at her face, Deana craned forward the last few muscle-cracking millimetres and took his fat red glans between her lips.

His taste was sublime, strong and salty, heavy with the semen of his earlier hidden climax, and sharp with the fresh, precursive juice that was now flowing freely. Deana suckled him like a starving baby, using her tongue as best she could with her neck held out at such a steep, uncomfortable angle.

But just as she heard him start to moan slightly her solace was cruelly denied her. Jake stepped back and as his swollen tip slid out of her mouth, he patted her on the head like a master rewarding a faithful but rather dim hound. She sobbed loudly, her vows to be silent and stoic all forgotten.

Jake was behind her now, she sensed, standing with Vida, and they were looking at the disgusting display of a champagne cork jammed in a shackled woman's bottom.

'Look at that, Kazuto,' Vida murmured, and Deana heard small sticky movements, then realised that Jake was being masturbated, just inches from her own insulted body. 'Isn't she exquisite? *Premier cul*, I'd say,' her tormentress went on, just touching the delicate and cruelly stretched skin around the wine cork.

Deana moaned and squirmed, hideously aroused again, and through the same peculiar 'distancing' heard Jake gasp in pure male suffering. 'Oh God, it's no good! I'll have to have her!'

Strong hands took hold of Deana's hips and tilted them, and at almost the same instant, something bulbous and silky butted rudely at the entrance to her vagina. With a rough uncoordinated thrust, he slid into her, then just stayed there; the thick, fat column of his cock lying parallel to the plug in her rectum.

Even in stillness the sensations were appalling. She was completely stuffed, completely stretched, her intimate orifices sealed and jumping, yet sending electric messages to the outposts of her much-abused body. Her nipples felt like aching stones, and her clitoris, pushed out by the obstructions within her, was so hot and swollen that she truly believed it might burst.

'I can't ... I can't ...' she whimpered, her voice rising to an animal scream as Jake began pumping inside her. There was too much. The cork was too big. *He* was too big. Her belly was going to explode, the pressures in her body were too great.

As her breath went out of her and her wild cry faded, her final aperture was filled. 'Suck,' ordered Vida quietly, pushing three stiffened fingers into Deana's gaping mouth.

Delirious, Deana saw fire behind her tightly closed eyes. She was just a thing now. A body. Their toy more completely than she'd ever imagined, her mouth and her bottom sealed at their whim while Jake's penis slammed remorselessly at her sex. He was shouting, she realised, wishing that she could. He was calling out obscene gibberish as he raced towards a high new climax: his second of the night and his first in the confines of her flesh. He was going to flood her any second now, just as she was flooding him with her juices, and wetting her thighs with the small spurts of urine that were being released without control from her bladder. As she realised she was peeing, she sobbed out piteously ... but not wholly from a feeling of disgust.

To wee herself was the very nadir of sensation, yet the raw, hot dirtiness of the act seemed to excite her shackled body even more. A great wrench of pleasure rushed crazily through the entirety of her loins – clitoris, labia, bladder and rectum – and centred in her vagina to grab at Jake's fast moving cock. And as *she* came, *he* let out a long male cry of release, and bored right into the very core of her.

As Jake finished, he pulled out quickly, and Deana felt him sway once and heavily against her then stagger almost drunkenly away. When her lips were set free by Vida she cried out, bereft with the loss of him, but also registering astonishment and wonder. He'd come, and come hard, but he was still thinking. Somewhere in the heart of his orgasm was consideration and tenderness. He could've slumped his full dead weight upon her and lain there to recover – but he hadn't. She could hear him behind her, panting, gulping in air, as devastated by the whole act as she was.

She could also sense him being supported and comforted by Vida; being assisted onto the *chaise* by his fellow dominant, while she, the submissive, the object, was left hanging across the bar, discarded. Her body was still encased in the hot leather corset and its strong, hard grip sustained her. Still stretched and secured, her rear still plugged by the wine-cork, she was a sorry mess of sweat and fluids. Jake's semen, her own juice and her urine ...

And yet against all that was reasonable and understandable, she felt exalted. Her spirit was flying and she could've lived in her bondage forever; content to exist only and indefinitely as a living receptacle of pleasure. An open, available body just waiting to serve Jake and his hungers ...

How beautiful she looked. How magnificent, how fine and how strong. She was shackled hand and foot, stretched tight across a bar, but even so, she'd risen up and beaten him. He could hardly believe it. Hardly believe the pleasure she'd just given him.

Jake lay motionless on the *chaise*, steadying his breathing and his heart, his bleary eyes still locked on the fabulous young woman he'd just screwed. His Dee. His proud, amazing Dee. She was a sobbing mess, but inside her was a steel-hard core that no-one would ever break, bow or bend. Least of all him.

He'd try though, he swore that now, even though he already knew full well that he'd fail. He'd take her and push her to the limit, and they'd both touch heaven in the process. The thought of how it might be made him harden slightly, even though he'd just had an orgasm, even though his penis felt wrecked.

As the blood began to mass in his groin, he wanted to take her again, immediately. Have his legs rendered boneless by her writhings and her groans, and his spirit destroyed by the power of her. She was stronger even than Vida, he realised now. And that was something he'd not thought possible. He was deeply devoted to his wild literary lady, and he knew he always would be in one way or another. But here was a woman who could match and surpass her. A woman who could fit like the last piece of a jigsaw into both Vida's life and his. The idea made his cock itch with lust and rear up like a foolhardy warrior who'd already fought a huge losing battle ...

As he watched her, he saw juices trickle down her thigh, and he wanted to leap off the *chaise*, run across the room and stroke her. He felt an intense urge to rub her bottom and her breasts, to kneel down and lick the fluid off her legs. But he knew that to do such things would reveal how much she affected him. She'd feel his trembling, know how weak and at risk she could make him. And it was still too soon for her to have that knowledge. The game had just started and there were many strange levels yet to travel ...

She still had to be humbled, here, tonight. Feel the love-pain of a beating, feel the pleasure of it, be shown the depths of pure shame.

These ideas of degradation made him focus on her bottom and its plug. Her puckered flesh was stretched out quite smooth around it, and he imagined how that same sweet hole would feel if it were gloved around him. For his part – and for his penis – it would be ecstasy. So tight and hot. Hotter with her than with any other woman . . . He considered then how she might react, and his cock lurched up to full erection.

Jake was no stranger to the rude extremes of the anus. To being plugged and screwed and all the while feeling scareder and scareder of disgrace. To feeling the wild, wicked surgings in the bowel, the grim, dirty terror that switched in an instant to pure, unbelievable pleasure. He knew that if he took her arse, Dee's experience would not be the same as his had been – when he'd been buggered himself – but there were some elements that would be common to both of them – and equally as pervertedly luscious.

'And shall we still punish her?' enquired Vida suddenly.

'Yes, I think so,' he said after a pause, his voice gaining strength as he realised he was almost recovered. 'I think it's a matter of principle . . . Don't you, Dee?'

The sound of her name was a shock. After her subjugation and shame, Deana had almost forgotten who she was. A person, a woman, who was now being *asked* whether she wanted to have pain inflicted on her body. Unlikely and inappropriate as it seemed, she did have a choice.

'Do it! I want it!' she cried, not giving herself a chance to renege. She could take it. She would. After what she'd had so far, she wanted everything.

'Good girl,' said Jake, his voice as soft as a zephyr. She sensed him moving behind her, then saw him come into her field of view, still next to naked with his tiny leather pouch askew and his genitals uncovered and insolent. His cock was already stiff again, and there were silvery streaks – dried semen – on the fudge-coloured plains of his thighs.

'Over to you now, Vida,' he said briskly, moving closer to Deana's face and filling her head with his strong pungent odours.

'My pleasure,' murmured Vida silkily. 'Bentley, I'll have the paddle now.'

Deana had almost forgotten the quiet maid was present, and for a moment she wondered what Bentley thought of all this. It was probably quite commonplace, though. The presence of a fully fitted out sex-room tended to suggest that Vida indulged in such scenarios frequently. And that Jake de Guile wasn't the only man – or woman – that she shared them with.

That, in a strange way, was a comfort to Deana. Jake and Vida were obviously close; but if Vida had other paramours, it meant that Jake was a free agent too. And might have room in his life for others, on a more than purely temporary basis . . . Others who were worthy of him. Partners who could take what he dished out. The pleasure as well as the pain.

Her musings were rudely interrupted when a pair of strong but very female hands took hold of the lobes of her bottom.

'She's very firm, very strong,' observed Vida, her voice detached and professional as she squeezed and mounded and made her assessment. 'Gorgeous muscle tone. She'll take a blow extremely well. And she's obviously very sensitive, so the level of pain should be considerable.' Her fingers dipped briefly into Deana's sexual furrow, starting at the stretched ring of her anus and cruising right down and around to, but not touching, her clitoris. 'I'm really going to enjoy this, Kazuto my love. I couldn't have asked for a better gift if I'd tried.' A single finger slipped deep into Deana's vagina for a second, then all manual contact was withdrawn.

'Show Dee the paddle, Bentley,' instructed Vida, and Jake stepped back to let the maid obey her orders and hold a strange yet familiar shaped object before Deana's suddenly fearful eyes.

She'd been something of a whizz at table tennis as a child, and she and Delia had played many a hard fought game with bats which resembled the object Bentley held out now. The paddle, as Vida called it though, was made out of menacing black leather, not innocuous rubber-backed wood, but in all other respects it was the same shape and size as a table tennis or ping pong bat.

'Have her kiss it.' Vida's voice was flat and steely now, as if she were settling into a deeper layer of her role and all the lightheartedness and fun in her was leeching away to leave only the cruel dominatrix behind. As Deana pressed her lips to the smooth leather surface, she wondered how many others had kissed it . . . then felt it sing across their pale naked rears in the service of Madam Mistry's dour pleasures.

'Do you want her gagged, my Lord,' Vida enquired as the paddle was passed back to her. After a moment, Deana sensed it hovering in the air above her bottom, as the dominant woman behind her did minute calculations of weight and speed and force.

'No, not yet.' Jake's voice was tight with excitement, an anticipation that Deana could unexpectedly empathise quite well. Deep in the heart of her anticipation, her trembling, and her very real fear of the pain to come, she found herself imaging the weirdest of visions. She saw Jake over this very same bar, his firm, muscular, backside quivering as hers was now, his erection standing out like a pole and sticky already with excitement. It was only an idea in her mind; yet she knew, somehow, that her instinct was true. Jake could give *and* take – he was standing before her now in majesty, but at other times he was just as willing to experience pain as he was to inflict or observe it.

'Very well. We begin.'

Almost before the words were finished, Deana felt a slash of hot agony explode across her taut left buttock. She screamed in anguish and surprise.

It was unbelievable. Unbearable. Beyond the power of her comprehension completely. In a flash all her ideas of bravery and pluck had disintegrated without trace. And it felt as if half of her bottom had disintegrated too, the whole muscular mass of it disappearing in a draft of red fire. She was crying like a child, and babbling unintelligible nonsense after only one stroke had been delivered.

She was gasping, fighting to pull in air, when the second blow landed – if anything, harder than the first. 'No! No!' she moaned, her anus clenching frantically on the cork as she rippled on the edge of control. Some thick molten substance was roiling about inside her, pushing hard at her previous limits. Her bowels churned, her labia stood out like fat, bloated leaves and her clitoris was ten times its normal size. She felt clear juice dripping from her sex, and she sobbed anew with shame when she realised she was wetting herself again.

The pain was intense, and felt eternal, but the most agonising part of it was the need to be touched between her legs. Throwing her body up off the bar, she jerked furiously on the wrist-cuffs, in a frenzy to caress her own clitoris.

'Please touch me,' she croaked, then cried out as two more strokes fell, hard and fast.

Tears were dripping from her eyes in a stream and then suddenly, right in the middle of her misery, a gentle hand was wiping her face with a feather-soft, rose-scented hand-kerchief. In a world of raw, blank pain there was also an angel to cherish her.

'There, there, sweetheart,' whispered the quietest, kindest, most heavenly voice in the universe. The cool fingers that went with it smoothed her face and hair tenderly, then touched their soft pads to her lips. 'Be a brave girl for me, Dee,' Jake whispered then replaced his fingers with his mouth and kissed her, like a priest giving unction to a heretic.

He sucked her tongue between his lips and kept sucking on it, deeply and wetly, holding her head between his hands as Vida laid blows across her bottom. Deana cried harder than ever, her tears drenching both her face and Jake's as the paddle rained down on her buttocks and desire gnawed her sex from within.

The pain of her beating was far worse than she had expected, but the horror of frustration was worse. She was suffering terribly, her bodily control all gone, but she would've offered to take a thousand strokes more for the touch of one fingertip on her clitoris.

'Please touch me,' she begged Jake when he released her mouth and started kissing her hot sweating face. 'Please! Please bring me off ... I can't bear it any more. Please touch me!'

'I can't, my darling,' he said, talking quietly as if to a dull-witted child, then licking at her fresh flood of tears. 'You have to suffer. And needing to come makes the punishment greater and deeper. Smacking your bottom is only a *small* part of your penalty.' With that he reached beneath her and delicately touched each of her pebble-hard nipples in turn. She moaned, and he smiled like a saint, his tiny caressing of her breasts only increasing the distress between her legs.

'Please ...' she whimpered.

'No, Dee, you must be a good girl,' he said quietly then started kissing her again, on her face, her hair and her lips.

And Vida resumed her dark endeavours too, employing every nuance of her undoubted skill and craft. Deana felt she was living in a surreal, multicoloured universe of pain and aching, unquenchable desire.

A coruscating triangle seemed to form, with three distinct nodes: the agony in her buttocks, the grinding tightness in her clitoris ... and the soft, loving pleasure at her lips where Jake continued his kisses.

She lost count of the strokes of the paddle. It was some time before she even realised that the beating had finished. All she did perceive was that after one particularly tender kiss on her forehead, Jake's lips left her face and his presence left her sphere of awareness.

'You've done a fine job, Vida,' Deana heard him say with genuine admiration; then realised – with a struggle – that her master and mistress were studying her bottom.

'I want my reward now, Kazuto,' said Vida in reply, her voice slightly frayed at the edges.

'Of course, my love, and where do you want it?'

'On the *chaise*, please, my Lord ... And I'd like this creature to watch us.'

'As you wish, my love. But do you think she's up to it?'

'She is,' said Vida more firmly. 'This one's made of tempered steel, my Kazuto. She's noisy, but she's taken far more than most others. You chose well here ...'

The sense of detachment and distance was even more intense than before. Deana felt as if she were listening to the dialogue of a film, and when she was released by Bentley, held upright and turned around she fully expected to see the action on a huge silver screen.

Numb, she allowed her wrists to be fastened behind her in the same steel cuffs she'd arrived in. She felt a sick, precarious moment as the cork was eased from her bottom, but it was quickly over and she felt almost relaxed as the surprisingly strong maid lifted her bodily in her arms and laid her face down across a pouffe. She rested there motionless for a few moments. With her eyes closed, and her breathing still heavy, she listened to Bentley's soft-footed retreat, and let the pain of her various torments recede.

When she looked up again, she almost believed she *was* watching a film.

A man and a woman – both of astounding, almost super-natural beauty – were pulling off their few scanty garments and kissing and caressing each other as they did so.

Curiously enough, Deana felt no jealousy as she watched Jake and Vida making love. In a diffuse and turned-about way she was grateful to both of them, and the pleasures of physical love seemed a fitting reward for their trouble. She also felt strangely privileged to be *allowed* to watch, even though the glorious sensuality of their entwining was a thorn in her own deep frustration.

At some time during Deana's moments of darkness, Vida Mistry had let down her coiled red hair. Loose now, it trailed across the *chaise* like a curtain of flame, and rippled as Jake moved above her. The beautiful authoress moaned long and plaintively as she was first mounted, then opened and taken completely. It was plain that the beating had aroused her as much as it had Deana ...

Crying out fiercely, Vida arched her slim body upwards to meet Jake's powerful thrusts. There was no doubt she was climaxing continuously, and had been since the instant he entered her. He too was visibly moved, his dark face contorting as he clenched his firm, brown buttocks and rode his squirming, shouting lover in a rhythm that was smooth but frantic.

Aroused and frustrated, Deana wept tears for the beauty before her. But even as she sobbed, the clear thinking artist within her applauded. Watching the heaving and bucking of

Jake and Vida, she planned a canvas she would paint sometime soon – a work for her own satisfaction, an immortalisation of two truly exceptional sensualists with their bodies bound together in sex.

I might even sell it to Jake himself! she thought suddenly, wryly realising that she *could* think at last. She was hurting and befuddled, and still desperately frustrated, but at least she'd recovered her faculties.

Mercifully, the embrace didn't last too long. With another great cry, Vida reared up again, her limbs flailing crazily while Jake found release in her body. He moaned himself, like a wounded bear, as his brown buttocks jiggled and pumped. Through a thick blur of tears, Deana watched the two of them slump down together, their obvious fulfilment a torch to her still-burning need.

But as she drooped forward over her pouffe, a chain of small sounds made her rouse and look up again.

Vida was curled up foetus-like on the *chaise*, her expression soft and silly and her beautiful eyes closed tight. She was quite obviously superbly satiated and insensible . . . but the man that had loved her wasn't!

Jake was on his feet. He was shaky, quite pale, and almost cross-eyed with fatigue; but even so he was walking slowly and carefully towards Deana where she lay on her pouffe. When he reached her, he knelt down behind her, and pulled her body backwards against his.

'Sweet brave Dee,' he murmured in her ear as he pushed himself hard against her.

Deana moaned, for reasons various and potent. His long, wet penis was nudging at the back of her thigh and his bushy pubic hair was a painful caress against the aching skin of her bottom. As was the hardness of his flat, sweaty stomach as he reeled her in tightly to his body. As best she could, she straightened her constricted fingers behind her and fondled all the flesh she could reach.

But as she touched him, all her torments faded, went vague, and were forgotten.

All memory of pain and frustration disappeared when his long, flexible fingers crept down over her belly and inveigled their way into the sticky-soft mat of her pubis.

And when a single one of those fingers – a brilliant bright genius of a finger – pushed inwards, found its target, then tickled it gently, Deana sobbed.

She sobbed, as her clitoris bloomed like a flower of love and her sex, her body and her mind all dissolved in a white ball of bliss . . .

11

Come into my Jacuzzi...

Does semen have any special nutritional qualities? wondered Delia as she sipped her mid-morning coffee.

She was being whimsical and silly, and she knew it, but the aromatic fresh-percolated flavour had made her think of something quite different...but just as delectable.

The orgasmic juice of a man.

She'd had more than her fair share of *that* last night, she observed, grinning in a smug sort of way that she'd never had cause to before.

Nectar of the gods, she thought, remembering how she'd taken it, direct from Peter's long prick. She could almost believe that it was semen that was making her feel good this morning. Fit and feisty. Bursting with naughtiness and energy.

It was funny though, but man's stuff was a bland brew in itself. She licked her lightly glossed lips and imagined them salty. Salt was the only distinct flavour she could remember; that, and a touch of bitterness. But it wasn't the flavour that made semen memorable, only the source.

Anyway, last night, after she'd bade a gentle '*au revoir*' to Peter, she'd had one of the best night's sleep of her life. She hadn't had a single sleepless moment about her promise to 'talk tomorrow' with Peter, and she hadn't even heard Deana eventually come home – sometime in the small hours of the morning.

Deana ... That was another thing.

When Delia had looked in before work, she'd found her sister sleeping as deeply as she had done. Deeper in fact, almost death-like. She'd been worried at first, but when she'd studied her slumbering sibling more closely, she'd realised her sister was smiling sweetly into her pillow, her face as pacific as a cherub's.

Deana had looked as fit and happy as she, Delia, felt; so there was nothing left to do but leave her to it and wonder. Wonder what Jake de Guile had done to create such contentment ...

Was he as good as all that, Deana love? thought Delia now, sitting at her desk and doing far more day-dreaming than was usual. She wondered what wild sexual scene had required that kinky corset. And whether Deana had got into trouble for wearing knickers with it.

We'd better have a long talk, love, she told the absent Deana whilst sipping her coffee. And as soon as possible. Something pretty special had happened last night and she needed to know about it. Before 'Dee' met Jake again.

Which could be tonight ...

Delia's stomach started quivering as her imagination revved into overdrive. It was so weird. She'd only just ditched Russell, and she now seemed to be involved with Peter, but she still couldn't stop wanting Jake. He made her body heat up, her blood pound and her hormones go crazy. And against all her previous inclinations, she loved it.

Jake was dangerous. He was a manipulator and a deviant. Yet there was something so utterly and sensually compelling about him that even the thought of him roused her.

She wallowed in her longing. Drooled like a pervert about mental pictures of his sleek brown body and the cool dark smoothness of his slender, muscular limbs. Her own sex rippled as she imagined the entry of his; the thick, unyielding push of his cock and the touch of his sensitive fingers on her most special places as he screwed her to mind-blowing bliss . . .

Dear Lord, had she got it bad!

When the inter-office post arrived, she was still fantasising and felt irritated at having to break off. She normally relished her office tasks, and loved her job. But today she had no interest in either.

At the bottom of the pile of letters and memos was a fax, and she was just preparing to fling it blithely in her pending tray when the signature pulled her up sharp and set her heart and her whole body pounding . . .

To Delia Ferraro, the facsimile read. *After reviewing your file, I find there are matters we must urgently discuss. I'll be working at home today and would be grateful if you could call around at your earliest convenience.* There was no endearment and no salutation, simply the crisp, angular signature. *Jackson K. de Guile.*

What kind of silly bugger game are you playing now, Jake? fumed Delia in the lift, willing it to speed up in its downward crawl – and not stop at every single floor as it appeared to be doing.

By the time she was in the foyer, she'd moderated her fury. She could hardly hit the roof with Jake for game-playing, could she? Not considering what she and Deana were up to . . .

And that's a game that's probably over, she thought resignedly when she saw Fargo waiting by the kerb with the limousine. He was holding open the rear passenger door, while the engine thrummed softly but powerfully in readiness.

She was sallying forth to meet her nemesis without a briefing of any kind, and without the slightest knowledge of what had happened to Deana last night. She could almost feel the game start to crumble . . .

If the roles had been reversed, Deana might well have been able to bluff her way through, but Delia knew *she* couldn't.

She was the oh-so-conventional one who'd been playing life far too straight for far too long. She'd already reached the limits of her meagre thespian talents, and there was nothing left to do but own up the minute she arrived.

Elf greeted her warmly at the dark blue door, although there was no hint in her exquisite Japanese courtesy of the simmering caresses they'd shared.

'Jake's in the Jacuzzi,' she said as Delia followed her along the hall and up the stairs. 'He'd like you to join him there.'

So much for reviewing her file.

At the top of the stairs they turned in the opposite direction to the one they'd taken on Delia's last visit. With a lovely smile and a gracious gesture, Elf ushered Delia ahead of her and into a bathroom that was even larger and more luxurious than the palace of ablutions she had visited last time. This one was a sumptuous, high-ceilinged, blue decorated chamber with a bubbling Jacuzzi at its centre – a large vat of fast-churning azure-tinted water that was currently occupied by Jake.

'That's all for now, Elf,' he said, dismissing his servant, 'I think Dee and I can fend for ourselves for the moment.'

Elf bowed slightly in the traditional style and with another of her beautiful, inscrutable smiles, backed out of the bathroom and left them.

'I see no files,' Delia said boldly, debating whether to come right out with her confession now or see if she could play for some time.

'Just kidding,' he said easily, popping up out of the pool a little way and revealing his muscular, water-sheened chest. His hair was loose again, hanging in a thick, dead-straight sheet to his shoulders, with odd strands plastered wetly to his face. 'Why not hop in with me?' he suggested, flicking his fingers up out of the roiling water. 'It's very relaxing, and you look a bit edgy.' He narrowed his long slanted eyes. 'I wouldn't have expected you to be hung up today, Dee. A session with Vida usually irons out the knots completely ... You ought to be on top of the world. I certainly am.'

Delia stared at him, at a loss. She remembered the soft little smile on the face of her sleeping sister ... and considered Vida Mistry's reputation. Oh God, what on earth had happened?

'I'm OK,' she said non-committally. 'I feel fine actually. Just things at work. Little snags. It's nothing really.'

'Just tell me what's happening and it's dealt with,' Jake said crisply, reminding Delia that this was her boss she was trying to flannel with imaginary workplace niggles.

'Thank you, Jake, but I can deal with it. It's my job,' she answered coolly, shifting from one court-shoed foot to the other, unable to stop looking at the vague brownish shape of his body as he floated serenely in the water.

'I'm sure you can,' he answered softly, his voice suddenly husky and cajoling. 'Now get your clothes off, woman, and get your lovely little body in this water!'

Her defiance crumbled. The water looked tempting and so did Jake. With an unselfconscious coquetry that was unknown in the Delia of a week ago, she began to slowly undress – peeling off each garment with a sense of mounting excitement.

She wasn't surprised that he watched her closely, but she was when he shot up from the water without warning while she still wore her white bra and pants. She froze with an atavistic fear when he grabbed her by the bottom, then pressed his dripping wet face against her midriff. His long-fingered hands were tight on her cotton-covered buttocks, his grip possessive and hungry.

For several moments he kissed and licked her as his fingertips kneaded and pummelled. His touch had a distinct assessing quality, as if he were feeling for some difference or change. He was handling her like a female animal he was planning to purchase. It was insultingly rude and demeaning, but to her horror, unbearably arousing.

With a small helpless cry, she wafted her hips toward him and grabbed for his silky-skinned shoulders.

'Yes!'

Jake's voice was strangely triumphant and his hands on her body were strong. With no further ado, he hauled her down into the water to sit on the shelved seat beside him, ignoring all her protests about the wringing wet state of her underwear and the imminent destruction of her hairstyle. Moving her and turning her to suit him, he brought his mouth down hard on hers, his tongue pushing lewdly for an entrance. The kiss was savage and mock-copulatory and as he stretched her whole mouth and jaw with the force of it, she felt his hands sliding deftly over the back of her head, removing the strategically placed hairpins and letting her long hair fall loose about her shoulders.

'That's better,' he murmured against her lips, fluffing at the sodden-ended waves and fanning them out with his fingers. That done, he plunged his hands back into the water, twisted her hips on the seat, then groped crudely at her body through her undies.

The way he handled her felt strangely adolescent. He was squeezing her breasts like a pair of plums, pinching her nipples until she squirmed and protested. When she bounced and tried to kick him, he swooped his hands down her body and took hold of her buttocks again.

'Does this hurt?' he hissed, his fingers gouging deep into the flesh of her bottom.

'Yes,' she whispered truthfully, wondering why on earth he was being so rough and gross with her, and wondering even harder why she'd suddenly started to enjoy it.

'How much?' he demanded, pushing and gripping so hard that her knickers went right in her crease.

Within seconds he was rubbing her intimately, one hand spread out across her bottom-cheeks for purchase, while the other played tunes on her sex through the thin cotton stuff of her panties. He was poking into both her orifices now, prodding at her swollen labia, flicking wickedly at her sensitive clitoris. It was so casual and vulgar it was gorgeous, and Delia's flesh started spasming and jumping.

'Oh . . . Ooh . . . Please,' she burbled. He was treating her badly, rummaging grotesquely at the most sacred part of her body, yet she was right on the edge of an orgasm.

'Do you want to come?' His voice dripped menace as surely as his hair dripped warm scented water, and without warning he pulled away his hands and let her bottom settle down on the seat. He laughed when she whimpered her loss.

Of her own volition, Delia moved towards him through the churning blue bubble, her body seeking out what it craved. He drew back, still laughing, and it suddenly dawned on her that this could well be the beginning of the end. Retribution-time. Game over.

While they'd been kissing and touching and close, she'd completely forgotten her deception. But now it all came back to her in a clear, adrenalin-fired rush. Bravely, she lifted her eyes to face his anger, but found *his* eyes were unreadable. Great deep unfathomable pools of hooded blue mystery . . . undivinable voids that spoke to her only of sex.

Unpredictable, delectable, infuriating sex.

Sex – the essence of everything that *was* Jake de Guile. It was his primary mode of communication; whether you were friend or foe, employee or lover. She had a strong suspicion that somehow, even the acquisition of his billions had been based on it. Quite how, in fine detail, she couldn't begin to imagine; but her gut, and her most intimate female instincts were completely and unequivocably sure of it.

But this ephemeral knowledge didn't solve any physical problems, and as she swayed in the water, her body was itchy and tingling with frustration.

'If you want to come, make it happen,' Jake suggested, reading her perfectly. As he spoke he slid down in the water and settled with the agitated surface just fretting at the line of his chin.

'I'm not sure I can,' she replied making her voice as small as possible, hoping he might not hear her in the watery hubbub of the pool. Oh God, if only she knew what Deana had done last night! Whether she'd done what Jake had just asked for . . .

Delia was accustomed to masturbating on her own and enjoyed it. She was secretly proud that she could pleasure herself so efficiently – but the act was strictly between herself and her fingers. No outsiders; no observers. And certainly no Jackson de Guile, Mr Sharp-eyes Incarnate, who she was now sure had sussed her duality . . .

'Now don't be defeatist, sweet Dee,' he chided, his eyes sparkling mischievously. 'It's easy. Shall I show you how?' He looked down into the slightly tinted water, and as Delia followed his eyeline, she saw the slender line of his hand meet the substantial, but bubble-distorted blur at his groin. 'The topography's different, of course. But the basic principle is more or less the same.'

It was an entrancingly sensual concept. Her lover – or should she say one of her lovers – was offering her lessons in practical self-pleasure. She didn't really need tuition, and she'd seen this phenomenon before . . . but the sight of Jake stroking himself had been so beautiful and stirring that only a fool or a terminal prude would not want to see it again.

'I ... Perhaps I will then,' she murmured, looking down into the water. She could just make out the long dark bar of his penis, erect and gently waving in the turbulence. Her own genitalia were hidden still, veiled by the thin sodden cloth of her pants. She slid her hands through the rollicking bubbles and started to reach round behind her.

'No! Don't! I've changed my mind.'

She glanced at him sharply. What was he playing at now? And if he knew about the game why didn't he say so instead of teasing and taunting? He might've 'changed his mind', but her body hadn't. She could feel her sweat glands kicking into action, her nipples getting hard as small pebbles, and her sex running slippery and wet as her own fluids joined those around her. Her sex wanted somebody's touch now – be it hers or his – and to stop at the very beginning would set frustration in cruel, grinding motion. But maybe that was just what he wanted?

There were shallow steps at the far side of the pool and Jake was already moving towards them. 'Let's do something else,' he said conversationally, emerging from the bubbles with water running down in a rude-looking stream from the end of his semi-hard cock. Unconcerned and utterly natural, he lifted a thick white towel from a stack of about twenty, and rubbed vigorously at his hips, his belly and his dark-red stiffening sex.

With his skin still moist and shiny, he flung the towel around his shoulders, leaving his lower body bare, and came slowly round to her side of the pool.

'Come on, Dee,' he said briskly, 'let's have you out of the water!'

Then, before Delia could protest, or question his action, he'd reached down into the pool, slid his strong hands under her arms and spirited her up and out of the water with little discernible effort. Disorientated, she found herself standing on the pool-side, dripping and still wondering exactly how she'd got there. Obviously, there was far more strength in those lean brown arms than a cursory glance might suggest.

Within seconds, she was being swathed in a sublimely soft towel of her own, rubbed with considerable energy and then made to stand like an awkward, reluctant child while Jake stripped off her bra and panties with a disturbing efficiency and detachment. Hardly glancing at her still damp body, he smoothed and arranged her wet, tousled hair, then dabbed at the smeary remnants of her make-up with cotton wool and a fine herbal lotion.

'There, that's better,' he said, sounding pleased with his efforts. He spoke, and was acting, with an easy calm that made him seem totally immune to her nudity . . . but down below his cock was saying otherwise.

He was fully erect now, his strong reddened shaft standing straight out before him and its tip thickly swollen and moist. He was as sexually excited as a man could possibly be but his face looked as placid as a guru's.

'Come along, sweet Dee,' he said, slinging aside his towel and reaching for her hand. 'Let's go and find ourselves a drink. It must be about that time.'

She half expected him to find robes or kimonos for them, but within seconds they were walking down the corridor. Delia's eyes were helplessly riveted on his long waving sex, and her own body was as naked as his . . . And as aroused.

The biggest surprise was that they even descended the staircase while nude, then strolled into a large, elegant salon-like room whose wide-open French window looked out onto a well-tended garden. She could see even Fargo out there – wearing shades and denim cut-offs now instead of his usual smart black – kneeling beside a flower-bed and ruthlessly eradicating weeds.

'Let's stay inside for now,' said Jake, leading her to a deeply upholstered, brocade covered chair and almost pushing her down into its depths. 'The sun's quite high and I don't want that lovely skin of yours to burn.' His fingers drifted languidly across the slope of her taut swollen breast, and she shivered at his super-cool smoothness. As he walked away, to a chair of his own, she admired the small, tight rounds of his perfectly formed masculine bottom.

Delia had seen no button pushed and heard no bell rung, but within seconds Elf joined them in the room, a heavy silver tray held effortlessly in her slender little hands. She smiled at Delia quite normally, as if she often saw women sprawled naked on the priceless antique furniture. It could be that she often did!

'Gin and tonic?' she enquired of Delia, hefting a sparkling cut-glass decanter when she'd set down the tray on the sideboard.

'Oh, please! I'd love one!'

The thought of that crisp, aromatic taste and the quicksilver punch of the spirit was irresistibly welcome. And when the drink itself came, the mix was perfect: as strong and bracing as Deana might have made when the pair of them had had a bad day.

As it was Delia took it and sank about a third of it immediately – deeply flustered by Jake's intent stare.

'You look as though you needed that.' His own very modest sip seemed to accuse her somehow, and piled on the pressure to confess and be done with it. 'Is there something you'd like to tell me?' he asked softly, putting his glass to one side and standing up again. From somewhere concealed, Elf had produced a robe for him; not the gossamer-fine silk kimono of the other night, but a fairly plain silver-grey cotton wrap that was in its own way just as seductive. Holding out his arms he allowed it to be slipped around his shoulders, but didn't bother fastening the sash. As the tension mounted, Delia half expected a robe to be produced for her too, but none was forthcoming. Taking a gin and tonic for herself, Elf retired to a ladder-back chair in the corner of the room, her smooth face devoid of expression.

Now was the moment to confess, of course, to own up to being a twin and a trickster ... but before Delia could speak, Jake suddenly seemed distracted. He strolled back across the room towards her, and stared down at some objects that lay on a large occasional table beside her.

Delia had barely noticed the table, and certainly not looked at its contents. But now she followed Jake's eyeline ... and felt her bare skin tingle with goose-bumps.

What she saw there was quite ordinary and familiar. A thick A3 pad of artist's drawing paper, and beside it a clutch of pencils. They were the sort of soft smudgy pencils that Delia saw every day in her own home: cluttering up the work surfaces, saving places in books, sliding down the sides of armchairs. She'd even seen a certain person stir her coffee with them.

'I've been thinking about what you said about being an artist, Dee,' purred Jake, his voice electric, 'and I've decided I'd like you to draw me ... Right now.' He paused, struck an attitude, then strode over to an opulent cushion-strewn settee and lay down. As he settled he let his long legs part and fall rudely akimbo, and between them his sex stood proud and red and if anything harder than ever.

'OK ... I'm ready,' he prompted, smiling. Almost laughing.

Oh God! Oh damn! Oh shit! There was nowhere to run to now ...

Delia had always reckoned there'd been a supernova in the constellation of Gemini in the fifteen minutes between her birth and her sister's. It was the only way to account for their different natural talents. Give Deana paper and pencils like those on the table and you'd get a witty character sketch, a sensual male nude, or even a line perfect Tom and Jerry in the space of five minutes.

But with the same materials, Delia was helpless. Even her stick-men were unrecognisable as such. She could write a detailed and incisive work-report. She could make a perfect cheese soufflé and an even better cocktail to wash it down with. She could rewire a plug in under two minutes, and she could even sing well enough to have once considered a musical career . . . but she couldn't draw to save her life!

It wasn't her life that depended on it now, but her hands were shaking as she reached out and picked up a pencil . . .

It was wicked of him to tease her like this. He knew that, but the process was so entertaining, and so stimulating, that he couldn't help himself.

'Well then, Dee . . . How about it?' Jake let his hand fall to his prick and he stroked it gently, thus increasing the area of her 'study'. 'I'd like to hang your work here.' He gestured expansively with his free hand, indicating this house that he liked well enough but didn't consider his home. 'Or perhaps in my place in Geneva. I'm sure whatever you do, it'll be the jewel of my collection.'

He was asking for art, but her lovely, scared face was a picture in itself. And her body too. Both told the proverbial story.

Her face was a captivating mix of apprehension, defiance and confused sexual excitement. Her body spoke unequivocably of lust. Hers, so clear in her pink, rosy blush and the superlative hardness of her nipples . . . And his, in all of him, when he looked at her sex and throbbed with desire. He wanted to come right now, just from the thought that a *second* woman – one equally and identically alluring – was being brought to him right at this moment.

The Ferraro twins. Doubly beautiful. Doubly intelligent and fiery. Interchangeable and matching in everything – even their strange body-heat – yet entirely and enchantingly different. He wanted to love them and be loved by them together. Have their two slender, hot-sweet bodies entwined and entangled with his. His erotic instincts were acute however, and even though it saddened him, he sensed that they'd find such a 'twin' scene abhorrent. They were prepared to play this sexy game of theirs, take turns and share him serially . . . but to kiss him, suck him and caress him in each other's presence? No.

That, he realised with wistful longing, was never going to happen. There was no point even opening a dialogue.

But there was still fun to be had with these two feisty, fabulous lookalikes. For him *and* for them. And as he watched the woman called Delia blush wildly and fumble with a pencil, he thought of her sister too and wondered if with her might lie a chance for something else. Something deeper . . . More lasting.

'It's no good. I can't do it,' said Delia, throwing down the pencil.

'But when we were in the gallery, Dee, you told me you were an artist,' Jake pointed out, his firm mouth curved into a demon of a grin. 'Surely I'm not so hideous that I strip you of your skills?' As he spoke he flexed his limbs again, and if anything made the pose even lewder. His fingertips moved steadily over his penis, caressing it to an even greater hardness.

He was quite, quite beautiful, thought Delia, wishing there were no complications, no games and that she could simply glide across the room, ease her own sex open with her fingertips and slip it down over his. She even wished she could *really* draw. There'd never be a better sight to record for posterity . . .

'I've never had the skills,' she said in a tiny, breathy voice

– hoping that if he didn't quite hear her, the deception might seem less heinous.

'I beg your pardon?' The devil-smile widened, and out of the corner of her eye, Delia saw Elf lean forward ever so slightly.

'I can't draw! I never could! And *I* never told you I could!'

He didn't speak this time; all she got was a questioning lift of his immaculate wing-straight eyebrows.

'The girl you met in the gallery was my sister, Deana Ferraro. There are two of us. We're identical twins. Deana and Delia ... Now are you satisfied?'

'Not quite,' he murmured, his hand still at work on his prick. It was extremely aroused now, hard and almost purple, the tiny eye opening and weeping out its juice. No, he wasn't satisfied, but he certainly would be soon ...

'Aren't you going to say anything? Ask me anything?' she demanded. His erotic calm was unnerving, the slow glide of his fingers perplexing and hypnotic.

'No. I'll let *you* tell me.' Shuffling slightly on the couch, he reached beneath himself and carefully cradled his balls. 'Go on, Delia. Let's hear it all.' At work on the whole of his genitals now, he let his head fall back against the cushions: his eyes closed, his lips slightly curved, and his long throat stretched taut and gleaming.

It was difficult to convey her account lucidly with a naked man masturbating in front of her, and Delia's words were a muddle. She was astounded by her own sexual candour, but she still stuttered and stammered and faltered – and wondered what had happened to the clear-voiced woman who gave such hot-shot managerial presentations.

Every now and again she clammed up dead in her tracks; especially when Jake moaned, or sighed, or arched his body in pleasure. He seemed supremely expert in teasing himself right to the brink, and on several occasions, Delia was certain that he'd pushed himself over it. That he was going to orgasm, ejaculate, and scream. But every time she stopped, and gaped open-mouthed in awed anticipation, he'd back off within a heartbeat of coming, quite blatantly slow down his hand-strokes and breathe deeply to contain his release.

'Are you listening?' she snapped suddenly, when he seemed unmoved by her graphic descriptions of her parting from Russell.

Jake's eyes flicked open, blue and glittery as he slanted her a penetrating glance. 'Of course,' he said smoothly, then began an embarrassingly verbatim repeat of that furious farewell screw – his hips shifting slowly and explicitly as he did so.

'Carry on then, my delicious Delia,' he said when he'd finished grilling her on the hot coals of shame, 'complete your story ... Tell me how long the two of you thought you could get away with this.'

'There's not much more,' she whispered. 'I ... um ... I saw Peter for a while last night, but nothing much happened.' Those black brows flicked again. 'And this morning, Deana was still fast asleep when I left. But she was smiling when I looked in on her, so—' She flashed him an enquiring glance of her own. 'So I presume she had a pleasant night with you.'

'I suppose you could say that ...' He chuckled softly, then before she could speak, respond or even really take in what was happening, he pumped his stiff flesh with one, two, three long strokes, and his semen shot out in an arc, flew high into the air, then fell back down onto his body.

'Although I doubt if the adjective "pleasant" does the experience full justice,' he resumed, unruffled, when his penis had finished its squirting and his pale silky essence lay in thick, fat drops on his belly. As she watched, ensorcelled, he massaged it into his skin like a cream or a moisturising lotion.

'But you can ask her yourself, if you're curious.' He paused and glanced at a small, but clear-faced clock that stood on the imposing marble mantelshelf. 'She's going to be here any moment.'

Swinging his long legs over the side of the sofa, he stood up, his penis swinging gently as he moved and still gleaming with the satin of his juices. 'So if you need to have an orgasm before she gets here, you'd better get on with it, hadn't you?' His smile was soft and taunting as he closed on her, his thin robe winging out on either side of him and concealing nothing. 'I could help if you like?'

He was right. After seeing what she'd just seen, she desperately needed to come. Somehow, or anyhow ... She didn't care. Her own fingers would do. Or his. Or even those of the delicately skilful Elf, who sat in silence and had taken in everything.

As the thoughts whirled in her mind, Delia also acknowledged the more subtle implications of his words ...

He was right again. She didn't want Deana to see her *en flagrante* – either at her own hands or his.

Close in everything, she and Deana had always discussed the joys and woes of their sex lives with absolute frankness and honesty. They also saw each other naked and half-naked around the flat.

But what they had always – and unspokenly – rejected out of hand was anything that hinted of a 'threesome'... One man with the two of them. In their youth, and in the past few days, they'd played their Gemini Game with a full-blooded eroticism and zest, but never, not even once, had they ever had sex with the *same* man at the *same* time.

They'd seen the longing for it many times, in the eyes of the men they'd dated. It was there more often than not, and it was in Jake's eyes right now. But the difference between Jake and others was that he seemed to sense her feelings. To understand that the ménage he wanted couldn't happen ... would never happen. And for *that* she could almost adore him.

'Delia?' he whispered, sliding elegantly to his knees before her, and taking the useless pencil from her nervous fingers. 'Do you want me to make you come or will you do it yourself? I think you maybe owe me a little show ... After the way you've tricked me.'

She nodded, acknowledging a sweet, sexual justice. She'd been on the point of masturbating for him in the Jacuzzi, so why not do it now? She and Deana *had* been trying to deceive him, to fool him. She was in his debt, and she owed him exactly what he wanted. She owed it to him now.

With as much grace as she could summon, Delia opened her thighs and showed him her soft pink furrow, fingering and combing at her lush brown curls to part them for his concentrated study.

Her sex felt hot to the touch, hotter than it had ever felt, her special intrinsic heat set alight by Jake's sapphire blue gaze. He murmured encouragingly as she unleaved her moist, swollen folds, then revealed her clitoris and the snug, little opening lower down. She was torn between her own need for a quick, hard orgasm, and a repentant desire to please Jake. Always the perfectionist, she tried for both, for sexual artistry; and sliding a finger from her left hand into her vagina, she attacked her aching clitoris with the other.

At the first touch, the pleasure surged and challenged her. She was half mad to come, but this was for Jake. She clenched the whole of her vulva, desperate to control the spasms that were already beginning inside her, twinkling in her deep sexual core and grabbing at the length of the finger embedded within her. Flung up by the long, tense muscles of her thighs, her hips rose high above the seat. Her heels gouged the carpet, and she whined out aloud when other hands joined hers at her crotch.

A spread palm slid beneath her bottom to support her, while another hand curved in to mirror hers, one finger pressed firmly against her anus as if it were trying to slide inside her, and lie parallel to the digit in her sex.

'Agh! Oh no!' she cried hoarsely when she realised that her moment was imminent. Her juices were streaming, gushing, bubbling. Flowing out of her vulva and seeping down to lubricate Jake's efforts. His probing was tender, yet unremitting, and with a swirl of his flexible wrist, he took advantage of the liquid environment and pushed his finger right home inside her.

The feeling of fullness was both beautiful and appalling. Delia squirmed, kicked out and rubbed her own body like fury. Her clitoris felt huge, swollen out from between her slick labia by the force of her pure, violent hunger. She lashed it with her fingertip, then screamed as huge waves of pleasure surged out from the first point of contact, and muscles she'd not known existed clamped down on the fingers within her. Crying and moaning and jerking, she felt Jake lean forward and over her, pressing his tongue into the niche of her navel to seal in the perfection of her climax.

And there, right in the centre of her bliss was a piquant and delicate sensation – the cool, silky swoosh of his soft, straight hair as it slid across her hot jumping belly . . .

12

Propositions

There won't be a bruise on her...

Yeah, true, thought Deana adjusting herself cautiously, but why the hell didn't you say it'd still hurt? Bitch!

Deana mostly went to work in jeans, and sometimes on her bicycle, but this morning both of these were out of the question. She'd tried putting on her Levis but given up; swearing out loud when the rough cloth chafed against her bottom, and astonished not so much by the tenderised rump she'd received, but by the way its soft glow still aroused her. She was drinking her coffee standing up now, because it seemed safest. Her shower had been long and difficult, mainly because she'd had to keep breaking off from washing to touch herself. Time and again, as the water had poured and streamed, her mind had filled with visions. Vida and Jake. The beam, the corset, the paddle ... And the unbelievable sensations of a beating.

The only garment she could tolerate below the waist now was a feather-light, layered chiffon skirt, and even that was exquisitely titillating, when worn, of necessity, *sans* knickers. There were four separate leaves to the skirt, and its colour was a strong, rich plum, but she was convinced that the sun would shine straight through it. A careful observer would see her body-shape easily, or maybe even the shadow of her pubis. That was if they weren't already ogling her nipples through the thin, soft stuff of her T-shirt.

Abandoning her coffee mug, Deana tempted fate for about the hundredth time since she'd woken up. Reaching around behind herself, she cupped the cheeks of her bottom and moaned.

Ow! Oh God! How could something so bad feel so good? How could she burn with so much more than just pain? She'd been beaten and exposed, her whole body humiliated, manipulated and shamed. It was so totally weak to feel this way. To crave punishment and the bending of her will. And yet, if Jake were to walk in right now, she'd be completely wet and ready for him, available for both the paddle or his penis.

You're in big trouble, Deana old love, she told herself seriously. Not only is the Gemini Game not a game any more, but it's spoiling you for all other men. For all other sex. At least the plainer, more normal sex she'd always been used to.

Throughout her all-young womanhood, Deana had thought herself daring and kinky. But now she knew she was a novice. All the times that Jake had fooled and played and toyed with her, displayed and hurt and humiliated her, all these moments had been the brightest times of her life. Like living in another dimension. A bigger and more vivid existence than she'd ever thought possible.

And the trouble was, now she'd seen a new way, she couldn't go back.

The temptation to 'go for it' was so strong she could taste it, and under normal circumstances she wouldn't have thought twice. She would have followed wherever Jake led. But there was Delia to consider. Delia who might also want to follow. Delia who was her flesh and blood far more than any normal sister would've been.

You want him all to yourself, Deana, don't you? she demanded of herself. It's OK to share him with Vida and her ilk, because they're so like him they almost seem a part of him.

But it's not so straightforward with Delia . . . She has your face, and your heart, and she's your greatest rival ever, even if you do love her dearly!

The only way not to think about the dilemma was to think about the sex. Deana had always been the Ferraro optimist, and despite the ache in her bottom and the turmoil in her mind, she couldn't help dwelling on the pleasure of last night, rather than the possible convoluted outcomes.

Those hours at Vida's, and the strip in the car beforehand, had been the weirdest of her sexual life, the culmination of a whole hot interlude of strangeness. Squeezing her abused flesh with her fingers, Deana moaned and tried to relive it all. As the images formed, and the muscles in her bottom protested, she felt her sex start to moisten and engorge. Edging along the side of the table she stood against, she pressed her crotch against its rounded-off corner, easing one ache as she developed and intensified another.

The memories were tactile, visual and aural. She remembered the gentle touch of Jake's lips against hers, as Vida had driven in the plug. She remembered the grace and beauty of his naked body as he'd thrust into his stern, exotic mistress. She remembered his soft moans as he'd allowed her to suck him. She remembered being screwed and demeaned and tortured, and loving everything about it. Especially the sly, heady knowledge that had come to her as she'd suffered. The instinctive recognition of a like mind, the internal revelation that Jake could 'take it' too when the time came. Take what she, Deana, could dish out. The idea that she might even outdo the mighty Vida was chilling. As seductive as a drug, but a thousand times more subversive.

She was rocking herself wildly now, working her clitoris on the table corner and making it throb as much as her bottom. Barefoot, she drove her warm, intimate flesh against the cool, inanimate melamine with the strong, flexing force of her toes.

She was just a woman in a kitchen rubbing herself off, but in her mind she was a queen clothed in majesty. A goddess of pain, thrashing her lover's bare bottom and making him squeal out with agony and pleasure. Strangely, her dream-self wore the same white corset as she'd worn last night – but this time it was a garment of power not submission. She wore boots with it, too, and long leather gloves. Her sex was left naked to be worshipped ...

As she flipped aside her weapon, a thin white leather-bound whip, her victim was miraculously released and turned towards her, his long blue eyes open wide with doglike adoration. Crouching before her, abject and striped, he raised his perfect pink mouth towards her vulva, and began, at her command, to lick.

In her dream the cunnilingus was the finest and sweetest she'd ever had, and in reality, her climax was dazzling. Jerking on her improvised sex-aid, she grunted and shouted with pleasure as she squeezed at the soreness of her buttocks. She was still wet and rippling when the mundane reached out and drew her back.

Someone was ringing her doorbell, leaning on the bloody thing in a non-stop, teeth-trembling trill.

'For Christ's sake!' she snarled, flipping down her skirt and marching along the corridor to the door, red pain still hectic in her bottom.

It wasn't who Deana had hoped it would be. Just her second choice ...

'Am I interrupting something?' enquired Vida Mistry suavely, her razor-sharp, jewel-green eyes zeroing in on Deana's rosy skin. The unmistakable mottling on her chest and her throat that signified she'd just had an orgasm.

'No! Yes! What the hell are *you* doing here?'

'Charming!' cooed Vida, sliding herself sinuously inside and strolling on down the corridor in the direction of the open kitchen door. Shaking with confusion, sex and anger, Deana stomped after her, muttering.

'I thought we were friends, Dee?' The outrageous dominatrix looked as different again this morning, as cool and unruffled as Deana felt hot and agitated.

And Vida was the one in white this morning, too. She looked as icy-smooth as a criminal in a baggy white linen man's suit, a white gangster's hat, and white patent leather loafers. Her scarlet hair was tucked away in a seductive, wisp-bestrewn pleat and her splendid breasts were contained in a red lace, underwired bra. She seemed to have forgotten about a blouse...

'Of sorts,' Deana conceded, thinking of the isolated moments of tenderness she'd experienced at this woman's pale hands. 'But I still want to know what you're doing here.'

'I'm here with a proposition, and on an errand. Jake gave me your address,' answered Vida succinctly, glancing around the kitchen, then homing in on the coffee percolator. 'May I?' she queried, taking a mug from the tree and nodding at the dark nutty brew.

'Go ahead,' said Deana.

Vida poured herself a half-mug of 'black' and drank it down in one long swallow. 'Mmmm... Yes! First of the day,' she murmured almost voluptuously, 'and now to business... I'll kick off with my proposition.' She dropped her tight, white-clad bottom onto a stool. 'Jake tells me you're an artist, Dee. How do you feel about illustrating a collection of my stories? I'm doing this sort of luxury collector's edition. Ritz and sleaze in one package... And I want some fairly raw but tasteful drawings to accompany my text. How about it?'

It was a fabulous opportunity and for about thirty seconds Deana was bowled over . . .

But then her critical faculties kicked in and she saw an anomaly. 'But Jake's never seen any of my work, and neither have you. My style could be completely unsuitable.'

'I shouldn't worry. Jake's got seven extra senses. He's probably looked inside your head and seen the way you draw.' Vida set her mug down with a disquieting silence and accuracy. 'And after last night, Dee, I *know* you'll understand what I need.'

Before Deana properly realised what was happening, Vida was on her feet and standing behind her. 'It's not exactly the sweetness and light tales I'm planning to anthologise, pretty Dee,' she whispered, her hands sliding down Deana's back. 'And I'm going to ask Jake to pose . . .' The strong, swift fingers slid further, then cupped and squeezed. Deana moaned as her buttocks seemed to sizzle, but her pleasure was far greater than her pain.

There was a delicious sense of complicity in the other woman's grip, and again, that sense of recognition. Vida Mistry had punished Deana last night, but unspokenly acknowledged her as an equal. Hidden antennae had signalled to each other, flashing the kinship of one dominant with another.

'What . . . What's your errand?' croaked Deana, leaving the question of the commission unanswered, because she sensed that of the two it was the lesser issue. She shimmied, showing her appreciation of Vida's clever fingers, while her own hand drifted helplessly to her groin.

'Oh, that's simple,' said Vida, digging delicately, then pushing and probing, 'I'm here to take you to Jake.'

As a sometime environmentalist, Deana knew little of cars and couldn't drive. What she did know, though, was that Vida's car perfectly suited its owner. It was Italian, vicious, expensive and red; and it seemed nicely apt that a sexual dominant like Vida should drive a vehicle so patently phallic.

Her driving was macho too. Suspended painfully in the low-slung bucket seat, Deana clung on for dear life as they shot into impossibly narrow traffic gaps, and Vida cut up other drivers with a fine disregard for road-craft, her high-gloss paintwork, or even the accepted rules of civilised behaviour.

The journey was a lot like the man they were travelling towards: fast, brilliant and terrifying. And it wasn't until she was ascending the steps towards a dark blue door familiar from only its description, that Deana realised how deeply the Gemini Game was in jeopardy.

This was Jake's home, and presumably he was in it now. But it was also highly likely that a man such as he was in constant contact with his business empire too, even while nominally 'off duty'. There was nothing to say he hadn't already spoken to a certain *Delia* this morning ... at work.

Yet, if he'd done that, why would he send Vida to the flat? Deana's thoughts started to spin and speculate, and she felt even more confused when Jake's servant, a beautiful, delicate-featured oriental girl, greeted her with a smile that was mischievous and intimate.

'He's waiting in the lounge,' murmured the slim, soft-spoken young woman – who Deana assumed must be 'Elf'. Deana answered with a nervous 'thanks' and followed Vida's long strides down the elegant, luxurious hall. At any other time, she would have loved to dawdle, look around, and assess the rest of Jake's art collection. But right now all the could think of was the Gemini Game ... And as Vida winked and pushed open a huge and gleamingly panelled door, Deana had the nastiest feeling it was all over ...

Within ten seconds, she *knew* it was over.

There were two familiar people relaxing in the deeply padded comfort of matching brocade chairs. Two people; one naked and one clothed, and each sipping what looked like gin and tonic.

The first was Jake – smiling and gloriously nude, his blue eyes glittering with a combination of triumph and sensual amusement. The second was Delia, wearing a rather pretty silver-grey robe, and despite being flushed and dishevelled, looking almost as amused as her host.

'Hi!' she said, shrugging her shoulders and toasting her glass towards Deana.

'Oh shit!' said Deana. Her fears were now realised, this had been inevitable, but somehow she still couldn't cope.

'Drink, Deana?' enquired Vida pleasantly, already with decanter in hand.

'Yes please,' she replied, her mouth dry. It was as good an opener as any ...

As she accepted the frosty glass, under the scrupulous gazes of both her sister and their stark naked lover, it dawned on Deana that Vida had just addressed her by her name. How long have *you* known? she wanted to ask, but just then, Jake rose from his chair and walked towards her, supremely untroubled by the stiffness of his prick as it bounced and pointed in front of him.

'Welcome to my house, Deana,' he said as he reached her, his voice warm, almost kind. He leaned close then, and as he pecked her on the cheek quite casually, she felt his hot flesh press hard through her skirt. 'Please, come and sit down ... I think we all need to talk, don't you?'

Meek for the moment, she allowed him to lead her to the chair next to Delia's. He smiled knowingly at her small distressed sound as she sat; and as she sipped deeply at the so welcome drink, Deana saw Delia staring at her curiously and frowning a silent 'what's up?'

'How long have you known?' demanded Deana, rounding on her naked tormentor rather than trying to explain her sore bottom to her sister.

Jake's eyes were so, so blue. Like alien rays they bored into her soul and silenced all questions and protests. 'I had a suspicion that something was amiss when I met you that night at the gallery,' he began without preamble. 'You were gorgeous, and I couldn't resist you, but you didn't quite conform to your dossier. In fact, apart from your face, you were barely recognisable . . .'

'What's all this about dossiers?' said Delia suddenly. 'I've seen my personnel file and it's strictly a CV and career summary. There's nothing about . . . about "personality traits". And all it says is that I've a sister. Nowhere does it say she's my twin.' Deana saw her sister's eyes narrow.

'OK, I admit it.' Jake laughed softly. 'I was looking for . . . shall we say . . . diversion. So I decided to invite some interesting people to my exhibition. Personnel files don't provide the sort of information I needed . . . So—' He tapped the side of his straight, elegant nose, 'I had to use other resources.'

'And what did these "other resources" tell you?' asked Deana. She hadn't needed Delia to tell her to take up the interrogation, it had just happened.

'When I arrived back here, I had another look at the file I'd "acquired",' Jake continued unperturbedly, surprising both of them by folding himself gracefully down onto the carpet at their feet. Sitting there naked, he continued to describe *his* game. 'And I realised it wasn't *Delia* Ferraro I'd screwed on the balcony, but her sister Deana. The artist . . .'

'I had a prior engagement. I didn't want to waste the ticket.'

Respect to you, Sis! thought Deana, impressed by her sister's super-coolness. Delia was handling all this with extraordinary tranquillity . . . but just how would she have coped last night? Deana wondered.

'I'd have done the same myself,' said Jake with a beautiful evil-imp smile, 'if I had a twin . . .'

'Doesn't bear thinking about,' observed Vida dryly from her place on the settee opposite.

'I take it one de Guile is adequate then, my dear?' he enquired without turning around.

'Plenty,' the authoress drawled, sipping her drink and grinning at the two Ferraros. Her expression was benign and conspiratorial, and Deana sensed her sister beginning to warm to the white-clad woman too.

'Kindly get on with it, Kazuto,' Vida went on, taking off her hat and flinging it accurately across the room to land on a side table. 'You know how I like all the details.'

And so Jake continued, his amusement unremitting as he outlined how he'd known all along that he was involved with twins. How he'd revelled in their contrasts and similarities, the sensuality of their dual nature, and their identical beauty that he'd found had some interesting individual distinctions.

It was these that he described with particular relish. These differences that Deana and Delia had never had knowledge of. Minute identifying marks – and differing responses – that made both of them blush as Jake outlined them in merciless detail.

'Between you, you're a beautiful paradox, my dears,' he said at last. 'So marvellously and tantalisingly alike yet at the heart of things so deliciously different.'

His pleasure in their diversity was eye-catchingly palpable. Throughout his description he'd been unselfconsciously stroking his penis, and now it was rigid, crimson-headed and trickling with clear, silky juice. Deana couldn't take her eyes off it, and she didn't need to look towards her sister to know that *she* couldn't either...

'And now, ladies, here's the deal.' His tone was endearingly chauvinistic, but even before he'd laid out his proposition, Deana had a deep-seatedly female feeling that it would be at least as irresistible as he was.

Without warning, Delia rose to her feet and smiled down at both of them. There was a strength in her sister that Deana had never seen before, and Delia's voice was level as she spoke. 'I heard this particular bit just before you arrived, Sis. I think I'll go and get dressed now, if nobody minds.' She looked enquiringly at Jake – who nodded, quite clearly impressed by her nonchalance.

'I'll come with you!' cried Vida, already on her feet and halfway across the large room. 'I could do with a freshen up. Come along, Elf, you can massage me.'

All this was bewildering, and Deana felt lost and abandoned. She looked urgently after Delia, and then nearly dropped the drink she was holding...

Delia had turned in the doorway, and when she caught Deana's eye, she winked outrageously, and mimed a very clear and distinct 'It's *your* turn!'

As the door closed behind them, Deana was flabbergasted. Whatever had happened to the seriously conventional and ever-so-slightly po-faced Delia Ferraro? The orderly young woman who frowned on her sister's sexual shenanigans and was prepared to settle for boring bed-play with an uninspiring dolt like Russell? Even if they had nothing else to thank him for, Jake had at least had an almost Promethean effect on Delia!

But could Delia cope with the wild-at-heart Vida? An unprincipled, amoral, domineering bisexual who was as likely to beat a girl's bottom severely as try to caress or seduce her?

'Don't worry, Deana,' said Jake taking the gin glass from her and putting it aside. He slid his hand slowly and soothingly up her thigh, rucking up her wafer-fine skirt as he traversed the smooth warmth of her skin. 'She's safe. Vida knows all about the differences between you, and despite everything, she will observe limits ...'

Deana could see that, on reflection. For all Vida's cruelty in the ritual mode, there was a warm core of kindness in her too. Last night, afterwards, she'd been as gentle and sweet as a cherub.

Jake's fingers were high on her leg now, near the crease of her groin, travelling and probing.

'What's this proposition?' she asked hoarsely, not much caring about plans and futures any more. This was the moment that mattered ... She looked down at Jake's long legs where he sat like a yogi on the carpet, and then at the thick vibrant staff of his cock which rose like a sword from the narrow brown cradle of his loins.

'Simple ... I want you and/or Delia to come and live with me in my home in Geneva.'

'What do you mean?'

The fingers slid further. 'Just what I said. I want you to live with me. Share my home. And my pleasures ...'

'You mean be your mistress ... your mistresses?'

'If that's what you want to call it. I just want you living in my house, and available to me. For sex whenever I want it.'

'Both of us?'

'Yes ... But not together. I don't think you'd like that, would you?' His fingers were almost in her curls now, flicking and feathering.

'That's outrageous, Jake!'

'What's outrageous?' he said, all innocence as he stroked at her sex-lips. 'It's only an extension of the games we've already played. I'd have you as you've been having me ... Turn and turn about. Serially ... Don't you like the idea?'

'But we'd be kept women. Sex toys,' she whispered as a fingertip pushed inwards through her intimate thicket and settled on her swollen-hard clitoris. She couldn't argue then because she could only moan. His touch was so slight that there was barely any motion at all – but she teetered on the knife edge of orgasm. She started wriggling, then cried out louder as her sore bottom pained her.

It was a hard, red fire in her muscles. A flame that set light to more delicate membranes, to folds and frills and crannies that were critically aroused already. She shouted as her sex leapt and she lost all conscious thought. Rolling and rocking where she sat, she ground her buttocks down hard against the brocade, and felt her sex-dew slither and slip ... Onto fingers that stayed doggedly in her groove no matter how violently she thrashed.

'You're such a hot creature,' he gasped, his finger stabbing deftly at her clitoris. 'So wild and hot and wet ...' She felt his hand clamp her firmly by the hip, holding her steady so he could rub and pinch and pound her.

Deana shrieked. Her pleasure was pain, and her pain was pleasure; and the two of them were surging like a dark, sweet syrup that roiled and bubbled in her belly. Beside herself, and babbling nonsense, she tore blindly at her thin, soft skirt – ripping it to strips in her need to grab her own seared flesh. Virtually sitting on her own trapped hands, she mortified her hot, aching rump in time to the waves of her climax.

She felt every part of herself in motion, her whole self balanced between Jake's pinching finger and thumb. He was controlling her utterly, pulling on a cord that stretched tight between her crotch and her soul ...

'No! No! No!' she howled, her legs flailing crazily despite his sure hold on her hip. Unable to stop herself, she wrenched at the cheeks of her bottom, reaching for a brand new kind of orgasm that bloomed in the heart of the first one. Her love-juice flowed out like a river.

'Give it up. Give it up. Give it up...' He coaxed, still jiggling, still teasing.

But at last, after a blank-white millennium of pleasure that bordered on madness, there was no more to give. Limp and half-senseless, Deana fell back against the chair, panting. She could barely think, but she could feel Jake's gentle hands moving: first on her brow, smoothing her hair, then on her loins and thighs, rearranging the ruins of her skirt.

'I suppose all that was to distract my attention?' she said eventually, her voice faint. 'To do my head in so I'd say "yes" and agree to be your sex slave, or whatever...'

Her eyes were shut, her eyelids too heavy to lift, but she felt Jake stand up and move away.

'No, that wasn't my tactic,' he said, returning and putting a glass in her hand. A glass that was cool and frosty. 'But if it's worked, I'm pleased.'

'No, it hasn't!' she shot back at him as the sharp gin brought back her wits. She opened her eyes, and discovered him watching her closely. He was cross-legged on the carpet several yards away, sipping his own drink, his penis still stiffly erect.

'This is the twentieth century, Jake, and we live in a suppos-edly civilised society. You can't just hijack women like some Arabian sheik with a harem.'

'But I'm not coercing you, Deana,' he answered reasonably, his blue eyes steady and calm. 'I'm asking. Asking the two of you to share my life for a while. For the purposes of compan-ionship and sex.'

'I give up!' cried Deana exasperatedly, taking another long

pull at her drink. When the glass was empty, she rose awkwardly, crossed the room and got a top up. She was going to end up drunk at this rate, but what the hell, this situation was surreal already . . .

'You talk about us sharing your "life",' she began again, her glass refreshed. 'But what about our lives? I know I'm a bit of a no-hoper. Mainly because I'm too lazy. But Delia has a top job! In your bloody company! I can't see her living the life of an odalisque. Lying around twiddling her thumbs all day and waiting for you to feel randy!'

'Fair enough,' he answered, 'but it wouldn't be purely sex. There'd be career opportunities for Delia, in my Swiss operation. A chance to wield real power, not just organising a bunch of secretaries and keeping an office in paper clips.'

'She does more than that!' protested Deana, who knew nothing of Delia's day to day work at all.

'I know,' he said with a shrug, 'but I still think she's capable of more.' His eyes met hers levelly. 'So are you, Deana my love. In a secluded environment you could really apply yourself. It may surprise you to know, but I've seen your work and I know that at the moment, you're wasted. I'd like to take you to Geneva and nurture you. Hold exhibitions for you. Bring you to the attention of discerning connoisseurs.'

'What . . . As an artist or a sex-pot?'

He grinned again. That strange, little boy smirk. 'Either can be arranged, but primarily I was thinking of art.'

'Why us?' she asked, changing tack.

An interesting phenomenon was taking place, one that Deana found both curious and thrilling. The more spirit and defiance she showed, the harder and hotter Jake's prick looked. 'There's nothing particularly special about Delia and I apart from the fact we're twins. You could have any woman you wanted from anywhere on earth. What the devil do you want us for?' She paused, drew breath. 'And you needn't think we'll do lookalike three-in-a-bed either! It's not on! Delia would hate it and so would I.'

'I'd be happy with just one of you,' he said quietly. 'You're both luscious, brilliant women in your own right. I want either of you or both, and I'm prepared to give you just about anything if I can have you. What's the problem?'

There was a tiny edge of vexation in his voice now – the sound of the mighty Jackson de Guile being thwarted, and feeling confused by it. Helpless, almost. Deana's excitement spiralled exponentially, especially when she noted the condition of his cock. He looked almost on the point of exploding . . .

'I don't understand it,' she went on, sipping her drink more airily now, and licking stray droplets from her lips. It was an old, old ploy, but she'd never known it fail. She almost laughed out loud as Jake's hot gaze locked in on her mouth. 'If you want someone to live in and play kinky games, why on earth don't you ask Vida? She's an expert. You wouldn't even have to train her.'

Jake laughed, and though the slight tension eased, his erection stayed proud as ever. 'I love Vida dearly,' he said. 'In fact anybody would, once they get to know her. But unfortunately, she's impossible to live with. We tried it once and we nearly killed each other.'

'Oh, so Delia and I are just your second choices!'

'Deana! Enough!' Jake's glass tipped over on the priceless carpet as he sprang to his feet, his eyes like fizzing blue coals and his cock swinging out like a club. 'Do you want to come to Geneva or not?'

'I don't know . . . I might do. I need time to decide.'

'All right! Now I give in!' he growled, his whole body a coiled sexual spring as he strode towards her. 'But if I give you as much time as you need, will you give *me* something now?'

'Yes, that's all right,' she said slowly, knowing. 'What do you want?'

'Relief for *this*, you witch!' he cried, hefting his heavy penis in his fingers and almost pushing it into her face.

'Of course,' she whispered.

Slowly and precisely, she placed her glass on the floor, then leaned forward ever so slightly and took his long silky cock between her lips ...

13

The Gemini Choice

After a weekend of virtual seclusion, Delia still hadn't made a decision.

It would have been easier to choose, she reflected, if Jake had been around all the time. His physical presence and beauty would have warped her judgement and dissolved her old-fashioned sense of duty. It would've made her say a quick, simple 'yes'.

But since that morning at his house, they'd seen nothing of him. He'd left them alone for a few days – to give them 'space', he'd said. It should have been an act of consideration, but for Delia, it only made things harder.

Deana had already made *her* choice. Made it instantly, she'd informed Delia dreamily. She was going to Geneva, come what may, but she wouldn't tell Jake until Delia had made her mind up too.

Delia envied her sister her decisiveness. How simple it must be, to know what you wanted with no second thoughts. To be positive and daring. Or maybe just a little bit crazy.

'I'm going, Delia,' Deana had said as soon as they'd had a chance to discuss it. 'I've got to, whether you are or not. He's dangerous, he's arrogant and he's manipulative . . . but he's done something to me. And more than just sexually. He's made me feel full of energy . . . excited. I can't really explain it. And I can't rest until I know if there's more.'

'Are you really sure, love?' Delia had asked, knowing it was an empty question. Deana had never back-tracked in her life, even if she knew without doubt she was wrong.

'Completely. But I won't tell him until *you've* decided too.'

There had been a few tears then, and a few sisterly hugs, but in moments Deana had been laughing off her doubts. 'And anyway, I'd be mad to turn down free board and lodgings in the lap of luxury, wouldn't I?' she'd said, with a grin. 'Even you charge me rent!'

'Which you don't pay all that often,' Delia had teased. At that moment, she'd been right on the point of saying, 'Yes, to hell with it, I'm coming too!' But she hadn't. Her cool sharp brain had murmured, 'Wait!'... and now she was *still* trying to make her decision.

It had been pointless coming in to the office today, she observed, looking listlessly out of the window. She couldn't manage her work choices either, and everyone seemed to be watching her curiously. As if they knew something.

Closing all her files and then throwing them back into her 'pending' tray, she felt relieved as she finally decided something. She'd take the rest of the day off! Her 'boss' could hardly sack her now, could he? Given the circumstances.

Back at the flat, she stripped off her clothes, and slid on the grey cotton robe she'd somehow managed to bring home from Jake's with her. Faint, evocative odours rose up from the fabric, and as she lay down on the settee, a drink at her side, she breathed in deeply and remembered...

Jake in the Jacuzzi and afterwards. Then later, Vida and Elf. That had been unexpected, but extraordinarily beautiful. She shuddered wildly, recalling how dressing – in their company – had been as sensual as taking clothes off. She thought of Vida's long white fingers, how bold they were, and how impossible to resist or gainsay. And *that* was yet another complication...

'I'll be glad when this is all sorted, and I don't have to drink so much,' she muttered, taking a sip of her wine. She'd felt like hitting the gin, but it seemed too early. Especially on an empty stomach. Swirling the pale golden fluid in the glass, she considered her dilemma yet again.

The trouble was that she liked her life as it was. Now Russell was out of the picture, there were friends she wanted to be with, things she wanted to do and try . . . Being whisked off to Geneva for a life of unremitting sex was a seductive idea, and if she'd been with Jake right now, and he'd asked her again, she would've said 'yes'. . . But he wasn't and she could see other options.

Jake was the most physically beautiful man she'd ever met. He was supernaturally potent, and almost mesmerically desirable when he even just *looked* at her. He was also, in his own bizarre way, quite kind. He was offering her a glut of pleasure and even a career advancement. But it just wasn't everything she needed. Perplexed, she took a sip of her drink, rolled back onto the settee, and stared at the blank, white ceiling.

Stared upwards and thought of a quiet night in with a friend . . .

Peter.

And there was another sound reason for refusing Jake. Deana had no 'relationship' ties here at home, but she, Delia, had Peter. A gorgeous and talented lover who lived in a shy man's skin. A slow, careful, artistic lover with clever fingers and a long, thick penis. A lover who would be at home now, working on his networked computer . . .

After pausing only to tie the sash of her robe, Delia made her way out through the back door and up the outside stairway that led up to the flat above.

'I . . . I was going to come down,' Peter said nervously as he let her in. His brown eyes were wide behind his glasses, goggling at her thinly clad body. 'I saw you come in. I thought you might be ill.'

He cared so much. How lovely. How lovely and unaccountably arousing.

'I've never felt better,' she said, advancing confidently and forcing Peter to step backwards in her wake. She'd taken the initiative last time, and the result had been fabulous. She could so easily do it again. 'You're not busy, are you?' Her question sounded brisk and purposeful, and she was thrilled by the feeling of power.

She eyed his casual shorts and T-shirt. Computing at home, he didn't have to dress up, so he probably had been working . . . Tough!

'Er . . . No, not really,' he answered, more excited, she sensed, than nervous.

'Good!'

Delia felt calm, but intensely aroused. In control of everything but her physical responses. A pink blush was washing through her face and throat, her nipples were puckered, and her sex was a pool of warm fluid.

'Good!' she repeated, flipping open her robe, then pressing the full length of her body against him. He gasped with surprise, but before he could protest, she'd pulled his soft mouth onto hers, and thrust into its depths with her tongue. Where his bare thighs were pressed along hers, he was shaking.

He was scared of her, she realised exultantly. In awe, but still desperately randy. His denim shorts rasped at her tender belly, but the discomfort was piquant. She pressed her moist flossy pubis against him, searching for his hardness; for the bulge behind his zip where his erection jutted out to greet her. He moaned, and she smiled against his mouth, grinding at his body with her hips and loving the way his penis lurched wildly in response.

'But Delia!' he protested when she freed his mouth.

'But nothing!' She dismissed his qualms by removing his spectacles and putting them aside. When she tugged his T-shirt off over his head, his face was an absolute picture. Lust and befuddlement fought a battle across its smooth pale planes. He'd been attacked by a bold sexual alien who'd snatched the body of his sensible neighbour, and he moved forward short sightedly to get a better perspective on her body. As he reached for her, she blocked him and brushed away his hands...

'What's going on?' he demanded, the beginnings of understanding in his warm, slightly unfocused eyes.

'Silence,' she said softly. 'Stay quiet and take your shorts and underpants off.'

He obeyed her clumsily, blushing when his penis flicked up against his belly.

Delia hid her smile of glee, loving what she saw but trying to maintain her cool aura. Peter really did have the most beautiful cock. A red-tipped, suckable lollipop of a cock... Knowing exactly what she wanted, she slid to her knees, pressed her breasts against his thighs and nuzzled her hungry face into his crotch. With his penis waving against her cheek, she licked the sweaty crease of his groin, then dove in deeper, pushing aside his shaft with her fingers so she could get to his testicles and suck them.

As she played with first one, then the other with her tongue and teeth, he whimpered. And then, when she enclosed both balls at once, and mock-bit him, he cried out piteously and his knees shook and swayed. Mouthing the wrinkled bag and the twin firm ovals within it, she savoured his rich gamey taste. He was a cleanly man, but it was some time since he'd showered and the day was hot. His skin was spicy with a strong, genital sweat and just the slightest hint of seminal musk – as if he'd come recently and not had a chance to wash.

Did you masturbate for me? thought Delia, worrying his balls with her lips as her saliva flowed freely around them. She could sense his prick getting more and more urgent. It was pressed against her face now, sticky and twitching, as hard as a shiny wooden bar. She wanted to suck it and taste it, but she also wanted to prolong the agony. Spin things out a bit. Enjoy herself with his body, his sex and his psyche; and use the lessons she'd so recently learned.

'Please ... My cock,' he moaned as she stroked her fingertips around his buttocks and down against the inslope of his thighs. She was still lightly chewing on his testicles, but avoiding any contact with his cock.

Using an erotic awareness she'd never realised she possessed, Delia dragged her nails along his bottom crease. Slowly and lingeringly, she scratched at his perineum and anus, balancing his pleasure against his fear of her teeth. He was gasping hoarsely now, his chest heaving like a bellows.

As his balls tightened ominously, Delia drew back without haste and studied her living creation. A man in desperate need of a climax. Peter, who stood before her with his feet braced, his knees slightly bent, and his hands clenched into fists at his side – white-knuckled with need and frustration. His eyes were tightly shut and there was moisture on his finely drawn face: beads of sweat on his lip and brow, and what just might be tears on his cheeks.

'Please,' he begged, through clenched teeth.

'Lie down on the floor,' she said, trying for a note of sternness, but sounding more excited than cruel. As he complied, she slid out of her robe and flung it aside, admiring his cock as it stood up vertically from his loins, its tip weeping clear fluid freely. She felt her pussy ripple crazily in readiness, as if calling to his beautiful intruder.

But instead of having mercy on the abject man before her,

she switched her tactics and squatted gracefully down onto his face.

The view from where she crouched was memorable. A flat, brown-furred belly, long, slim, steel-tense thighs, the red swaying tower of his cock.

'Lick,' Delia Ferraro ordered quietly, 'lick everywhere and don't slack!'

A long while later, she rose from the rug, her body glowing and sated.

'I've got to make some phone calls,' she whispered to the stupefied man she'd just mastered. 'But I'll be back in a little while . . . You can fix me a drink when you recover.'

Smiling wistfully, Delia reached for the phone and dialled her sister's agency. She was missing Deana already, but she knew her decision was the right one.

I suppose it's better this way, thought Deana, pacing up and down the pavement outside the agency she no longer worked for.

This way there'd be no time for tears and protracted heart-wrenching farewells, and no chance to question her decision or tell herself she was a fool.

All it had taken was two telephone calls. One that she'd received; and one that she'd made.

Delia had said, '*Arrivaderci*, Deana. And promise you'll give him hell for me!'

Jake had said, 'That's wonderful. I'll send a car for you in fifteen minutes and a courier will collect your passport. You won't need anything else.'

Glancing down at her plain workaday watch, she pondered this statement. All she had with her was a canvas ex-army bag containing tissues, purse, a few scraps of make-up and an inexpensive body spray. All she had on was a thin pink cotton summer frock, loose and short-sleeved, and beneath it a small pair of knickers. The watch and her scrappy old sandals completed the sum total of her 'going-away' outfit ... but she had a feeling that even these paltry few items wouldn't stay with her all that long. That she was poised on the brink of shucking off her old life completely ... along with every single thing that went with it.

Squinting out into the street, she saw a familiar long black shape come gliding towards her, forging its way through the heavy city traffic as if surrounded by a *Star Trek* force-field. When the rear passenger door was exactly in front of her the limousine stopped, and in the wink of an eye, a tall, blond, black-clad figure was at her side and assisting her into the car. When she was safely installed, Fargo returned to his place behind the wheel – and it was several seconds before Deana realised that he hadn't said a word.

Alone on the luxurious rear seat, with smoked glass between her and the secretive chauffeur, she felt a momentary pang of alarm ... And then almost jumped out of her skin at an unexpected high-pitched beeping. She looked around in a panic for its source.

Beside her on the seat was a blue, leather covered box about twelve inches by eight, and a state-of-the-art portable phone. Picking up the slim, tiny unit, she flicked it open, just as she'd seen Delia do with hers, and murmured a tentative, 'Hello?'

'Hello again, sweet Deana ...' Jake's voice purred out of the tiny speaker as clearly as if he'd been sitting beside her. 'Are you ready for your adventure?'

'Yes,' she said trying to project more confidence across the ether than she actually felt. It was one thing to agree to the theory of a life of pure sex, but now came the practical and the physical.

'Are you ready for *me*?' The emphasis on the pronoun was

unmistakable, and as she heard it she realised that she was ready. Ready for him, and completely ready for sex . . .

God alone knew how many miles away Jake was, or whether he was at his house, some airport or other, or even in transit as she was, but he still had the ability to stir her. Looking down, she saw her nipples like small dark cones peaking clearly through her thin, pale dress. She felt the ache of the process itself . . . The way the buds of her breasts were getting harder and more sensitive as they prepared for the touch of Jake's fingers.

'Did you hear me, Deana?' he enquired, his light soft huskiness losing none of its power across the airwaves. 'Is your body rousing? Are you wet? Does your vagina feel empty without me?'

'Yes,' she whispered, not sure if the phone could pick her up.

'Better make sure, Deana. Test yourself . . . Take your panties off and push two of your fingers inside yourself . . .'

Lost for words, she did her best to obey, still clutching the slim black phone in one hand while struggling with her clothing with the other. After what seemed an age of shuffling and wiggling, her white cotton panties lay accusingly on the sleek, dark, leather-covered seat. Beside the mysterious box . . . She moaned, not quite sure whether she wanted to continue, then lifted her skirt, eased apart her thighs and pushed the first and second fingers of her free right hand into the slippery wetness of her sex.

'Did they go in easily?' enquired the persistent, disembodied voice.

'Yes.'

'Good. Now work them in and out. Cover them with your juices, then taste yourself . . .'

It was the same order he'd given on that first night, and her sex felt just as snug and clinging as it had done then. She was right on the point of orgasm, and wanted desperately to touch her clitoris, but she knew that if she did, she'd come immediately and Jake would know. His hi-tech phone would give him her screams the instant they left her lips.

That he had the knowledge shouldn't matter. Especially when they'd shared so much already and he was about to take over her life. Everything about her was his now . . .

So why did she still need an 'edge'? A piece of herself that was solely and always her own . . .

'Tell me how you taste,' he prompted.

'Salty,' she whispered, 'musky . . . Not strong.' She licked her fingertips, then – unbidden – put them back where they'd been. Her inner walls quivered as they stretched.

'Yes, that's right,' his voice encouraged from the phone.

Deana started wildly, pulling her fingers from her body with a vulgar slurp and wondering where the camera was placed. She stared suspiciously at the slim, dark device in her hand, then shook her head. It was a sophisticated piece of technology but she didn't think it had 'eyes' as well as 'ears'.

'Can you see me?' she demanded, smoothing down her skirt and still staring intently around her.

'Only in my mind.' Jake's soft, silky chuckle was so intimate he seemed to be beside her. A tantalising thought occurred . . .

'Where are you, Jake?'

'In transit, sweet Deana. Just like you. Only slightly closer to our destination. I was already on the move when you called.'

A dozen questions swarmed in Deana's brain. How had he known she'd accept? Where were they flying from? And who was driving Jake, if Fargo was driving her? There was nothing that could change things now . . . but she still asked. 'Are you alone?'

'Elf's here. But I'm like you . . . Isolated. Set apart by sound-proof glass.'

'Good,' she murmured into the mouthpiece, her questions replaced by ideas. Sexy, outrageous ideas. 'Are your trousers open?'

'I'm naked from the waist down.'

The words were slightly breathy, as if he were panting. She imagined him resplendent on the back seat of a car such as this . . . Legs splayed open, touching himself.

As she eased up her skirt again, she heard a rustling sound down the line, then an electronic click. When Jake spoke again the quality of his voice was different, still clear but bigger and more echoey.

'Deana,' he said, sounding as if he were struggling for precision against difficult odds. 'You see the intercom unit in front of you? Well, if you flip down the panel to the left and fit in the mobile phone, you'll find everything that much easier.'

Curious, she followed his instructions, and when she'd slotted the phone into place with a barely audible click, she heard Jake's next words from everywhere around her . . .

'That's better,' he said, the sound conveyed to Deana through high definition speakers. '"Hands free" now, Deana. Free to touch and explore . . .'

Deana said nothing, but in her mind she saw *his* hands. Long, brown, narrow-fingered hands. Folded tight round his flesh and slowly and rhythmically moving.

'Do you see the leather-covered case, Deana?' he asked, gasping softly and confirming her suspicions. The catch in his voice betrayed him. She'd heard it before, in his moments of utmost pleasure.

'Yes.'

'Open it up.'

She obeyed him – and it was her turn to gasp.

The velvet-lined case contained several unusual items. One was patently valuable, the others were less so, but all in their own way, breathtaking.

Wide-eyed, she lifted up the most costly of the objects: a narrow, elegant collar-like confection of soft white leather, fastened with a small buckle of what looked suspiciously like platinum and studded alternately along its length with baroque pearls and diamonds. She supposed it was symbolic of her new erotic status, but it was hard to imagine the average 'slave' wearing anything so priceless and beautiful. Without hesitating she buckled it round her throat.

The other things she wasn't so sure of . . .

A small glass tub contained a clear lubricating substance, and beside it were two gleaming, black latex sex-toys. One was about eight inches long and moulded as a gross but rather finely crafted penis; the other was shorter, rounder and disgustingly bulging and flanged. It made Deana quiver and remember the feel of the champagne cork.

'Do you like my gifts?' came the ragged voice from the speakers. 'They're to welcome you to a new life, Deana. Will you try them for me? Now?' Only his electronic presence was with her, but still she saw his eyes. His lovely slanted eyes, hot and blue in the tinted glass gloom of the car's dark interior. They speared her from inside her own mind, making her flesh echo *his* yearning, and ache for his reality.

She hardly needed the lubricant, but even so there was a certain voluptuous discomfort while inserting Jake's instruments of lust.

And as she moved and rustled on the seat, he bombarded her with increasingly desperate pleas for information. Questions about how wet she was, how open. How swollen her labia and clitoris were.

Deana said not a word. She knew that he knew she'd obey

him – and put his dark, infernal toys inside her. But in a relationship built on games, she now had an urge for a new one.

By denying him the description he craved, she could drive him inside his own imagination – as he'd driven her into hers. She granted him a sigh as the dildo slid deliciously into her vagina, and a harsh, unforced groan as the anal plug breached her bottom. But there was no running commentary and no detailed catalogue of pleasure. She obeyed his every obscene instruction, but gave him no means knowing it . . .

Jake's cries were animal and desperate. And as Deana lay on the seat in a foetal, panting ball, she could sense him doing the same, miles away. As she fought the rippling surges in her bottom, her loins and her belly, she heard *his* shouts and yelps of elation . . . interspersed, strangely enough, with his own complete description of what *he* was doing to himself.

The images were amazing.

She'd no way of knowing what Jake was wearing, but her mind showed him clad in a pure white shirt; its dazzling high-gloss pallor making his brown body look browner, and his prick look magnificent, purpled and dark. It rose like a staff from his naked groin and the lush black tangle of his pubic hair . . .

'Yes!' he shouted triumphantly, his slim, imaginary hips lifting up and humping the shadows. 'Oh God, yes, Deana, I'm going to have you! All of you this time. Every inch. Every curve. Every crevice. Every fold. I'm going to screw every hole of your sweet sexy body and you're going to come until you beg me for mercy! I'm going to lick you until you scream . . . You're going to be the best screwed woman on earth and you're going to love it! Every second of it!'

It was an extravagant claim, but as she scrubbed at her clitoris with her fingertip, she knew that this man could fulfil it . . . He could probably extract all these unthinkable acts from her and more ... but only because he was beautiful enough for her to *let* him.

Deana laughed aloud, her body bouncing madly on the seat as her flesh clamped and pumped around the dildoes. She could've come from the touch of her own fingers; she could have come simply from the obscene images of Jake and herself that flashed like slides through her brain; she could've come from the hard rubber masses that abused both her vagina and her rectum ...

But it wasn't any of these that had finally tipped her over.

It was power ... Her own power. Sweet and hot and drugging. She was coming because she had power over herself and power over Jake. No matter what he screamed and ranted.

And as she lay in the back of a dark speeding limousine, sweating, pulsating and shaking, and listening to a man's grunting cries of release, she knew their contest had barely begun.

I can't take much more of this heat, she remembered thinking, a million years ago in a stark white art gallery, when she'd been pretending to be someone else.

But now she knew she'd been wrong. She was crazy Deana Ferraro – Deana the fearless – and she could take anything and everything and just grow stronger and stronger and stronger.

Any act, any challenge. Any outrage or perversion. She could take it all, any heat that Jake cared to kindle. The question was, could he take the same heat from her?

And on that thought, she climaxed again ...

Visit the Black Lace website at
www.black-lace-books.com

**FIND OUT THE LATEST INFORMATION AND TAKE ADVANTAGE
OF OUR FANTASTIC FREE BOOK OFFER! ALSO VISIT THE SITE
FOR . . .**

- All Black Lace titles currently available
  and how to order online

- Great new offers

- Writers' guidelines

- Author interviews

- An erotica newsletter

- Features

- Cool links

**BLACK LACE — THE LEADING IMPRINT OF
WOMEN'S SEXY FICTION**

**TAKING YOUR EROTIC READING PLEASURE
TO NEW HORIZONS**

LOOK OUT FOR THE BLACK LACE 15TH ANNIVERSARY SPECIAL EDITIONS. COLLECT ALL 10 TITLES IN THE SERIES!

All books priced £7.99 in the UK. Please note publication dates apply to the UK only. For other territories, please contact your retailer.

Published in March 2008

CASSANDRA'S CONFLICT
Fredrica Allen
ISBN 978 0 352 34186 0

A house in Hampstead. Present day. Behind a façade of cultured respectability lies a world of decadent indulgnce and dark eroticism. Cassandra's sheltered life is transformed when she is employed as governess to the Baron's children. He draws her into games where lust can feed on the erotic charge of submission. Games where only he knows the rules and where unusual pleasures can flourish.

To be published in May 2008

BLACK ORCHID
Roxanne Carr
ISBN 978 0 352 34188 4

At the Black Orchid Club, adventurous women who yearn for the pleasures of exotic, even kinky sex can quench their desires in discreet and luxurious surroundings. Having tasted the fulfilment of unique and powerful lusts, one such adventurous woman learns what happens when the need for limitless indulgence becomes an addiction.

To be published in June 2008

FORBIDDEN FRUIT
Susie Raymond
ISBN 978 0 352 34189 1

The last thing sexy thirty-something Beth expected was to get involved with a sixteen year old. But when she finds him spying on her in the dressing room at work she embarks on an erotic journey with the straining youth, teaching him and teasing him as she leads him through myriad sensuous exercises at her stylish modern home. As their lascivious games become more and more intense, Beth soon begins to realise that she is the one being awakened to a new world of desire – and that hers is the mind quickly becoming consumed with lust.

To be published in July 2008

JULIET RISING
Cleo Cordell
ISBN 978 0 352 34192 1

Nothing is more important to Reynard than winning the favours of the bright and wilful Juliet, a pupil at Madame Nicol's exclusive but strict 18th century ladies' academy. Her captivating beauty tinged with a hint of cruelty soon has Reynard willing to do anything to win her approval. But Juliet's methods have little effect on Andreas, the real object of her lustful obsessions. Unable to bend him to her will, she is forced to watch him lavish his manly talents on her fellow pupils. That is, until she agrees to change her stuck-up, stubborn ways and become an eager erotic participant.

To be published in August 2008

ODALISQUE
Fleur Reynolds
ISBN 978 0 352 34193 8

Set against a backdrop of sophisticated elegance, a tale of family intrigue, forbidden passions and depraved secrets unfolds. Beautiful but scheming, successful designer Auralie plots to bring about the downfall of her virtuous cousin, Jeanine. Recently widowed, but still young and glamorous, Jeanine finds her passions being rekindled by Auralie's husband. But she is playing into Auralie's hands – vindictive hands that drag Jeanine into a world of erotic depravity. Why are the cousins locked into this sexual feud? And what is the purpose of Jeanine's mysterious Confessor, and his sordid underground sect?

To be published in September 2008

THE STALLION
Georgina Brown
ISBN 978 0 352 34199 0

The world of showjumping is as steamy as it is competitive. Ambitious young rider Penny Bennett enters into a wager with her oldest rival and friend, Ariadne, to win her thoroughbred stallion, guaranteed to bring Penny money and success. But first she must attain the sponsorship and very personal attention of showjumping's biggest impresario, Alister Beaumont.

Beaumont's riding school, however, is not all it seems. There's the weird relationship between Alister and his cigar-smoking sister. And the bizarre clothes they want Penny to wear. But in this atmosphere of unbridled kinkiness, Penny is determined not only to win the wager but to discover the truth about Beaumont's strange hobbies.

To be published in October 2008

THE DEVIL AND THE DEEP BLUE SEA
Cheryl Mildenhall
ISBN 978 0 352 34200 3

When Hillary and her girlfriends rent a country house for their summer vacation, it is a pleasant surprise to find that its secretive and kinky owner – Darius Harwood – seems to be the most desirable man in the locale. That is, before Hillary meets Haldane, the blonde and beautifully proportioned Norwegian sailor who works nearby. Intrigued by the sexual allure of two very different men, Hillary can't resist exploring the possibilities on offer. But these opportunities for misbehaviour quickly lead her into a tricky situation for which a difficult decision has to be made.

To be published in November 2008

THE NINETY DAYS OF GENEVIEVE
Lucinda Carrington
ISBN 978 0 352 34201 0

A ninety-day sex contract wasn't exactly what Genevieve Loften had in mind when she began business negotiations with the arrogant and attractive James Sinclair. As a career move she wanted to go along with it; the pay-off was potentially huge.

However, she didn't imagine that he would make her the star performer in a series of increasingly kinky and exotic fantasies. Thrown into a world of sexual misadventure, Genevieve learns how to balance her high-pressure career with the twilight world of fetishism and debauchery.

To be published in December 2008

THE GIFT OF SHAME
Sarah Hope-Walker
ISBN 978 0 35234202 7

Sad, sultry Helen flies between London, Paris and the Caribbean chasing whatever physical pleasures she can get to tear her mind from a deep, deep loss. Her glamorous life-style and charged sensual escapades belie a widow's grief. When she meets handsome, rich Jeffrey she is shocked and yet intrigued by his masterful, domineering behaviour. Soon, Helen is forced to confront the forbidden desires hiding within herself – and forced to undergo a startling metamorphosis from a meek and modest lady into a bristling, voracious wanton.

ALSO LOOK OUT FOR

THE NEW BLACK LACE BOOK OF WOMEN'S SEXUAL FANTASIES
Edited and compiled by Mitzi Szereto
ISBN 978 0 352 34172 3

The second anthology of detailed sexual fantasies contributed by women from all over the world. The book is a result of a year's research by an expert on erotic writing and gives a fascinating insight into the rich diversity of the female sexual imagination.

Black Lace Booklist

Information is correct at time of printing. To avoid disappointment, check availability before ordering. Go to www.black-lace-books.com.
All books are priced £7.99 unless another price is given.

BLACK LACE BOOKS WITH A CONTEMPORARY SETTING

❏ THE ANGELS' SHARE Maya Hess	HRAM978 0 352 34043 6	
❏ ASKING FOR TROUBLE Kristina Lloyd	HRAM978 0 352 33362 9	
❏ BLACK LIPSTICK KISSES Monica Belle	HRAM978 0 352 33885 3	£6.99
❏ THE BLUE GUIDE Carrie Williams	HRAM978 0 352 34132 7	
❏ THE BOSS Monica Belle	HRAM978 0 352 34088 7	
❏ BOUND IN BLUE Monica Belle	HRAM978 0 352 34012 2	
❏ CAMPAIGN HEAT Gabrielle Marcola	HRAM978 0 352 33941 6	
❏ CAT SCRATCH FEVER Sophie Mouette	HRAM978 0 352 34021 4	
❏ CIRCUS EXCITE Nikki Magennis	HRAM978 0 352 34033 7	
❏ CLUB CRÈME Primula Bond	HRAM978 0 352 33907 2	£6.99
❏ CONFESSIONAL Judith Roycroft	HRAM978 0 352 33421 3	
❏ CONTINUUM Portia Da Costa	HRAM978 0 352 33120 5	
❏ DANGEROUS CONSEQUENCES Pamela Rochford	HRAM978 0 352 33185 4	
❏ DARK DESIGNS Madelynne Ellis	HRAM978 0 352 34075 7	
❏ THE DEVIL INSIDE Portia Da Costa	HRAM978 0 352 32993 6	
❏ EQUAL OPPORTUNITIES Mathilde Madden	HRAM978 0 352 34070 2	
❏ FIRE AND ICE Laura Hamilton	HRAM978 0 352 33486 2	
❏ GONE WILD Maria Eppie	HRAM978 0 352 33670 5	
❏ HOTBED Portia Da Costa	HRAM978 0 352 33614 9	
❏ IN PURSUIT OF ANNA Natasha Rostova	HRAM978 0 352 34060 3	
❏ IN THE FLESH Emma Holly	HRAM978 0 352 34117 4	
❏ LEARNING TO LOVE IT Alison Tyler	HRAM978 0 352 33535 7	
❏ MAD ABOUT THE BOY Mathilde Madden	HRAM978 0 352 34001 6	
❏ MAKE YOU A MAN Anna Clare	HRAM978 0 352 34006 1	
❏ MAN HUNT Cathleen Ross	HRAM978 0 352 33583 8	
❏ THE MASTER OF SHILDEN Lucinda Carrington	HRAM978 0 352 33140 3	
❏ MIXED DOUBLES Zoe le Verdier	HRAM978 0 352 33312 4	£6.99
❏ MIXED SIGNALS Anna Clare	HRAM978 0 352 33889 1	£6.99
❏ MS BEHAVIOUR Mini Lee	HRAM978 0 352 33962 1	

☐ PACKING HEAT Karina Moore   HRAM978 0 352 33356 8   £6.99

☐ PAGAN HEAT Monica Belle   HRAM978 0 352 33974 4

☐ PEEP SHOW Mathilde Madden   HRAM978 0 352 33924 9

☐ THE POWER GAME Carrera Devonshire   HRAM978 0 352 33990 4

☐ THE PRIVATE UNDOING OF A PUBLIC SERVANT   HRAM978 0 352 34066 5

     Leonie Martel

☐ RUDE AWAKENING Pamela Kyle   HRAM978 0 352 33036 9

☐ SAUCE FOR THE GOOSE Mary Rose Maxwell   HRAM978 0 352 33492 3

☐ SPLIT Kristina Lloyd   HRAM978 0 352 34154 9

☐ STELLA DOES HOLLYWOOD Stella Black   HRAM978 0 352 33588 3

☐ THE STRANGER Portia Da Costa   HRAM978 0 352 33211 0

☐ SUITE SEVENTEEN Portia Da Costa   HRAM978 0 352 34109 9

☐ TONGUE IN CHEEK Tabitha Flyte   HRAM978 0 352 33484 8

☐ THE TOP OF HER GAME Emma Holly   HRAM978 0 352 34116 7

☐ UNNATURAL SELECTION Alaine Hood   HRAM978 0 352 33963 8

☐ VELVET GLOVE Emma Holly   HRAM978 0 352 34115 0

☐ VILLAGE OF SECRETS Mercedes Kelly   HRAM978 0 352 33344 5

☐ WILD BY NATURE Monica Belle   HRAM978 0 352 33915 7   £6.99

☐ WILD CARD Madeline Moore   HRAM978 0 352 34038 2

☐ WING OF MADNESS Mae Nixon   HRAM978 0 352 34099 3

BLACK LACE BOOKS WITH AN HISTORICAL SETTING

☐ THE BARBARIAN GEISHA Charlotte Royal   HRAM978 0 352 33267 7

☐ BARBARIAN PRIZE Deanna Ashford   HRAM978 0 352 34017 7

☐ THE CAPTIVATION Natasha Rostova   HRAM978 0 352 33234 9

☐ DARKER THAN LOVE Kristina Lloyd   HRAM978 0 352 33279 0

☐ WILD KINGDOM Deanna Ashford   HRAM978 0 352 33549 4

☐ DIVINE TORMENT Janine Ashbless   HRAM978 0 352 33719 1

☐ FRENCH MANNERS Olivia Christie   HRAM978 0 352 33214 1

☐ LORD WRAXALL'S FANCY Anna Lieff Saxby   HRAM978 0 352 33080 2

☐ NICOLE'S REVENGE Lisette Allen   HRAM978 0 352 32984 4

☐ THE SENSES BEJEWELLED Cleo Cordell   HRAM978 0 352 32904 2   £6.99

☐ THE SOCIETY OF SIN Sian Lacey Taylder   HRAM978 0 352 34080 1

☐ TEMPLAR PRIZE Deanna Ashford   HRAM978 0 352 34137 2

☐ UNDRESSING THE DEVIL Angel Strand   HRAM978 0 352 33938 6

BLACK LACE BOOKS WITH A PARANORMAL THEME

- ❑ BRIGHT FIRE Maya Hess — HRAM978 0 352 34104 4
- ❑ BURNING BRIGHT Janine Ashbless — HRAM978 0 352 34085 6
- ❑ CRUEL ENCHANTMENT Janine Ashbless — HRAM978 0 352 33483 1
- ❑ FLOOD Anna Clare — HRAM978 0 352 34094 8
- ❑ GOTHIC BLUE Portia Da Costa — HRAM978 0 352 33075 8
- ❑ THE PRIDE Edie Bingham — HRAM978 0 352 33997 3
- ❑ THE SILVER COLLAR Mathilde Madden — HRAM978 0 352 34141 9
- ❑ THE TEN VISIONS Olivia Knight — HRAM978 0 352 34119 8

BLACK LACE ANTHOLOGIES

❑ BLACK LACE QUICKIES 1 Various	HRAM978 0 352 34126 6	£2.99
❑ BLACK LACE QUICKIES 2 Various	HRAM978 0 352 34127 3	£2.99
❑ BLACK LACE QUICKIES 3 Various	HRAM978 0 352 34128 0	£2.99
❑ BLACK LACE QUICKIES 4 Various	HRAM978 0 352 34129 7	£2.99
❑ BLACK LACE QUICKIES 5 Various	HRAM978 0 352 34130 3	£2.99
❑ BLACK LACE QUICKIES 6 Various	HRAM978 0 352 34133 4	£2.99
❑ BLACK LACE QUICKIES 7 Various	HRAM978 0 352 34146 4	£2.99
❑ BLACK LACE QUICKIES 8 Various	HRAM978 0 352 34147 1	£2.99
❑ BLACK LACE QUICKIES 9 Various	HRAM978 0 352 34155 6	£2.99
❑ MORE WICKED WORDS Various	HRAM978 0 352 33487 9	£6.99
❑ WICKED WORDS 3 Various	HRAM978 0 352 33522 7	£6.99
❑ WICKED WORDS 4 Various	HRAM978 0 352 33603 3	£6.99
❑ WICKED WORDS 5 Various	HRAM978 0 352 33642 2	£6.99
❑ WICKED WORDS 6 Various	HRAM978 0 352 33690 3	£6.99
❑ WICKED WORDS 7 Various	HRAM978 0 352 33743 6	£6.99
❑ WICKED WORDS 8 Various	HRAM978 0 352 33787 0	£6.99
❑ WICKED WORDS 9 Various	HRAM978 0 352 33860 0	
❑ WICKED WORDS 10 Various	HRAM978 0 352 33893 8	
❑ THE BEST OF BLACK LACE 2 Various	HRAM978 0 352 33718 4	
❑ WICKED WORDS: SEX IN THE OFFICE Various	HRAM978 0 352 33944 7	
❑ WICKED WORDS: SEX AT THE SPORTS CLUB Various	HRAM978 0 352 33991 1	
❑ WICKED WORDS: SEX ON HOLIDAY Various	HRAM978 0 352 33961 4	
❑ WICKED WORDS: SEX IN UNIFORM Various	HRAM978 0 352 34002 3	
❑ WICKED WORDS: SEX IN THE KITCHEN Various	HRAM978 0 352 34018 4	
❑ WICKED WORDS: SEX ON THE MOVE Various	HRAM978 0 352 34034 4	
❑ WICKED WORDS: SEX AND MUSIC Various	HRAM978 0 352 34061 0	

To find out the latest information about Black Lace titles, check out the website: www.black-lace-books.com or send for a booklist with complete synopses by writing to:

Black Lace Booklist, Virgin Books Ltd
Thames Wharf Studios
Rainville Road
London W6 9HA

Please include an SAE of decent size. Please note only British stamps are valid.

Our privacy policy
We will not disclose information you supply us to any other parties. We will not disclose any information which identifies you personally to any person without your express consent.

From time to time we may send out information about Black Lace books and special offers. Please tick here if you do <u>not</u> wish to receive Black Lace information. ❏

Please send me the books I have ticked above.

Name ....

Address ....

....

....

....

Post Code ....

Send to: Virgin Books Cash Sales, Thames Wharf Studios, Rainville Road, London W6 9HA.

US customers: for prices and details of how to order books for delivery by mail, call 888-330-8477.

Please enclose a cheque or postal order, made payable to Virgin Books Ltd, to the value of the books you have ordered plus postage and packing costs as follows:

UK and BFPO – £1.00 for the first book, 50p for each subsequent book.

Overseas (including Republic of Ireland) – £2.00 for the first book, £1.00 for each subsequent book.

If you would prefer to pay by VISA, ACCESS/MASTERCARD, DINERS CLUB, AMEX or SWITCH, please write your card number and expiry date here: ....

....

Signature ....

Please allow up to 28 days for delivery.